THE DOCTOR'S PREGNANCY SECRET

BY
LEAH MARTYN

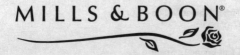

MILLS & BOON®

First published in Great Britain 2007
Harlequin Mills & Boon Limited,
Eton House, 18-24 Paradise Road, Richmond, Surrey TW9 1SR

© Leah Martyn 2007

ISBN-13: 978 0 263 85258 5

Set in Times Roman 9¾ on 10 pt
03-0807-65655

Printed and bound in Spain
by Litografia Rosés, S.A., Barcelona

THE DOCTOR'S PREGNANCY SECRET

CHAPTER ONE

IT WOULDN'T be for ever, Fliss consoled herself, letting her gaze linger, before she finally closed the door on her inner-city high-rise apartment. But already she was beginning to doubt her sanity in making the decision to leave the lifestyle she'd grown to love and take a job in a country hospital.

Her mouth tightened. Damn Daniel. All these changes she'd been almost forced to make were down to him. Fliss suppressed a sigh. Calling her former lover 'an opportunistic rat' didn't help. What was done was done. Now her best chance was to look forward and not back. And hope this change of direction would give her a sense of purpose again.

She'd let her apartment for six months and most of her furniture had gone into storage until she'd sorted out her living arrangements in Mt Pryde. Which at the moment looked like being the doctors' accommodation at the district hospital.

Fliss gritted her teeth. She *wouldn't* look back. The thought stayed resolutely with her as she began wheeling her suitcase along to the lift. Thank heavens, that was the last of it. Already her sporty little hatchback sedan was packed to bursting with the bits and pieces she couldn't live without indefinitely.

Hauling her case across the concrete floor of the basement car park, she thanked her lucky stars she'd rejected the offer of a kitten last Christmas. At this rate, the poor creature would probably have had to travel on the roof!

At last, seated more or less comfortably in the driver's seat, she belted up, settling her sunglasses across her nose and starting the engine. It was roughly a two-hour drive to Mt Pryde, which would make it around noon when she arrived there. She'd head straight to the McNeals' place. Jo and Brady had invited her to lunch.

Fliss's spirits began to lift as she hit the country highway. It was that tender time between summer and early autumn that went largely unnoticed in the city. But out here every paddock seemed ablaze with the sunny gold of wattle blossoms contrasting vividly with the soft opalescence of the sky.

A dry smile nipped her mouth. If she really went overboard with her imagination, she could easily place the whole picture within the pages of a tourist brochure.

Perhaps her move to the country wouldn't be so bad after all. And it didn't have to be for ever. Just until she had her head on straight again after the mortal blow Daniel had delivered her.

But she vowed it would be a long time before she'd trust a man again.

She made a sound of annoyance in her throat. She'd have to stop giving Daniel space in her head. He'd proved himself a cheat and a liar. But until the hurt went away, it would be so good to have Jo close by to lend a sympathetic ear.

Fliss smiled reminiscently. Jo was one of her dearest friends. Along with Sophie, of course. The three of them had shared an apartment when they'd done their medical internship, then their residencies. They'd had a ball. But they'd studied resolutely too and had encouraged one another through ruinously long hours at the hospital, finally celebrating hard when at last they'd become fully qualified.

And now it all seemed light years ago. But thank heavens they still kept in touch. They were more like sisters than best friends, Fliss decided.

And after Daniel, it was Jo who had helped her sort herself out and steer her life in this new direction. Fliss recalled one of the many phone conversations they'd had until she'd finally got herself together and acted.

'I'm only considering this because I'm desperate,' Fliss had maintained heavily.

'All I'm saying is, apply for the job! You need to get out of that place, Fliss. I mean, do you really want to be at the sports clinic when Daniel shows up for his weekly massage?'

'He wouldn't dare!' Fliss's throat had gone dry at the prospect. 'Would he…?'

'If he's got as much hide as you've told me, I think he would.'

'But you're asking me to come to the bush, Jo. What am I going to *do* there?'

'You'll work, of course, like everyone else here. And Mt Pryde is a reasonably sized country town, barely a two-hour drive from the city, and we actually do have running water and electricity,' Jo had ended pithily. 'Besides which, the hospital is crying out for senior medical staff with a bit of nous.'

Fliss had snorted. 'I didn't show much *nous* falling for that sleaze Daniel, did I?'

'Water under the bridge, sweetie,' Jo had said gently. 'You weren't to know he was practically leading a double life.'

'Jo, I was gutted…'

'I know…' Jo was all sympathy. 'But perhaps changing location and taking on a challenging job will give you a whole new outlook.'

'I suppose it might. OK…' Fliss's sigh of resignation came up from her toes. 'What do I have to do to get an interview? '

'Initially, put in a call to Queensland Health,' Jo responded helpfully. 'They'll have all the rural vacancies on their computer files. Tell them the one you're interested in and go from there.'

'I mightn't get it, of course.'

'Flissy, you'll walk it.'

'Jo, I've worked in sports medicine for years. I've probably forgotten everything I ever learned about emergency medicine.'

'Don't you dare give up on this,' Jo warned. 'I've worked with you in Casualty. You're a smart lady. You don't go into paralysis when a quick decision has to be made. And workwise, think what a complete change it'll be.'

Fliss groaned. 'That's what I'm afraid of.'

'You're too young to be afraid of change,' Jo chastised her friend lightly. 'Look on it as an adventure.'

'Mmm.' Fliss sounded less than impressed. 'So, if I get the job at the hospital, where would I live? Can I rent a nice place in the town?'

'Rentals are a bit tight at the moment apparently. As a stopgap you could possibly live in at the hospital.'

'Oh, please!'

'Actually, the accommodation's not bad. Refurbished only recently. On the other hand, you could come and stay with Brady and me. We've a spare bedroom.'

'No way, Jo.' Fliss was adamant. 'You're only newly married. I wouldn't dream of it.'

Jo and Brady had been married for only a few months. When they'd met, Brady had been a single father with a baby son and determined to go it alone. Jo had had other ideas and after a swift, intense and some times rocky courtship, the two had finally got themselves sorted, had had a lovely wedding and Jo had become small Andrew's proud stepmum.

'You'd be on hand to babysit for us sometimes,' Jo said practically.

'I'd be happy to do that anyway. That's if I end up in your neck of the woods.'

'You know, it might be fun,' Jo encouraged.

Silence.

'This is all so difficult for me, Jo…'

'I know it is, sweetie,' Jo commiserated quietly. 'But, please, just take the first step. And Brady and I will be here for you, don't forget that. You'll be among friends.'

Fliss seemed to be thinking. 'If I do get the job and come to live in Mt Pryde, you won't go lining me up with odd men, will you?'

'I don't know any *odd* men!'

'You know what I mean,' Fliss warned.

'OK, I promise. No odd men.'

'All right. I guess I'll give it a try, then.'

'Good for you,' Jo said warmly. 'Now, keep me posted.'

'I feel sick!' Fliss wailed her unease.

Jo clicked her tongue. 'Just do it, Fliss, OK? Life is meant to be lived, for heaven's sake! Now, get off the phone and start living yours!'

'You always were the bossy one, Josephine.' Fliss managed a half-laugh. 'Takes me back to our training days.'

'Well, we're all grown up now,' Jo said dryly. 'And I was never the bossy one. You were!'

For the first time Fliss laughed naturally. 'I guess I was. OK, as of now, I'm taking charge of my life.'

'Good,' Jo said succinctly. 'I can't wait for you to get here.'

Now Fliss glanced at her watch. She was making good time. Another hour and she'd be in Mt Pryde. And about to experience whatever working in a rural hospital had in store for her.

Callum O'Byrne shifted his weight more comfortably into the base of his chair and began opening his mail. Frowning slightly, he extracted the contents from the large envelope that had arrived by express delivery.

'Terrific!' he muttered, when he saw the law firm's name at the top of the page and realised he was holding his divorce papers. Kirsty hadn't wasted any time in dumping their marriage. Not that they'd had a proper one in years, really.

Well, if that's what she wanted, he wouldn't hang about. It wasn't as though they'd had to reach any kind of settlement. In the final wash-up, they'd wanted nothing in a material sense from one another. And what they *should* have given to each other emotionally, they'd let founder. And now it could never be reclaimed.

Unclipping his pen from his shirt pocket, he began signing where his solicitors had indicated, realising as he did so that he was severing the last link between himself and his former wife. But perhaps he should be looking at it in a more positive way. In simple terms, they were setting each other free.

Stuffing the newly signed papers into the envelope provided, he sealed the flap and aimed it across the desk into his out-tray. Maddie could shove it in the post with the rest of the mail when she got around to it. As if he'd conjured her up, his secretary-cum-everything knocked and came in.

'Morning.' She placed a mug of coffee on his desk. 'Don't forget you have a meeting over at the council offices at nine-thirty.'

Callum groaned. 'I thought it was *next* Monday.'

'Sorry. It's today.'

The senior registrar turned his head up in a frowning query. 'This is the one where I have to plead for extra funding for more residential places for our aged folk, isn't it?'

Maddie nodded. 'Someone from the department of Health and Ageing is supposedly attending and the mayor has asked for you to be ready with some facts and figures.'

'Ah, yes. I'm going to have quite a bit to say about things in general. Now…' He looked around blindly. 'Where did I put my notes?'

Maddie pointed to the manila folder on the desk in front of him. 'I typed them up for you on the weekend. I think I managed to sort out your shorthand. But have a quick read through them and make sure I haven't missed anything.'

'What would I do without you to cover my butt, Mads?'

'Not sure.' Madeleine Curtis gave the semblance of a long-suffering smile. 'Probably you'd spend all your time out in Casualty and never set foot in your office at all. By the way, you haven't forgotten you've a new MO starting today, have you? Dr Felicity Wakefield?'

Yes, he had. Completely. But he certainly remembered the lady herself. He frowned a bit, recalling a river of dark hair, a pair of big soulful brown eyes and a wide mouth that had looked made for smiling. But she hadn't done much of that, if his memory served him right.

'Of course I haven't forgotten,' he bluffed, raising a hand and kneading the back of his neck. 'But perhaps I should run through her CV again. Do you have it handy?'

'It's all on your computer, Callum.' Seeing his baffled look, Maddie shook her head resignedly. 'Want me to show you again how to access the file?'

'Please. Perhaps I should get one of those textbooks for dummies,' he growled, moving aside so Maddie could reach out towards the keyboard.

'It's only practice. And when do you ever give yourself time for that?'

'I'm a doctor, not a technocrat,' he grumbled. 'I hate these things!'

Maddie touched a few keys expertly. 'There you are. And there's something else…' She hesitated. 'Although it's probably not a good time to tell you, with everything else you have on your plate.'

'Not going to leave me, are you?'

Maddie clicked her tongue. 'As if. The thing is, management have cut my hours back to three days a week.'

'Oh, for Pete's sake!' Callum frowned in consternation. 'Did they say why?'

'Lack of funding. But at least I'm allowed to choose which days I'll come in. We'd better have a chat about that later, I guess.'

Sweet heaven. Callum felt a surge of anger grate rawly in his throat as he swallowed. How did these bureaucrats expect rural hospitals to keep functioning when they persisted in slashing ancillary services all over the place? 'How will you manage with a salary cut?' His direct look spelt concern.

'Jeff's still full time with the ambulance base, thank goodness. But Sam and Jacob are out of their school uniforms again,' she added frankly. 'And being twins, it's not like we can hand them down, is it?'

'I guess not.' Callum's mouth turned down at the corners, his thoughts turning dark for a moment. He and Kirsty could have had a couple of kids by now, if only… He stopped the unproductive thought with a quick shake of his head, telling Maddie instead, 'I'll keep my ear to the ground. There might be an opportunity for some extra hours you'd be able to tap into.'

'Thanks, Callum.' Maddie gave a taut little smile and left quietly.

Nursing his mug against his chest, Callum stared into space. Life was a pain in the nether regions sometimes. He began draining his coffee slowly, his thoughts miles away. Finally, with a long sigh that was a mixture of cynicism and resignation, he put his mug aside and dragged his concentration back to the matter in hand.

His new medical officer.

He began speed-reading the screen in front of him. He wished now he'd had more of a chance to speak informally with her. But on the day she'd come for her interview, he'd been called to an MVA and had managed to be present for only the tail end of the proceedings.

And when he'd finally got there, he discovered the panel the Health Department had appointed had gone ahead and offered her the job in Casualty without even waiting for his input. And he'd had quite a bit he'd wanted taken on board.

For starters, the applicant's background in sports medicine was light years away from emergency medicine. But, then, on the other hand, they were desperate for senior doctors in rural hospitals so could they really afford to be unrealistic in waiting to find exactly the right person to fill the vacancy? Lifting a hand, he stroked a finger between his brows, his mind full of speculation as he continued to absorb the contents of the file.

Felicity Wakefield's credentials were impeccable. He couldn't dispute that. But one had to wonder why the lady had left her state-of-the-art city clinic to come and work in a permanently under-funded country hospital.

Well, maybe she'd shape up and maybe she wouldn't. Callum blew out a sigh as he clicked off the file. It went without saying, though, he'd have to keep an eye on her. But with his present workload, how on earth was he going to find the time…?

A discreet knock on his door cut short his train of thought. 'It's open,' he called, and brought his head up with a swiftness that bordered on impatience. 'Ah, Dr Wakefield.' She was early, he thought, waving an arm and beckoning his new medical officer in. Scooting his chair back, he rose to his feet and held out his hand towards her. 'Glad you could make it.'

Fliss blinked and blinked again. Lord, he *was* as big as she'd remembered. At least seven or eight inches taller than her five feet six. And with a rugged set of facial features that was intensely masculine.

With her training in sports medicine, Fliss had an eye for musculature, and O'Byrne measured up. Really measured up. Ignoring the odd twist in her heart and reminding herself she was off men at the moment, she lifted her chin and met the senior registrar's assessing cobalt blue eyes as coolly as she could. 'Dr O'Byrne. Hello again.'

'It's Callum.' A dark brow arched impatiently. 'Take a seat. Are you all settled in?'

Almost defensively, Fliss pulled back from the intensity of his gaze and cursed the awareness that feathered right up her backbone. She ran her tongue around the seam of her lips. 'In the doctors' accommodation for the moment.'

'Anything you need?'

Got a couple of years to listen? she felt like saying but sanity prevailed and she responded instead, 'Everything's fine.'

But far short of what she was used to, he'd bet. Leaning back in his chair, Callum folded his arms and narrowed his gaze over her. She was a looker all right. *Very* easy on the eyes. But today all that dark hair had been gathered up and swept into a braid that draped neatly over one shoulder. He'd liked it better flowing free…

Oh, for crying out loud! Since when had he noticed what women did with their hair? He held back a bark of self-derision at his adolescent ogling.

'The accommodation's fine,' Fliss said thinly, missing nothing of his blatant scrutiny. Please, heaven, don't let him be another sleaze, she pleaded silently. 'And I imagine I'll find a house or a flat in time. Where do *you* live?' she asked boldly, matching him stare for stare.

'Out of town a bit, on acreage.' He snapped his gaze away and rocked his body forward, placing his hands precisely on the desk in front of him. 'I'm sorry I wasn't here for the whole of your interview. I had an emergency.'

'Yes, I knew that. Motor vehicle accident, wasn't it?'

He seemed surprised she'd remembered. His eyes narrowed and darkened. 'Three teenagers. One dead at the scene.'

'Oh.' Fliss winced. 'How awful for the families involved.'

'And for the medical officer who had to break the news to them.' Callum's mouth moved in a grim twist. 'Welcome to emergency medicine, Felicity. Think you'll be able to cut it?'

Fliss felt the nerves in her stomach tighten. It seemed Callum O'Byrne had already assessed her capabilities and found her wanting. Without the semblance of a trial. 'I'm here to pull my weight,' she said, the faintest challenge in her voice. 'I don't expect any special treatment.'

'We understand each other, then.' Callum's gaze ran clinically over her again, before he abruptly swung up from his chair. 'I'll give you the tour.'

'No need,' Fliss had some satisfaction in informing him. 'I was here quite early. Jess and Anita showed me where everything is.'

Thank heaven for his senior nurses. He nodded. 'We have a pretty good staff here at the moment. But folk come and go a bit, especially the MOs.'

Fliss sent him a cool look. 'How long have you been here?'

'A bit over a year.'

'So you must like the place—or the place likes you?'

His chuckle was unexpected and a bit rusty. 'And maybe it's because I have nowhere else to go just now.'

Oh, that sounded sad. Fliss put her head on one side. Perhaps O'Byrne was in some way a refugee from circumstances, just as she was. Almost covertly her eyes slid over his hands. No wedding ring and no telltale shadow where one might have been recently. Oh, well, life happened and perhaps he had a story. Like her. 'We have a couple of residents, I believe.'

'Ah, yes.' Callum snapped himself back to attention. 'Nick Rossi and Simon Gallant. They're both shaping up well, Simon especially. Nick needs to start stretching himself a bit more. But we'll lose them after their residencies unfortunately. They'll go after positions in the city to gain more experience. But at least I hope they'll have found their time with us here worthwhile.'

Fliss touched a finger to her chin. 'I'm afraid I never felt the urge to do a stint in the country before now.'

'I gathered that from your CV.' Callum lowered himself to the corner of his desk. 'We do the best we can with limited facilities.

Max Birrell is our general surgeon and most of the GPs have visiting rights at the hospital. But, of necessity, the staff of the ED have to be the backbone of the place. We try to be flexible with time off but sometimes we have to go the extra mile for our patients.' He looked moodily at her. 'All things considered, it might be best if you stick close to me for the first little while.'

And maybe she'd just surprise him where that was concerned. Fliss's mouth tightened. She'd headed up her own department in her last job, for heaven's sake!

'Have you had breakfast?'

'In the canteen,' Fliss said, stepping quickly through the door while he held it open. 'The food was very good.'

'We're gradually getting there with the hospital's entire refurbishment,' was the SR's dry reply. 'I eat there quite a bit myself.'

'And there I was imagining you out in your bush retreat, cooking up a storm on your Aga.'

He actually laughed. 'Sorry to disappoint you but I have a modern electric stove. And when the mood takes me, I bake bread.'

Fliss had her wide-eyed look. 'Probably a new way to get rid of stress, is it—all that pounding of dough?'

'Gives you strong wrists,' he asserted with a deadpan expression. 'It's a fascinating process. I'll show you some time, if you're interested.'

This was a ridiculous conversation, Fliss thought, with the man who was technically her boss. And surely he wasn't serious? For a few embarrassing seconds she delayed answering. And then realised she wouldn't have to answer at all—Charge Nurse Anita Lloyd was hurrying purposefully along the corridor towards them.

'Emergency call from the ambulance base, Callum,' Anita said without preamble. 'A steel beam's fallen on one of the workers out at that new factory development on the Emerald Hill Estate. Jeff Curtis is there with the ambulance but he wants the workman assessed before they move him.'

'Nick can go,' Callum said, referring to their resident.

'He's in the middle of a suturing job on one of the workers from the cannery.'

'Simon?'

'Not back on until tonight,' Anita said. 'You're it, I'm afraid.'

'Damn.' Callum glanced at his watch and frowned. 'I'm due at a meeting over at the council offices shortly. It's imperative I be there. I've got to put the case for funding for more places for our aged folk.'

Fliss took in the situation in a glance. He was obviously torn. 'I'll do your meeting.'

'You?'

Fliss's small chin came up. 'I'm quite capable of deputising for you. Either at the meeting or at the accident site.'

'No. I'll go to the accident,' he offloaded quickly. 'Don't want to throw you in at the deep end on your first day.'

'So I'll do the meeting.'

He hesitated for a second, as if deliberating whether or not he could let her loose on this very important mission, and then said gruffly, 'OK, then. Thanks, Felicity.'

'Fliss.'

Callum felt his pulse tick over. *Fliss?* Of course, Fliss. 'Take my notes,' he said, his voice carefully neutral. 'Maddie will get them for you. Better still, she's up to speed with everything so take her with you.' His eyes clouded for a moment. 'You've met Madeleine Curtis?'

'When I came for my interview. '

'Just don't let the bureaucrats ambush you,' he emphasised. 'We need this money.'

'Don't worry, I'll get your money. If all else fails, I'll resort to girl power.'

Callum tore his gaze away from her smiling mouth, feeling his hormones tuning up like the Sydney Symphony Orchestra. Oh, good grief! The ink on his divorce papers was barely dry. Lifting a hand, he scrubbed lean fingers impatiently across his cheek-bones. 'Whatever works,' he said shortly, before he turned and began moving swiftly away up the corridor.

But as he quickened his steps towards the casualty department, he was dogged by an awareness, a longing that had lain dormant for longer than he cared to remember. He yanked his thoughts up short with a barely discernible shake of his head.

Hell, after all this time he'd probably be like a bull in a china shop. A very large bull at that and in a very delicate china shop.

CHAPTER TWO

FLISS found Maddie in her cubby-hole next to Sister's office and told her what had been decided about the meeting. 'Callum said you should come with me.'

'He did?' Maddie touched the tiny locket at her throat. 'Well, as long as you wouldn't feel I'd be looking over your shoulder or anything.'

Fliss's laugh was a bit off key. 'Look all you like. To tell you the truth, I'll be flying by the seat of my pants for the most part. I'd be really glad of your support.'

'You've got it.' Maddie looked pleased. 'Pop back into Callum's office while I grab us a coffee. Then we'll go over the notes for the meeting.' She glanced at her watch. 'We've a little while before we need to leave for the council offices.'

'So, what do you know about aged-care facilities in general?' Maddie asked several minutes later. They were sitting side by side at Callum's desk with the notes he'd prepared in front of them.

'Probably not nearly enough,' Fliss said candidly. 'But I'd assume that most older folk would rather stay in their own surroundings. I know my gran did.'

'Spot on.' Maddie nodded approvingly. 'And in rural areas the need is more urgent because we don't have the luxury of unlimited facilities to choose from. So, in turn, that means if there aren't sufficient places locally, older folk in need have to up stakes and move elsewhere, sometimes miles away from family and friends.'

'So obviously it's very stressful for all concerned.'

Maddie nodded. 'But, then, of course, we have the other alternative—elderly people having to wait for someone to actually die before they can access a place in a local nursing home.'

'That's appalling!' Fliss frowned over the information in front of her. 'Mt Pryde looks like a particularly prosperous district. Surely we can do better for our senior residents.'

'Oh, I'm so glad you feel like that, Felicity.' Maddie tilted her auburn head and smiled. 'This has been Callum's hobbyhorse for ages. Wouldn't it be something if you could swing a miracle for us today?'

'Hey, we're in this together,' Fliss countered quickly. 'I'd feel like I was about to swim with sharks if you weren't here to give me all this background information. And call me Fliss, please, Maddie. Felicity is such a mouthful.'

'No worries.' A smile nipped the secretary's mouth. 'I like shortened names myself. But not *everyone* does, of course,' she emphasised.

'Hmm…' Fliss tapped a finger to her chin. 'Is there a message for me there, I wonder?'

Maddie's mouth turned down in a clown-like smile. 'Possibly.'

'Ah.' Fliss gave a low husky laugh, warming to the other's light humour. 'So I should steer away from calling a certain person Cal, then?'

'Mmm—might be a good idea,' the other returned gravely, before her grin burst out spontaneously. 'But on the whole Callum's fairly easy to get along with,' she said seriously. 'And he's been great for the hospital. Personally, I hope he stays and stays.'

'Is there any reason he may not?' Fliss felt a tinge of unease. Part of her reasons for coming to Mt Pryde had been to claw back some stability in her life. She didn't want to begin feeling unsettled on her first day in her new workplace.

'I have no idea,' Maddie admitted. 'Callum plays all his personal cards very close to his chest. But we've got right off the track. I'm supposed to be briefing you, not gossiping.'

'Let's just say you were filling me in about hospital politics,' Fliss countered with a quick smile. 'But, Maddie, I do need some hard data to take to this meeting. Some facts and figures I can present as urgent reasons for more funding.'

'I can help you there.' Maddie whipped over several pages of the report until she found what she wanted. 'Callum beavered away until he got firm numbers that can't be refuted by the bureaucrats.'

'Let's see…' Fliss's eyes swooped down on the report. 'OK, Mt Pryde has twenty-five people who can expect to wait for six months for high-dependency care. Almost double that number waiting a year or more for low-dependency care. And respite care for many is so scarce as to be almost non-existent. Right, that's enough to be going on with. I have the gist of it, I think. And if I strike a blank spot, I'll flannel like mad.'

Maddie looked impressed. 'Are you good at that?'

'I've had my moments,' Fliss returned with a grin. Shooting upright, she began gathering up the notes for the meeting. 'Now, do we have a briefcase I can put this paperwork into so I can at least look professional?'

'You bet.' Maddie flicked another glance at her watch and swung off the chair. 'I'll just get one. And to make things quicker and easier, we'll take my car.'

'Oh, heavens, it all looks very official.' Fliss's heart gave a downward lurch as they joined the delegates making their way into the conference room.

Maddie chuckled. 'What did you expect? Farmers in cloth caps and chewing bits of straw?'

'Oh, ha!' With a small defensive action Fliss raised a hand and settled a strand of hair behind her ear. 'Who's the *suit* with the tan and the pewter hair?' she whispered. 'Do you know?'

'Marcus Jones.' Maddie whispered back. 'He's from the Department of Health and Ageing.'

'So he's the one I have to convince?'

'Or impress. Oh, there's Selina Edmonds!' Maddie urged Fliss forward. 'She's the delegate for the local seniors. Come and meet her. She's an absolute gem. Apparently she's almost ninety, would you believe?'

'You're kidding!' Fliss looked on in admiration as the feisty-looking little lady settled herself on one of the chairs at the long table. 'And I love her purple hat.'

Maddie made the introductions and Selina patted the chair beside her. 'Sit next to me, dear,' she said to Fliss. 'And tell me why you're here exactly.'

Fliss looked sharply at Maddie, who only grinned and explained, 'Selina's a former head teacher of a girls' secondary college.'

It figured, Fliss thought wryly, and tucked herself in beside the elderly lady. Quickly she explained the reasons for Callum's absence and that she was deputising for him.

'I see.' Selina nodded slowly. 'So we'll have to depend on you to present a strong case to access this funding, won't we?'

Oh, lord. Fliss felt her mouth dry. Was she going to flunk this first test placed on her by her new rural community? 'I'll do my best,' she said carefully.

'It's never easy, getting money out of government coffers,' Maddie chimed in supportively. 'But I imagine, as usual, Selina, you'll have something pertinent to say, won't you?'

'Certainly, I'll be adding my voice. There's no point in hoping for things unless you get out there and kick butt, as you young ones say. I may not have many years left, but I intend to die going full blast.'

Fliss hid a smile. 'I think there's every chance you will, Selina.'

The elderly lady hitched a slender shoulder. 'The Grim Reaper is going to get us all one day. I just don't see the point of sitting in my bonnet and shawl and issuing an invitation for him to call.'

Maddie's soft laughter rippled. And then she sobered quickly. 'Uh-oh. I think the meeting's about to start.'

Selina tutted gently, 'The meeting is about to *begin* dear. Only horses start.'

Two hours later, Fliss was back in the Casualty department. The place was humming. She looked around her, returning Nick's casual salute as he disappeared into one of the cubicles. But there was no sign of Callum. Was she supposed to report to him or not? she wondered. Then again, perhaps he was still at the morning's accident scene.

Her tummy rumbled, reminding her it had been ages since she'd had breakfast. She'd have to ask about the protocol for meal breaks. Lord, it was like the first day at a new school, she thought, helping herself to a drink at the water cooler.

'Oh, Fliss?'

Fliss looked up to see the charge nurse hurrying towards her. 'Problem, Anita?'

'I wonder if you'd look at a patient, please? A sixteen-year-old high-school student. Practically howling with pain from muscle cramp. One of teachers has just brought him in.'

'That's right up my alley.' Fliss took the patient notes. 'Where is he?'

'I took him straight to the treatment room.'

'Excellent. Let's have a look, shall we? And do we have a name, Anita?'

'David Drummond.' Anita made a resigned small face. 'Pre-season football training's on the go again.'

'With related injuries,' Fliss countered with a dry smile. 'I know them all by heart.'

Anita swished back the curtains on the cubicle. 'This is Dr Wakefield, folks,' she announced.

'Hi.' The teacher offered a quick smile. 'I'm Claudia Mason.' Her eyes flicked to the lad on the treatment couch. 'This is David.'

'Hi, David.' Fliss's keen glance went to her patient. He was a sports-fit, good-looking lad. And obviously right out of his comfort zone, spreadeagled on a treatment couch, with three females looking on. 'How are you feeling now?' she asked.

The young man blushed and made faltering eye contact. 'Right leg's really sore,' he mumbled.

'Muscle still cramping?'

'Not so bad now. Miss Mason thought I should get it checked out.'

'The pain seemed quite intense.' The teacher explained. 'And David's been complaining about cramp during the normal sports period at school. That's why I thought we should try to get a handle on it. Um, I'll wait outside, shall I?'

'If you'd feel more comfortable,' Fliss suggested.

'I think I would.' The young teacher threw a questioning look at her student. 'You'll be OK, won't you, David?'

'Of course he will,' Anita jumped in diplomatically. 'Dr Wakefield's specialty is sports medicine. David couldn't be in better hands.'

Fliss turned to Claudia. 'We'll have a chat after I've examined David, if that's OK?'

The young woman nodded and turned to leave. 'Great. Thanks.'

'Coffee-machine is in Reception, if you'd like a cup,' Anita offered helpfully, holding the curtains back so Claudia could slip through.

'Now, David, let's see what we have here, shall we?' Fliss's trained hands began to move experimentally over the lad's calf muscle, feeling the telltale knotting beneath her fingers. The cramping had obviously been quite severe and the muscle was taking its time to come good again. 'Just let me try something here, David,' she said, stretching out the calf muscle to its full length and holding it for a second.

'Ouch!' David started up off the couch and then fell back.

'Sorry about that.' Fliss made a small face. 'Do you get pain in your shin?'

'Sometimes.'

Methodically, Fliss began massaging the muscles on the sides of his calf away from the shin bone. 'Are you doing your warm-up and flexibility exercises before training?'

Her young patient looked sheepish. ' Most of the time.'

'Not good enough,' Fliss said with mock-severity. 'You have to do them *every* time and before your games as well.'

Feeling the tautness of the muscles beginning to relax at last, Fliss carefully lowered the boy's leg onto the couch. 'How long have you been playing soccer?'

'Since I was about ten.'

'What position do you play?'

'Striker.'

Fliss raised a brow. 'Got a good turn of speed, have you?'

The youth looked up sharply, obviously surprised at the calibre of the question. 'I can move a bit.'

'Hoping to turn professional one day?'

David's smile flashed briefly. 'That'd be awesome. It feels a lot better now,' he added awkwardly. 'Thanks, Doc.'

'You're welcome.' Fliss turned to the charge nurse. 'Anita, we'll need to get some heat on to that leg now, please. And *you* champ, have to take it easy for a week or so to give your muscles time to recover. Think you can manage that?'

'I guess…' For a moment the lad fiddled with his watch band and then looked questioningly at Fliss. 'Why do I get cramp, do you reckon? Most of the other guys don't have a problem.'

'It could be due to a number of things,' Fliss said carefully. 'If you're overdoing your training, it could be you're placing way too much stress on that particular muscle.'

'I train every day after school,' David admitted slowly. 'You have to, if you want to be the best. Goals don't kick themselves.'

Fliss's mouth twitched. 'No, I imagine they don't. But on the other hand, you don't want to risk getting cramp every time you play and having to be taken off the field.'

The boy looked as though he'd just been handed a life sentence. 'I'm not burnt out, am I?'

'At sixteen?' Fliss raised a chuckle. 'Don't think so. But young and all as you are, you're going to have to start taking care of your body. Especially if you hope to make your living from sport in the future. That makes sense, doesn't it?'

'Yep.' The boy nodded. 'So, what should I do?'

'Ease back on your training for a while and see if that muscle responds. If it doesn't, it may mean it's exhausted or lacking nutrition. In that case, the only option is to rest it until it recovers. And it will.' She smiled reassuringly then busied herself with the small trolley that Anita had prepared and began transferring the heat probes to the affected muscles. 'How's your diet?' she asked. 'Eating plenty of fruit and veg?'

'I guess. Not too keen on vegetables. But I don't eat junk food.'

'That's a plus,' Fliss approved with a smile. 'And what about protein-supplement drinks? Tried any of those?'

'Sometimes.'

'Have them more often, then. They'll give you energy.'

David looked at the pretty doctor and grinned shyly. 'I'll ask Mum to get some when she buys the groceries.'

'Excellent.' Fliss turned to wash her hands and to pass on a few instructions to Anita. Then, with her hand on the curtain, she looked back at her patient. 'I'm going to have a chat to your teacher now, David, but if you have any more problems with cramp, come back and see us and we'll do some more investigation, all right?'

The boy gave a trapped kind of smile and relaxed back onto the pillows. 'Thanks, Dr Wakefield—for the advice and stuff.'

'Take care of yourself.' Fluttering a wave, Fliss stepped backwards out into the corridor.

And right into Callum O'Byrne's arms.

'Oh, lord!' she gasped, overcome with embarrassment and trying to right herself. 'Sorry.'

'For what?' he countered dryly, levering her smartly upright and removing her thick braid of silky hair, which was tickling his nostrils. 'Have you done something…?'

Fliss's actions to free herself came to a sudden halt and her dark eyes, just centimetres from his blue ones, hazed over. Was he trying to be cute? She felt colour warm her cheeks and throat. 'Did I hurt you?' she asked stiffly.

'I think I'll survive. Do you normally walk backwards, Dr Wakefield?'

'Uh, no. Not usually.' This was beyond ridiculous. Fliss kept her chin high. 'I didn't expect to find you loitering around outside the cubicle.'

'Loitering!' He made a sound halfway between a snort and a laugh. 'I don't loiter! I was merely attempting to look in on you to see how you were doing.'

'Checking up on me, you mean.'

Callum merely raised an eyebrow. 'You seem a bit tetchy. You obviously need some food inside you.' He looked at his watch. 'And you're due for a break. Why don't you join me for lunch in the canteen?'

Now she felt foolish. And about six years old. She lifted a shoulder in capitulation. 'All right, then. But first I need to have a word with my patient's teacher, Claudia Mason. She was concerned enough to bring him in.'

'What's his problem?'

'Muscle cramps. Apparently he's been getting them frequently during his sports sessions at school and at his football games. I've left Anita monitoring some heat treatment for him.'

'Good.' Callum nodded and then added gruffly, 'I'll go ahead and order our lunch. What would you like?'

She blinked at the swift change of conversation. 'What's likely to be on the menu?'

'It's Monday, so the main dish will probably be a stew of some kind.'

Fliss's mouth flattened in a grimace.

'Pasta, then?'

'Better.' She bit back a smile. 'Thanks.'

His blue eyes lit briefly. 'Quick as you can, then. There's bound to be an emergency or two waiting to happen as we speak.'

As Callum strode towards the hospital canteen, he felt the nerves of his stomach mimicking the on-off cycle of a tumbledryer. The last time he'd felt like that had been when he'd faced up to the fact his marriage was history. Now, almost guiltily, he found himself remembering how it had felt to have his arms around a woman again. And even if it had happened by accident and been over in a second, holding Fliss Wakefield had felt good.

Better than good. He'd wanted it to go on and on.

Did he? Where had that idiot idea sprung from? He was losing it. Nevertheless, a few minutes later, he found his gaze hovering impatiently on the entrance to the canteen, until the lady herself hurried through and made her way carefully between the tables to join him.

'Everything's sorted,' Fliss said, slipping into the chair opposite him. 'The food looks great,' she rushed on, giving him a fractured little smile. 'And I'm ravenous.'

Well, surprise, surprise, Callum thought darkly. He was too. But it had nothing to do with food. Hells bells. He tried to get a grip on his wayward thoughts. He was always so focused in the course of his working day but almost from the moment Fliss Wakefield had fixed him with those big soulful eyes with their tangle of charcoal lashes he'd felt himself off in la-la land.

Dreaming.

'I got you a side salad as well,' he heard himself say brusquely.

'Thanks. Mmm…' Fliss sniffed appreciatively. 'Even your stew smells good.'

'It usually is,' Callum said economically. He made a sharp gesture towards her food with his hand. 'Don't stand on ceremony.'

They made desultory conversation as they ate. 'I assumed Claudia Mason was the sports teacher at the high school,' Fliss said. 'But she tells me they don't actually have one on staff.'

'No, they don't.' Callum concentrated on his stew. 'They share one with several other schools in the district. Kyle van der Bleik comes once a week and takes all the students class by class so it's very full on.'

'He wouldn't have time to give much individual attention, then?'

'Probably not. You're wondering how your patient's cramps could have been overlooked?'

'Mmm.' Fliss picked up a crisp curl of lettuce and popped it in her mouth. 'And Claudia told me the boys' football coach isn't accredited either. One of the dads gives up his time to put them through their paces.'

'It's a country town,' Callum said pointedly. 'Professional coaches are a bit thin on the ground.'

'I realise that. I'm thinking there may be some way I could help.'

'I see.' Callum's look was softly amused. 'What did you have in mind?'

'For starters, I could put together an appropriate exercise programme for the team.' Fliss's face was alive with purpose. 'Monitor their fitness, even be their support person at their matches. What do you think?'

'I think you should be careful you don't spread yourself too thinly.'

In other words, don't get involved. Well, that wasn't her way at all. She thought of David and his earnestness towards making himself into a champion and said determinedly, 'Youthful hopes and dreams should be nurtured. I intend to do what I can.'

Callum's brows rose slightly. 'It's up to you. Just make sure it doesn't interfere with your real job.'

'Thanks for the advice, Dr O'Byrne,' she countered, her brittle gaze coming up to meet his and finding his eyes running discerningly over her. Again. 'But I actually do know how to prioritise my time.' Probably far better than he did, Fliss fumed silently. If what she'd gathered from the hospital grapevine in just a few short hours was true. That he hung around the hospital far longer than he needed to. But then, on the other hand, perhaps he didn't have anything or anyone to get home for...

'I'm merely suggesting emergency medicine is a little different from what you've been doing,' he defended calmly. 'We can't always be sure where we'll be at a given time.'

'Dearie me,' Fliss mocked sweetly. 'And there I was imagining we shut up shop at six o'clock and all went home to our own little beds.'

To her chagrin, he had the temerity to laugh. Heartily. Showing a set of perfectly kept teeth.

Fliss dipped her head. Damn the man. For the first time in a long time she felt out of her depth. And just when she thought she'd had his personality sorted, Callum O'Byrne had sprung another surprise. It seemed the good doctor had a sense of humour—a dry one admittedly. But it was there.

And somehow, in ways she couldn't explain, it made her feel vulnerable around him.

'Maddie said you put up a good case for our funding this morning.'

Fliss blinked uncertainly. So he was handing out compliments now. 'I didn't get anything definite,' she offloaded guardedly. 'The request has to go to the cabinet apparently.'

'But they listened. That's the main thing. And you were never going to come away with an open cheque.'

'Would've been nice, though,' she replied, something wistful in her tone. 'Must be awful to have nowhere to go when you most need it.'

'Oh, please…' Callum tipped his gaze up to the ceiling. 'Don't go there—not on a Monday.'

Before Fliss could summon a response, both their pagers bleeped and they were on their feet. Fliss found herself almost running to keep up with Callum's long strides as they hurried back to Casualty.

'What's up?' Callum came to a halt at the nurses' station and rapped the question at Troy Davies, who was replacing Anita for a split shift.

'We've had an emergency call relayed from the ambulance base,' the charge said. 'There's been an accident at Trail Farm. One of the new boys has taken a motorbike without permission and come to grief.'

New boy? Fliss looked a question between nurse and doctor. 'So, is this place a boarding school or something?'

'Trail Farm is a rehab centre for troubled youths,' Callum enlightened tersely. 'What details do we have, Troy?'

'Apparently, the kid went riding off into the wild blue yonder and collected a single-strand wire fence. At speed. Profuse bleeding to the right side of his neck.'

'Young idiot.' Callum's mouth clamped into a thin line. 'He could have decapitated himself. '

'Can we expect arterial damage?' Fliss asked, her mind flying ahead, mentally preparing for what lay ahead.

'The base didn't know for sure,' Troy said. 'He was reported missing fairly quickly and a couple of the staff tracked him down. They're bringing him in and the ambulance has gone out to meet them.'

'Right.' Callum straightened away from the counter. 'Let's hope they've kept him sitting up or we could be dealing with a massive bleed. Whatever, I don't like the sound of it so would you alert Theatre, please, Troy? And better check whether Penny Chou is in the hospital precincts.' He turned to Fliss. 'Penny is our anaesthetist.'

Fliss nodded. She knew that. She'd met Penny at Jo's wedding. 'So, do we have some idea of the ETA?'

'Trail Farm is about ten Ks out of town,' Callum said. 'If the guys cane it, they should be here directly.'

'So we'd better get cracking. What nurses are available, Troy?'

The charge nurse made a face as he picked up the phone. 'Apart from me, no one. Jess is with Nick, attending to a frail aged lady who took a tumble down the steps at the town hall after bingo, and both our nursing assistants have gone home sick—tummy bug apparently. I've called Admin and they're trying to get us someone from another department.'

'Fat chance.' Callum scrubbed a hand around the back of his neck. 'Could we recall Anita?'

Troy looked doubtful. 'She mentioned the hairdresser and something about foils. So probably not.'

'Oh, come *on,* guys!' Whatever was called for, Fliss just wanted to get stuck in. 'Let's get a bit of triage going, shall we?'

She was right, of course. Callum felt the tension easing out of his shoulders. His new registrar was already making a difference. He'd managed for so long with an impossible workload, it would take some getting used to the fact he could now share it. With confidence.

He swung into action. 'Troy, if no one else is available, get Maddie to wait with a wheelchair for the ambulance. Fliss, would you run a check over what'll we need in Resus, please? I'll just make doubly sure Theatre is up and running. They may need to call someone in. Let's just hope we don't get another emergency on the back of this one,' he added grimly, as he took off down the corridor towards the theatre suite.

Fliss felt an unfamiliar adrenaline rush as she got things ready for their patient. And suddenly everything she'd ever learned in her emergency rotation came rushing back. She could do this, she thought with something like pride, and almost at once heard the wail of the approaching ambulance.

A minute later Callum hurled himself into Resus and went to wash his hands. 'Are we organised?'

'We are.' Fliss watched the interplay of his muscles as he washed his hands vigorously. 'And we have a name now—Scott Owens, aged fifteen. Condition groggy but conscious.'

'That's something, I suppose.' Callum elbowed the taps off and reached for a length of paper towel. 'Theatre could do with an extra pair of hands so I'll be there for the next little while.'

'You're a surgeon?'

'In another life. These days, I scrub in only when I'm needed.'

He snapped on a pair of gloves. 'So, while I'm in Theatre, you're in charge, Dr Wakefield.'

'Fine,' Fliss responded looking him straight in the eye. And thought darkly that if he dared ask her whether she could cope, she'd land one right on his shins.

But he didn't, and within seconds there was the unmistakable crunching sound of a wheelchair arriving and suddenly the doors to the Resus were flung open.

'OK, on my count,' Jeff Curtis said and the injured youth was transferred to the treatment couch. 'And keep him sitting up.'

'Thanks, guys.' Callum whipped out his stethoscope. 'We'll take over now.'

'Is someone with Scott?' Fliss wanted to know.

'Yeah, Doc. Tony Buchan, the manager, came in his own car.'

'Ask him to wait, please, Jeff.'

'Will do. But Troy's on it anyway.'

'Thanks.' Fliss turned to Callum. 'How's Scott looking?'

'Breathing seems OK.' He tossed the stethoscope aside and very carefully removed the temporary dressing from around the youth's throat, examining the wound with a swift eye. 'Aorta is intact. You'll be OK, son,' he said, as the boy's eyes fluttered opened and closed again. 'Clamps, please, Fliss.'

Fliss handed him the instrument, resembling a cross between a pair of scissors and a pair of pliers, and watched as he systematically began a temporary closure of the wound.

'Would you dress it now, please?'

Fliss was ready with several thick pads to staunch any residual bleeding. 'He's ready for oxygen.' She looked sharply at Callum. 'Eight litres a minute?'

'That should do it.' Callum made a moue. 'Let's get him on an oximeter as well and see what that tells us.'

Fliss worked automatically, dovetailing with Callum as they carried out the emergency procedures with quick precision. The probe was in place on the injured boy's finger, allowing them to monitor the amount of oxygen saturation in his blood.

'There's no time to wait for a cross-match. That'll have to come later.' Callum was already preparing an IV line. 'We'll run Haemaccel in the interim. Re-check for any bleeding, please, Fliss.'

'Some seepage but it's holding.' Fliss replaced the loose

dressing. Taking a reading from the oximeter, she reported, 'Oxygen sats ninety per cent.' She began scribbling on Scott's chart. 'What's his BP doing, Callum?'

'Let's see. BP a hundred over sixty. Pulse one-twenty. Respiration twenty-four. I'll get the drugs.'

When Callum returned with the painkiller and anti-emetic, he saw Fliss had already hooked their young patient up to a heart monitor. The little box like a clock radio would keep them apprised of Scott's heart rate. And in the case of a sudden bleed the team would be immediately alerted.

'Good work.' He looked fleetingly at Fliss before injecting the prepared drugs. 'I'll escort him to Theatre now. Thanks for your help.'

Fliss began putting the resus room back to rights. Ordinarily there would have been a nursing assistant on hand but today it was obvious everyone had to get outside their normal duties and pitch in.

When she was more or less satisfied she had left everything in order, she went back to the nurses' station. 'Mr Buchan still about?' she asked Troy.

'Waiting in Reception.' The charge handed over the notes. 'I got what history I could but he'll obviously want to speak to you in more depth about Scott.'

'Thanks.' Fliss's eyes flew over the information then she looked up. 'I'll have a chat to Mr Buchan now, Troy. For privacy, we'll use Callum's office.'

'Call me Tony, Doctor,' the manager said, as they settled in chairs near the window. 'This is a bad business,' he added worriedly. 'We go all out to provide a safe environment for the boys.'

'I'm sure you do,' Fliss said diplomatically. 'But it can't be the first time a lad has pushed the boundaries, surely?'

Tony's mouth drew in. 'Of course not. But we take our professional role seriously. After all, the boys are in our care.' He sent a slightly trapped look at Fliss. 'What's the prognosis on Scott? I believe you attended to him when he was brought in.'

'Along with Dr O'Byrne.' Fliss nodded. 'Very fortunately the main artery escaped damage but there'll be quite involved surgery to repair the injury caused by Scott's collision with the wire. I understand he's relatively new to Trail Farm?'

'Only arrived a couple of weeks ago. And like all our newcomers, Scott was still finding his way.'

Fliss frowned a bit. 'How are the boys sent to you, Tony?'

'They're referred from the courts. We only take non-violent cases.'

'And what was Scott's misdemeanour?'

'Nothing that endangered lives. But he'd been cautioned three times and that's the cut-off point for the magistrate.'

Fliss looked down at the notes. 'I understand Scott is cared for by his paternal grandparents. Why is that?'

Tony lifted a shoulder in a shrug. 'His mother and stepfather are substance users. There's been Family Services intervention countless times apparently, especially as there are two younger siblings. The upshot was Mr and Mrs Owens approached the court for legal custody until, hopefully, the mother and stepfather sort themselves out.'

So Scott probably had quite a bit of anger and frustration tucked away inside his head, Fliss thought sadly. But practical things first. 'Have his grandparents been notified?'

'I've spoken to his grandmother myself. I've explained someone will get back to her when we know more.'

'I'll do that,' Fliss volunteered. 'Meanwhile, is someone from the family able to be here for Scott?'

Tony scraped a hand around his jaw. 'The grandparents live in Brisbane but I should think they'd want to come if they possibly can. Scott being taken away from them has hit them pretty hard.'

Fliss thought for a moment. 'While Scott is in hospital, it would probably be best if either Dr O'Byrne or I liaise with the family.'

'If you think it's appropriate,' the manager said slowly. 'We'll have to put in a report to our relative departmental head, of course, but I'd like to keep the local media out of it if that's possible—for all our sakes. But mostly for Scott and his family.'

'I think we can manage that.' Fliss got to her feet, indicating the interview was at an end.

Tony offered his hand. 'Thank you for your direct approach, Dr Wakefield. I'd like to assure you that even if we do run a tight ship, it's a fair one and we've had more successes than failures among the lads who've come to us.'

'We'll keep in touch,' Fliss said as she saw him out. 'And I'd like to come and have a look at Trail Farm some time, if I may.'

'Certainly.' Tony spared a brief smile. 'We've nothing to hide.'

Fliss was thoughtful as she finished writing up the notes on Scott. She wondered whether Trail Farm had a decent sports programme for the boys. The competitive nature of team sport was a sure-fire way of deflecting the aggression peculiar to adolescent males and giving them a different focus. She'd have a chat to Callum about it. Meanwhile, there was something else she needed to do. She picked up the phone to call Jo at her GP surgery.

CHAPTER THREE

'OH, HI, sweetie!' Jo responded eagerly. 'I've been wondering how your first day's going.'

'Let's say better than I feared,' Fliss said carefully.

'And Callum? How are you getting on with him?'

Fliss's laugh was forced and she wondered why she felt a little rush of adrenaline at the sound of his name. 'All right, I think.'

'Well, that's a turn up. I'm so pleased for you, Flissy.'

'Yes, well, don't get carried away, Josephine. It's early days yet. And by the way, this isn't a social call.'

'It's not?'

Fliss chuckled. 'No. I'm looking for a speech therapist. Does Mt Pryde have any such person?'

'Laura Sabatini at the school,' Jo said promptly. 'She has extra qualifications beyond her teaching degree. But Callum should know all that.'

'I expect he does. I'm just making my own inquiries and getting a feel for things.'

'And you don't want to have to run to him for every darn thing.'

'You know me too well,' Fliss said ruefully. 'Anyway, better go. Thanks, Jo.'

'Any time, honey. Came and see us soon, hmm?'

'I will. Bye.' Fliss replaced the receiver and then got to her feet. She needed coffee.

She found Nick Rossi in the staffroom. He was standing at the window, nursing a carton of chocolate-flavoured milk. 'Energy hit.' He grinned and slurped the last of the contents down and then aimed the carton with deadly accuracy towards the bin.

Fliss made a face. He was such a boy! Nice though. Blond and good looking and probably breaking female hearts all over Mt Pryde. 'I'll settle for a coffee.' She made her way to the filter machine.

'How's it going?' Nick asked, planting himself against the wall and folding his arms.

Fliss shrugged. 'Pretty good. Very different than I'm used to but interesting for all that. Do you have a specialty you want to go for after your time here?'

'Nah.' He shook his head. 'I'll leave that for the heavy hitters. I really want to do my GP training, include a rural component and head bush again. Become what they're calling now a "rural generalist".'

'Crikey,' Fliss said mildly. 'I'll have to start reading my medical journals to keep up with the new terminology. You're enjoying your time here, then?'

The resident nodded. 'I'm learning a lot and Callum's a good boss. I just hope I can get into a decent GP program somewhere.' He sent Fliss one of his lopsided grins. 'I don't have anyone in high places to go to bat for me.'

'You'll make it,' Fliss said wisely. 'If you want it enough. By the way.' She changed topics deftly. 'Do you know anything about Trail Farm?'

'Never been there.' Nick shook his head. 'But Callum has. Whenever they've called for a doctor, he's gone out there. Ah—that's me,' he said ruefully, as his pager beeped. 'Catch you later, Fliss.'

A dry smile curved Fliss's mouth. 'I'm here for six months, so you probably will. Yell, if you need a hand.'

Fliss was barely halfway through her coffee when Jess popped her head in. 'Could you see an infant, please, Fliss? Looks like nappy rash to me but the Mum's frantic. And *young*,' she added with a roll of her eyes.

Fliss got to her feet and tipped the remains of her coffee down the sink. She glanced at her watch. 'Shouldn't you be gone?'

'Just about to,' the RN said. 'But don't worry, we're on track for a full complement for the late shift. Troy will be here until six and Leanne and Tammy have just arrived.'

She'd never had to concern herself with staffing problems until now, Fliss realised with something like guilt. She'd taken so much for granted in her upmarket clinic in the city… She sent a wry smile towards Jess. 'I guess I'll get around to putting the names to all the faces eventually.'

'It's awful, being new in the zoo,' Jess agreed, a wry smile tickling the corners of her mouth. 'But I bet by this time next week you'll feel like you've been here for a hundred years.'

'As long as I'm not looking like it,' Fliss said. 'I'd frighten the patients.'

They stopped by the nurses' station and Jess handed Fliss the notes for her new patient. 'Zoe Fielding, aged six months. Mum is Emma.'

'Thanks, Jess. You take off.' Fliss knew the nurse had a little one to collect from school. 'I'm sure I can manage one small patient on my own.'

'OK, thanks. See you tomorrow.' Jess waggled a couple of fingers in farewell and took off towards the staffroom.

Fliss swished back the curtain of the cubicle and went in. She greeted the young mother and introduced herself. 'And this is Zoe, I take it?'

Emma nodded and bit her lips together. 'I've really stuffed up. She's in such a mess—'

'Well, let's have a look, shall we?' Fliss turned her attention to the infant. Jess had obviously removed the nappy and the little one was kicking happily, her bright gaze darting everywhere like that of a small bird's. Fliss's look became soft. Apart from the angry red areas of skin around her bottom, the baby looked healthy and well cared-for. A real poppet, in fact. 'How long has Zoe had the rash, Emma?'

'A week or more.'

'So, any changes in her care that would account for it?' Fliss asked. 'Like a different soap perhaps?'

The young mother shook her head. 'But I've had to switch from disposable to cloth nappies,' she explained after a minute. 'And we're living at the caravan park and the laundry facilities are pretty pathetic—'

'So maybe you're not able to wash them as thoroughly as you like to,' Fliss finished for her. 'Is there a reason you have to use the cloth nappies?'

'I simply can't afford the disposable nappies.'

OK, let's find a way around the problem, Fliss thought practically. Get some history. 'Tell me a bit about your situation, Emma,' she said kindly, noticing the young mother looked tired, her fair hair tied back in an untidy knot.

Emma pressed her hands between her jeans-clad knees, her

throat constricting as she swallowed. 'We're pickers,' she explained. 'We follow the crops, pick what's in season. Here in Mt Pryde it's beans and carrots. But this year, we only have my husband's wage 'cos I have the baby. But we love her to bits and we wanted her.' Emma's eyes filled suddenly and she flipped her hands against them almost fiercely. 'But we've credit-card debt and Shane's pay just doesn't stretch to disposable nappies.' She took a jerky breath. 'How bad is she, Doctor?'

'Not so bad we can't fix it.' Fliss smiled. 'But you were wise to bring her in. And just so you know, most nappy rashes are a normal part of babyhood. It's not a sign of neglect on the part of the parents.'

'Oh.' Emma's shoulders slumped as though all the fight had suddenly gone out of her. 'I thought you might have to report me or something.'

'Heavens, I hope we're about healing, not policing.' Fliss reached out a finger and gently stroked the soft skin of Zoe's cheek. 'Right now, though, we need to get this little one more comfortable. For starters, don't use any soap for the moment.'

'OK…' Emma bit the underside of her lip. 'If you think it's best.'

'Soap can remove the natural oils that protect the baby's skin,' Fliss explained. 'But you could use one of the baby-bath liquids that don't contain any soap ingredients.'

'So, will I put something on the rash itself, Doctor?'

'Yes, but I'm sure we'll have a sample of cream in our dispensary here that will be suitable. And while I'm about it, I'll see if I can chase down a way for you to have access to a supply of disposable nappies.' She put a hand on the young mother's shoulder and squeezed. 'We'll sort this out, Emma,' she affirmed gently. Or my name is not Felicity Wakefield, she added with silent determination.

Fliss went straight along to Maddie's office. She'd been impressed by the secretary's local knowledge and practical thinking and as the hospital had no social worker on staff, Fliss guessed that if there was a way through this dilemma, Maddie would know about it. Without breaking doctor-patient confidentiality, she gave Maddie the gist of the situation. 'I want to help this young family, Maddie,' Fliss said earnestly. 'And disposable nappies would save the mum so much washing.'

'Absolutely.' Maddie made a face. 'I don't know how our mothers coped with those wretched cloth things. But they seemed to, of course, and we're all here to tell the tale,' she finished with a dry little laugh. 'Anyway, to get back to the problem in hand. If you think this mother's need is genuine, you can give her a note for the community aid shop. It's right at the end of the main street as you go up the hill towards the park.'

'And they'll supply her with the disposables nappies?'

'As well as secondhand clothes and furniture, they also carry a range of basic grocery and household items. Any folk experiencing hardship can access them as long as they have a referral from a registered service provider. And if folk can afford a nominal payment, that's fine too. All donations gratefully received, as they say.'

'That's brilliant, Maddie.' Fliss's mouth turned up in a quick smile. 'I'll get onto things straight away.'

On her way back to the emergency department Fliss ran into Callum coming from the opposite direction. She drew to a halt. 'How did things go with Scott?'

'Pretty well. Once we'd cleaned him up and got in there, there wasn't as much damage as we'd feared. But enough to keep him quiet for a while. Uh, could you spare a few minutes for a chat?'

'Yes, of course. I'm just finishing with a patient,' Fliss said. 'Where will I find you?'

'My office?' The corners of his mouth compressed ruefully. 'I've some notes to write up.'

Thirty minutes later Fliss tapped on Callum's door and went in. 'I pushed the boat out and got us a hot chocolate from the canteen. Comfort food,' she said with a stilted little laugh as she handed the disposable cup across to him.

'Thanks,' he acknowledged gruffly. He eyed her a bit warily, seeming surprised and even a bit taken aback. and Fliss wondered how long it had been since anyone had done a simple act of kindness for him. Apart from Maddie, of course. 'How did you guess I needed this?'

Fliss sent him a guarded smile. 'Put it down to my powers of observation.' Hooking one foot casually behind the leg of the chair, she cradled her cup between her hands and said, 'While you were in Theatre, I had quite a chat to Tony Buchan. What kind of operation does he run?'

'He seems a straightforward kind of guy. Tries really hard with all the lads.'

'Nick said you've some knowledge of Trail Farm.'

'I'm the designated MO for the place so, yes, I've been there off and on. The facilities are good and the staff professional.'

'How long do the boys stay?'

'Depends. The kids are there mainly because they're marginalised in some way. There are no hard-core offenders. The programme embraces a kind of outreach structure. The staff try to set the lads some challenges that will increase their self-esteem and they stress teamwork. They're counselled as a matter of course.'

Fliss looked thoughtful. 'What if their families don't want them back?'

'Mostly, they do. But where not, a suitable foster placement is found for them.' Callum drained his chocolate and threw the container into the bin under his desk. 'Thanks for that.' He looked at her through half-closed eyes. 'It really hit the spot.'

Fliss palmed away his thanks, saying, 'Could we liaise with Scott's grandparents? I understand from Tony they have to travel from Brisbane but I'd like to encourage them to be here for him.'

'Fine with me,' Callum said mildly. 'I'll brief you about his surgery and fill in any gaps you need to cover. As a matter of course, we'll need to have a speech therapist review his swallow in a few days.'

'That's Laura Sabatini, right? I've already teed her up.'

'You've been busy. Or do they call it being pro-active these days?'

'Probably.' Fliss's response was touched with dry humour. 'I feel as though I haven't stopped learning today.'

'Coming back for more tomorrow, then?'

'You bet I am. I believe in honouring contracts, whatever it takes.'

A tight little smile drifted around Callum's mouth. At that rate, the lady opposite him would probably not be too impressed to learn he'd officially *ended* his marriage that very day. But he'd had no choice. Well, that was his story anyway.

'Something in your face tells me you don't entirely agree with my philosophy, Callum.' Fliss's look contained the faintest challenge.

He gave a hard laugh. 'Crystal balls now, is it, Felicity?'

'Never felt the need.' Fliss propped her chin on her upturned hand and smiled across at him.

A tiny flicker of uncertainty appeared behind Callum's eyes. Heck, this conversation was taking on the weirdest overtones and he didn't know how to deal with any of them. He pulled his feet back under his chair, folded his arms across his chest and groped for something sensible to say. 'Uh, how's your accommodation shaping up?'

'We talked about that this morning,' Fliss drawled, a hint of mischief in her brown eyes. 'And it's fine—or it will be once I've feng shui'd it.'

Callum arched an eyebrow. 'I guess that's good, is it?' He couldn't help the smile that crept over his face. Fliss smiled right back and their smiles dallied for a moment, then caught and held—and suddenly the room was full of something neither of them understood.

Fliss blinked uncertainly. Her body felt full of electricity, tingly, strange. And Callum's laughing eyes were warming her from head to toe. Oh, boy! She wasn't nearly ready for this complication.

Neither was Callum. Were they flirting? Hell, was there even such a word nowadays? An odd beat of silence fell between them. And Callum, feeling right out of his comfort zone, turned his head to break the sudden tension, his gaze going out through the picture window towards the blue hills that ringed Mt Pryde. He took a deep breath to steady himself. 'Are you ringing Scott's grandparents or am I?' he asked abruptly.

Fliss looked startled. It was as though he'd dropped a very large, very black curtain and cut off their light-heartedness. Well, she could deal with that, if she had to. She knew now that Callum O'Byrne had a light side to his personality. But for some reason he seemed almost afraid to let it show. She wondered why.

She rose to her feet. 'I'll read through your notes from the surgery, then call them, if that's all right with you.' Before he could answer, she lifted her chin and said lightly, 'Why don't you take an early mark? You look bushed.'

'Do I?' he replied blandly.

'Yes.' Fliss had already noticed the charcoal shadows beneath his eyes and the way he'd rolled back his shoulders several times during their conversation, denoting a bone-crunching weariness.

'Who's the boss here?' Callum got to his feet, his height seeming to tower over her.

'You, Dr O'Byrne,' Fliss said sweetly. 'But surely you know how to delegate? I'll check on Scott before I leave, even though there's a competent night sister in charge, and I'll stay until Simon comes on duty. And if anything unmanageable occurs, you're only a phone call away.'

Callum stifled a hoot of raw laughter. The only thing unmanageable around the place was his new registrar. But she was right. He was whacked. He'd been there since five that morning. 'OK, you win.' He gave in, dragging his hands through his hair and locking them at the base of his neck. 'I do have animals to feed anyway.'

Animals? Fliss looked uncertain for a second and then recalled he'd said he lived out of town on acreage. 'I see.' But, of course, she didn't. She was a city girl through and through. 'So what kind of animals do you have? Cows, sheep—er, goats?'

'No.' He laughed. 'Not even close. I look after Australian native animals for the wildlife association.'

'And, what does that entail?'

'I'm not a full-time carer so I take only what I can handle. Some of the animals have been injured in some way and need only to be kept quiet while they heal. Others are poorly for various reasons. Basically, I keep an eye on them, make sure they're fed and safe. And for health reasons, I don't bring any inside the house.'

Fliss caught her bottom lip on the edge of a wry smile. 'So you don't sleep with a possum tucked into your pyjama top, then?'

'Even if I wore a pyjama top—not a chance.' He grinned, showing those beautiful white teeth once more. 'And I don't carry a fruit bat in a sling around my neck while I cook dinner either.'

'I'm sure that's a great relief,' Fliss said, as she gathered up his notes and headed for the door. With her hand on the knob, she turned and shot him an impish grin. 'For the fruit bats, that is.'

Callum felt very odd as he watched her departing back. She'd left in her wake a whole chain reaction of emotions that scared the life out of him. With painstaking care he'd spent the past months weaving a safety net around his innermost thoughts and feelings. But now... He whipped his jacket off the back of his chair and shrugged it on. Now he needed to get out of the place, to breathe in some fresh air.

And get his head on straight.

Next morning Fliss was in the emergency department early. Nevertheless, Callum was already there. She gave a hiss of frustration. The man may as well bring in his bed and park himself in Casualty permanently. 'Morning,' she said, as their paths intersected. 'Quiet night, would you believe?'

'Well, I wasn't called in so I assumed it must have been.'

'Animals OK?' Fliss asked innocently.

Callum looked at her a bit warily. 'They're doing fine.' Which was more than he was, he thought edgily. Even a good night's sleep hadn't taken away his odd sense of unreality around Fliss Wakefield.

And she looked good enough to eat. And so feminine, with her pristine white shirt and long denim skirt that nearly touched her ankles. And her hair today wasn't confined so much, just gathered into a loose pony tail at the base of her neck…

'Seen all you need to?' Fliss chirped unblinkingly.

'Was I staring? Sorry.' Callum dipped his head to check his watch, disgusted to hear the huskiness in his voice. He firmed it up with his next question. 'Did you get onto Scott's grandparents?'

'I did. They were leaving Brisbane around eight this morning so I imagine they'll be here ten-ish.'

'They're both coming, I take it?'

She nodded. 'And Scott's sister and brother—Megan, who's thirteen, and Ty, who's ten.'

'Why on earth are they bringing the children? A hospital is no place for kids unless they're sick.'

Fliss's bottom lip thinned. 'They've no one to leave them with. And Scott's mother has no relatives who are close enough. And according to Cathy Owens, they don't care anyway.'

Cathy? Good grief was she on first names with the grandmother already? And why was he not surprised? He looked at her measuredly. 'Point taken. Do you want us to see them together or would you like to take over Scott's care yourself?'

'That's very generous of you, Callum,' Fliss responded frankly. 'But I think it needs both of us. And you're the boss. You should be there. Um, there was just one more thing…' In an almost nervous gesture she unlinked her hands from around her middle and ran them down the side seams of her denim skirt.

Callum's mouth curled into a rueful smile. 'Hit me with it, then.'

'The Owens family don't have a lot of money and Cathy said they could only afford to stay one night at the motel. Ideally, I think they should be here for Scott until he's discharged from hospital.'

'So you want to have a whip-round?'

Fliss made an impatient tut. 'Of course not. But there are unoccupied rooms going begging in the doctors' quarters. I—wondered if we could put the family up there for the few days of Scott's hospitalisation?'

Callum was looking at her hard. 'Do you have this boots-and-all approach to everything, Doctor?'

She coloured faintly and laughed a bit off key. 'I guess I do. So, is it OK, then?'

'Let me run it past management.'

'We could claim extreme hardship—couldn't we?'

'Leave it with me,' he reiterated firmly. 'I'll get back to you.'

He'd begun to move away but she went swiftly after him. 'As soon as you can, please, Callum.'

He turned and looked briefly over his shoulder. 'This is insane,' he growled but Fliss could see the glimmer of a smile hovering around his mouth before he swung back and began to stride towards his office. Presumably, to make the all-important phone call.

A suturing job on a young chef who had cut herself badly while trying to debone a chicken kept Fliss busy for the first part of the morning and then Anita approached with a worried look. 'Old chap's just been brought in, Fliss. Found lying on a seat outside the post office. Looks like he spent the night there.'

'Right. Do we have a name?' Fliss asked as she made her way along to the next cubicle.

'Karl Riebel, seventy-one,' Anita said. 'No sign of alcohol abuse, from what I can ascertain.'

So, just a poor, sick old man, Fliss thought as she began her examination. Karl was obviously suffering from exposure and dehydration. 'Cough for me now, please, Karl.' Fliss dipped her head, listening. There was something brewing all right. 'You've a few rattles in there. Where are you living at the moment?'

'Nowhere much, lovey. I just doss down wherever I can.'

'I see.' Fliss looked concerned. 'I'll just check your tummy now.' She began to palpate the elderly man's stomach for any hardening that could indicate a problem with one or more of his internal organs. 'That seems fine. When did you last eat, Karl?'

The old man coughed and shook his head. 'Didn't feel like anything…'

Fliss drew Anita aside. 'How are we for beds?'

'One or two available,' the charge said. 'Are you going to admit him?'

'Yes, I'd like to. He needs to be on antibiotics and we need to get his fluids up as a priority.' She returned to her patient. 'I'm going to keep you in, Karl. You have a chest infection. Is there anyone we need to notify?'

The old man crimped his lips like the edges of a Cornish pasty as he considered this. 'No family.'

So, no family and no fixed address. Fliss scribbled quickly on the chart. 'Do you get a pension, Karl?'

'Dunno—might, I suppose. A lady from the government came to see me one day when I was living at a hostel in Brisbane. We filled out some forms, like. She said I'd get some money but nothing happened.'

'Most benefits are paid into people's bank accounts these days, Karl. Didn't this person tell you how to get access to your money?'

'Might've, but it was all over me head.'

'So, how do you manage?'

Karl looked distressed and his eyes began filling. 'I—usually get a bed with the Sally Army. And they give us some tucker and sometimes a bit of a handout…'

'OK, sweetheart, don't fret.' Fliss patted him briefly on the shoulder. 'We'll give you a shower now and pop you into bed. In the meantime, we'll get onto Social Security and see where your benefits have disappeared to.'

The old man coughed again, his chest heaving with the effort. 'Ta, lovey.'

Delegating the patient's care to Anita, Fliss hurried along to Maddie's office and popped her head in. 'Could you spare a minute?' she asked hopefully.

Maddie made a wry face. 'Seeing as I'm about to cram five days work into three, what's one more minute? Something I can help you with?'

Fliss gave her details of their patient. 'Could you begin a ring-around and see if we can get a trace on Karl anywhere? But rather than calling Social Security and being put on hold for an hour, try the Salvation Army's main office in Brisbane first. Karl might have had someone to advocate for him there. Whatever, we've got to find out where his pension money's gone.'

'Poor old man.' Maddie shook her head. 'Now, there's a clear case for more aged-care funding, if ever there was. I mean, he should be being looked after.'

'You'll get no argument from me about that,' Fliss countered a bit grimly. 'Let's know how you go, please, Maddie.'

'Leave it with me.' Maddie had her determined face on. 'I'll hound people until I get some answers.'

'Thanks, Mads. You're a star.'

Fliss glanced at her watch as she hurried along to Reception. It was nearly ten o'clock. The Owens family should arrive shortly. She found Callum waiting for her.

Oh, good, she thought, he must have sorted everything.

'I'm sorry, it's not good news,' he said quietly. 'Management won't OK the use of hospital accommodation for unauthorised personnel.'

'But the Owenses aren't *personnel*!' Fliss exploded in an angry undertone. 'They're the family of a very vulnerable patient. I would have thought they need all the support we, as health professionals, can give them.'

'Hold your horses,' Callum said mildly. 'There may be a way we can still help. All the money from our fundraising efforts goes into a designated account for emergency purposes. Along with several others, Maddie and I are authorised to co-sign cheques. We can arrange for the family's motel bill to be paid. That way, they can stay as long as they need to.'

Fliss looked torn. 'But won't that get you into trouble with management?'

'I don't see why.' Callum lifted a shoulder dismissively. 'I'm using my discretionary powers.'

'Hmm.' Fliss didn't look convinced. Perhaps she'd acted rashly and precipitately, almost pushing Callum into a course of action he would rather not have taken...

'Hey, don't look so worried.'

Fliss caught her lower lip. 'They might sack you.'

'You don't seriously believe that, do you?' Callum drew himself up to his full six feet two. 'Fliss, I've coped with heads of government all over the world. I'm not about to be intimated by a bunch of penny-pinching bureaucrats.'

'OK.' She laughed a bit hollowly. 'Thanks for going to bat for our little family.' She spun her gaze around the precincts. 'They should be here by now, shouldn't they?'

'They arrived a few minutes ago.' He grinned disarmingly. 'I found them in the car park and took them straight through to my office.'

Well, he was a swift worker! Fliss blinked a bit. 'Perhaps I should get them a cup of tea—and what about the children?'

'I've just sent them up to Maddie, and the grandparents have been provided with tea and scones.' Callum took her elbow and began steering her towards his office. 'All you have to do is sit in on the meeting and continue being the very fine doctor you are.'

Fliss was still glowing under his praise as they sat around his desk with Jim and Cathy Owens.

'Everyone's been so kind.' The grandmother's hands were clasped tightly on her lap.

'This is all a bit foreign to us.' Jim linked the two doctors with his forthright blue gaze. 'We brought our kids up right. Never thought something like this would happen with our grandson.'

'How is he?' Cathy cut in, as though she couldn't wait another second to find out what was happening with Scott.

Callum spread his hands on the desktop in front of him. 'Scott's surgery went well, Mrs Owens.'

'And when can we see him?'

'Steady on, Cath.' Jim placed a calming hand on his wife's forearm. 'Let the doctors tell us what's what first.'

'Don't be alarmed when you see Scott,' Fliss came in gently. 'Because of his injuries, he has to be nursed sitting upright in bed.'

Cathy's eyes widened momentarily in apprehension. 'W-will he know us?'

'Of course, but he won't be able to speak for the next couple of days.'

The grandparents looked sharply at each other in alarm. Then Jim asked quietly, 'He'll be connected to tubes and so on, will he?'

Callum came in authoritatively. 'Scott has an IV line in. Part of its function is to run medication into his system for pain relief. And he has a nose tube as well.'

'Oh… I never thought…' Cathy's hand went to her own throat.

'We can't take a chance on Scott vomiting,' Fliss explained. 'As you can imagine, that kind of exertion would be very painful for him with the wound to his throat so new.' Not to say downright dangerous, she tacked on silently.

The grandparents looked stunned, their eyes going from Callum to Fliss and back again. Cathy bit her lips together, then asked fearfully, 'He will be all right though—?'

'Of course he will.' Fliss gave the firm assurance.

'He's never been in hospital…' Cathy beat back tears with the heels of her hands. 'Our son, David—Scott's dad was killed two years ago in a mining accident.'

'Amanda hooked up with some no-hoper,' Jim growled. 'Never liked him. And I was right. Now she can't take care of her own kids. And we're left with all the responsibility. It's not fair.'

'But we love them all dearly,' Cathy came in quickly. 'Jim's just upset.'

'You're both reacting to the shock of it all,' Fliss said sympathetically. 'But, honestly, in a couple of days, things will start looking much brighter for Scott.'

'Dr Wakefield's right.' Callum leaned back in his chair and folded his arms. 'Scott's recovery may seem a bit slow at first but when he's up to taking his food again, things will seem more positive.'

'When will that be, Doctor?' Cathy asked shakily. 'When will he be able to eat?'

'We'll have a speech therapist review his swallow in a few days' time. And if there's no problem and we're happy with the rest of his progress, he'll be able to start on a puréed diet. We'll upgrade that as he tolerates it.'

'I see…' Cathy began to dab her eyes with the tissues Fliss had unobtrusively provided. She turned to her husband. 'That all makes sense, doesn't it, love?'

Jim nodded. 'Thanks both of you for explaining things,' he said gruffly.

Cathy favoured them with a watery smile. 'Can we see Scott now?'

With the merest nod of approval from Callum, Fliss got to her feet. 'I'll take you up myself.'

CHAPTER FOUR

CALLUM lifted his razor and swiped the last of the shaving gel from his jaw. No callout again last night. He could get used to this, he thought, leaning over the basin to wash his face. As he straightened he looked in the mirror, a welter of unfamiliar emotions engulfing him. And as for the goofy grin that kept breaking out all over his face—well, he didn't know what to do about that at all.

'Fliss…' Just breathing her name aloud brought the release of his pent-up feelings. He hadn't been able to stop thinking about her. In fact, his head was full of images of her. Her face was so mobile, so expressive of the emotions she was feeling. She hid nothing from the world.

'Oh, get real,' he muttered, taking a towel from the rail and blotting his skin dry.

He was letting himself get sidetracked by a pretty face. That's all it was. And as for trying to get close to the lady… He snorted ruefully. It would be like trying to capture a sunbeam.

But he couldn't stop the spring in his step as he strode into the casualty department some thirty minutes later. His buoyant mood didn't last long. Within seconds he was frowning over the notes from the night shift. Well, he would see about that, he decided, making straight for the staffroom.

He found his registrar and resident standing very close, their heads together and cackling over something in the local paper. Callum felt his stomach curl into an uncomfortable knot. 'Where's Simon?' he rapped, without preamble.

Both heads turned as one and both sets of eyes stared blankly.

'Just gone off duty.' Fliss was the first to regain her poise. 'I took handover.'

'And it's not all you took, Dr Wakefield.'

Fliss blinked uncertainly. 'Sorry?'

'My office, please.' Callum inclined his dark head curtly. 'As soon as you can. And Dr Rossi, don't you have something useful to do? Why do you think we pay you?'

Watching his retreating back, Fliss fancied she was still dodging the invisible bullets he'd fired. She looked at Nick for enlightenment. 'What was that about?'

The resident shrugged. 'Don't ask me. But the big man's obviously got a burr under his saddle about something. This is where I make myself busy, I reckon.' With that, Nick peeled himself away from the wall and beat a hasty retreat.

Fliss's stomach was churning as she made her way along the corridor to Callum's office. Where did he get off pulling rank like some kind of sergeant major? Fuming and wondering what on earth she was supposed to have done, she pushed his half-open door and went in.

'Sit down.' Callum turned sharply from where he'd been peering out the window.

Fliss walked towards his desk and slowly and deliberately placed her hands along the back of one of the chairs. 'I'd rather stand, thanks. And I don't appreciate being spoken to like an intern, especially in front of another member of staff.'

'And I don't appreciate being kept in the dark about another admission from Trail Farm. I'm the medical officer for the place. I should have been called.'

'Simon wanted to,' Fliss informed him stiffly. 'But I was here, checking on Scott. I stepped in and assisted Simon with the patient.'

Callum stood, arms folded, and stared at her. 'Ronan Clark's asthma is being managed.'

'Well, it wasn't being managed last night. It was a bad attack and it frightened the life out of him.'

'I'm up to speed with the boy's history. You should have called me. You took liberties.'

Seeing the hard look to Callum's mouth, his uncompromising body language, Fliss responded coolly, 'I've treated many asthmatics. Every area of sports has its share of them. I knew what I was doing.'

'I should have been called,' he said stubbornly.

Fliss gave a little shake of her head. For heaven's sake, he was acting like a small child whose toy had been taken away. She sought to explain again. 'Look, I was five minutes away and you were five kilometres away. It made sense for me to treat the patient.'

Of course it did. With a jagged sigh Callum turned and leaned his shoulder against the window. He was being pedantic and pathetic. And seeing her cosying up with Nick hadn't improved his mood. Hell! Suddenly, he felt as though he'd been hit between the eyes. Surely he wasn't jealous?

With this new knowledge he stared at her, his jaw working. 'Did you ascertain any reason for the attack?'

Fliss shook her head. 'Nothing definite. But when I was examining him I found a yellowing residue of bruising under his ribcage. I intended to talk to you about it this morning.'

'So, what are you saying?' Callum threw her a narrowed look, drawn by the intensity of her expression. 'That there's a problem at Trail Farm and someone's beaten him up?'

'I think two admissions in two days is a cause for concern, don't you?'

Callum went quiet for a few seconds and then said, 'I'll have a chat to Ronan. He may open up and give us a clue. You were right to be concerned.'

Fliss's mouth pleated into a wry little twist at the corners. She guessed if that was his best effort at an apology for jumping all over her, it was all she was going to get. 'If that's all, I need to get on. I want to have a word with Maddie about Karl Riebel.'

'Yes—yes, that's fine. Go ahead. Uh, thanks.'

Well, you handled that beautifully, O'Byrne. Callum ploughed a hand through his hair in frustration. She was running rings around him, challenging him in all directions. Her patient care was flawless, her coping skills nothing short of inspirational. In fact, she was performing like a thoroughbred to his plodding draught horse.

He swore under his breath. He had to stop dreaming like an adolescent and pick up his game. If something was amiss at Trail Farm, he'd better find out. These youngsters could be in jeopardy.

'Morning, Maddie.' Fliss popped her head into the secretary's office. 'Any joy about Karl's pension?'

Maddie beckoned her in. 'I was about to come and find you.

Just had a call from one of the Salvation Army hostels in Brisbane. It seems Karl did have a visit from Social Security while he was staying there. The manager said they'd arranged for him to use the hostel as a fixed address but by the time the paperwork arrived from the DSS, he'd moved on. They kept it there in the hope he'd come back but when he didn't, they notified the department.'

'Who promptly put the matter into the "too hard" basket,' Fliss replied.

'Well, to be fair,' Maddie said, 'there probably wasn't a lot more they could do.'

'S'pose not…' Fliss tapped her finger against her chin, thinking. 'So, who has the actual paperwork now? Do we know?'

Maddie's mouth pulled down. 'It's sitting in a mail rack at the hostel, from what I gathered. I guess we could ask them to read-dress it, care of our postal box here. That way, we could make sure Karl got it.'

'Good thinking,' Fliss approved. 'In the meantime, I'll make sure our Karl doesn't do a runner. I'll leave it with you, Maddie.'

'No problem.' With a purposeful look Maddie picked up the phone.

'So, did you manage to talk to Ronan?' It was almost an hour later and Fliss caught up with Callum as he was making his way back to Casualty from the wards.

'Uh, yes.' He didn't slow his stride. 'If you can spare a minute, I'll bring you up to speed.'

'It's quiet just now,' Fliss said. 'I was on my way to the canteen for a coffee.'

'Then I'll join you. But I'll pass on the coffee and have a green tea instead.'

When they arrived at the canteen, Fliss said, 'I'll get our drinks. You bought lunch the other day. Oh, fancy a muffin?'

Muffins didn't come near to what he really fancied, he thought grimly. But the safer option won by a mile. 'Fine, thanks,' he said shortly. 'I'll get a table by the window.'

'They're apple and cinnamon.' Fliss placed the little tray with their drinks and warm muffins on the table in front of him a couple of minutes later. 'And let's not hang about. I'm starving.'

His chuckle was a bit rusty. 'Must be the country air.'

'Must be.' She smiled, activating the tiny dimple in her cheek.

Callum felt a curious swirl of pleasure, watching her enjoy the simple repast. She had such natural charm and he felt guilty about the way he'd jumped all over her earlier. He'd been a real grouch. And he liked to think he wasn't like that usually. But the fact was Fliss Wakefield had got to him, got right under his guard. And he had no idea what to do about it.

The hint of a disconcerted frown passed over his face. Hell, he was so out of touch…

Over the rim of her coffee cup, Fliss sneaked a glance at Callum.

He was such a hunk of manhood. He gave her goose-bumps and she felt all bubbly inside when she was this close to him. Like she'd drunk too much champagne.

But she had to wonder why he wasn't married or at least in a permanent relationship. But on second thoughts he gave every impression of being *married* to the hospital. He needed to lighten up. She took a mouthful of her coffee and felt it warm her insides. Would he bolt if she asked him out for a drink some time? Maybe she could at least try and see what happened…

'Fancy a trip out to Trail Farm this afternoon?'

Callum's question cut across Fliss's thoughts and she jerked her head up enquiringly. 'You're onto something?'

'Ronan's running scared. And I think he's has good reason to be.'

'Did he name names?' Fliss leaned forward, her expression intense.

Callum nodded.

'Oh, please.' Fliss met his gaze fearfully. 'Not staff, Callum?'

'No. Another boy, called Phoenix.'

Fliss's look sharpened. 'Is that his real name? What's going on there? Some kind of mafia?'

'That's not as far-fetched as it may seem,' he responded grimly. 'I had to really work on Ronan before he'd tell me anything. Gently, of course,' he stressed, tight-lipped. 'Apparently, this Phoenix character is a bully, likes to throw his weight around—which is considerable. He's been leaning on several of the boys to steal money from Tony Buchan's office to get smokes and alcohol.'

'But how?' Fliss frowned slightly. 'There's no way he could get into town to buy them unless he walked. And surely he'd be missed?'

'Oh, he had all that covered,' Callum affirmed darkly. 'He had some of his gang drive up and bring the goods. They met at one of the farm's boundary fences and exchanged the forbidden loot for the cash.'

'That's bizarre!' Fliss shook her head in disbelief. 'How could he get away with it?'

'The boys are out and about much of the day on various activities,' Callum explained. 'It's easy enough to bunk off and be back before you're noticed apparently—if you know what you're doing.'

'But how did the lads get in to actually steal the money?'

'They have a woodwork shop at the farm. Bully boy discovered early on that one of the screwdrivers would open the lock on the sliding window of Tony's office from the outside. But only wide enough to let a small person climb through.'

Fliss felt a lurching sensation in her stomach. 'Ronan has a rather small stature, doesn't he?'

'And Scott.'

'Oh, Callum.' Fliss felt sick at the implications. 'So when the boys refused to do what he wanted, he beat them up?'

'Or threatened to. Which is what he did in Scott's case.'

'And that's why he took off?'

'According to Ronan.' Callum scraped a hand across his cheekbones. 'Thank heavens this Phoenix character has been there only a matter of weeks or who knows what havoc he might have wreaked before he was sprung?'

'This is appalling.' Fliss's voice snapped with anger. 'What are the staff doing? Are they deaf, blind and stupid?'

'Someone needs to be held to account certainly.'

'And why was there cash lying about in the first place?'

'Trail Farm's steering committee conducts a regular art union with a new home as the prize each time. It's advertised nationally. I've bought tickets myself. But unfortunately people continue to send cash for tickets, despite being told not to. It's kept in Tony's office until someone comes into town to bank it.'

'Well, that's just asking for trouble. But surely Tony would notice if some of it went missing?'

'Apparently, our bully boy was cautious. He'd already intimidated a couple of the lads into doing what he wanted but instructed them to take just enough to pay for what he needed. But then they jacked up so he tried his luck with Ronan and Scott.'

'And that was his big mistake.' Fliss glanced at her watch. 'Shouldn't we get out there, then, before someone else is targeted?'

'There's no rush.' Callum frowned into his cup of tea. 'I've already rung and spoken to Tony. I should think the police will be there by now and young Phoenix will be off the premises by the end of the day.'

Fliss's mouth folded in on a grim smile. 'That news should turn Ronan's asthma around. Have you told him?'

'Just about to. Uh, Fliss, I just want you to know I appreciate your vigilance.'

She flapped a hand in dismissal. 'You'd have noticed the bruising yourself if you'd been the one to examine Ronan.'

'I don't know whether I'd have linked the two cases as suspicious, though.' Callum's voice was clipped. 'It took a fresh pair of eyes and an objective approach.'

'That's what I'm here for, isn't it?' she insisted quietly. 'And don't start beating yourself up, Callum. You've been run off your feet for months.'

His smile was a bit forced but at least it was there. 'If I haven't said it before, it's good to have you here.'

'What time do you want to go to Trail Farm?' Slightly embarrassed by his praise, Fliss changed conversational lanes deftly.

'Barring emergencies, we could try for four o'clock.'

'Fine.' Fliss got to her feet. 'I'll have a word with Scott's grandparents. They should know what's been happening to their grandson. Unless you…?' She stopped, a question in her eyes.

'No, you go ahead.' His spun his arms to half-mast and stretched. 'You seem to have taken them under your wing.'

They left the canteen and began making their way slowly back to the casualty ward. 'I really am sorry about earlier,' Callum said. 'I overreacted.'

'Forget it.' Fliss twitched a shoulder. 'I don't usually bear grudges. Oops, there's my bleep. See you.'

He watched as she tore away, appreciating the way she moved like a gazelle. He silenced a self-berating bark of laughter. Heck, he appreciated *everything* about her. In just a few days he was already captivated by the emotion and energy she put into her work. She was such a free spirit. And it had been an age since he'd met anyone who'd even begun to stir his senses like Fliss.

But how did he get to know her? His brow furrowed. Obviously, they needed to spend time together away from the hospital. Doing what, though? His mind flipped through the options. Perhaps he could ask her out for drink. Or a coffee. Better still, invite her to his place for a home-cooked meal. She must be getting bored with the canteen by now.

A jab of apprehension suddenly attacked him in the chest. What if she politely told him to get lost? Surely she wouldn't, though— would she? Pushing back panic he didn't understand, he hurried his steps towards the wards to tell his young patient he was now safe from any more bullying.

They went in Callum's Land Cruiser.

'Tony does know I'm accompanying you?' Fliss flipped the query to him as they reversed out of the hospital car park and headed for the exit sign.

'Yes.' Callum checked the road was clear before turning out into the tree-lined street. 'He said there may be time for a quick tour.'

'How long has the centre being operating?'

Callum thought for a second. 'Probably just over a year. They've done pretty well in a relatively short time.'

'Are they having an in-house inquiry about this bullying business?'

'I imagine so.' Callum's mouth firmed. 'I don't have figures on the ratio of staff to residents but maybe they'll need to employ extra people.'

'As long as they're properly trained,' Fliss emphasised.

'That's part of their mission statement, to employ appropriately qualified people. And they come under the umbrella of the relevant government department, so they're monitored.'

'How often, though?'

Callum screwed his mouth into a moue of amused resignation. She was like a terrier with a bone. 'People are more tuned into the running of these kinds of establishments nowadays. It's more than their job's worth not to keep an eye on things.'

'Someone's slipped up here, though…' Fliss let her voice trail away. It bothered her a lot when children were exploited or unhappy for any reason. They were so vulnerable…

'Why the big sigh?' Callum turned his head a fraction and sent her a slow, lazy smile.

Fliss blinked, feeling the shock waves of its aftermath right down to her toes. It was like the sun coming out. Shame he didn't do it more often. She licked her lips and answered spontaneously,

'When I come up against things like this, I just want to get all the troubled kids of the world and gather them into a giant cuddle. And I know it sounds weird and whacky so don't laugh,' she warned.

'I wasn't about to.' His tone was edged with empathy. 'I felt much the same when I was working for Médecins Sans Frontières.'

Fliss swallowed. If he'd worked for Doctors Without Borders, he must have experienced scenes of the most awful kind. Perhaps that was why he had such a serious side to his personality. Perhaps...

'That's the turnoff for Trail Farm up ahead,' Callum said shortly, cutting off her introspection. 'We're just five minutes away.'

'Good.' Fliss found herself leaning forward, eager for her first glimpse of the place. Callum pulled into the forecourt and she took only seconds to release her seat belt and swing out of the car onto the gravelled surface. She looked interestedly around her. The buildings were of timber construction, all bungalow-type dwellings and positioned in a semi-circular arrangement. They were like ordinary, everyday cottages, pleasantly painted in green and white, and each had its own spacious verandah. Her spirits lifted.

Callum had come to stand beside her, watching the play of emotions across her face as she took in her surroundings. His mouth curved into a wry smile. 'You expected concrete structures and bars on the windows, didn't you?'

'I didn't know what to expect,' she huffed, and took a little step away from him. 'But this is good, isn't it, Callum?'

'Yes.' His mouth drew in. 'That's why this episode will have hit the staff pretty hard. So don't rock the boat, hmm?'

She put a hand on her heart. 'As if I would! I'll leave all the talking to you,' she added innocently.

He laughed shortly. 'And if I believed that, I'd believe someone has just donated an MRI scanner to the hospital. Ah.' His gaze lifted towards the main office building. 'Here's Tony now.'

'Thank you both for coming.' Tony shook hands with them. 'You'll be pleased to know our troublemaker is off the premises. He should never have been sent here.'

'So, inappropriate placement, then.' Callum was blunt.

'It would seem so.' Tony planted his hands on his hips. 'I understand it was your vigilance that sorted the problem so quickly, Dr Wakefield.'

'I happened to be the MO on duty at the time,' Fliss said with a little shrug. 'I'm sure Callum would have come to the same conclusions if he'd been the one to examine Ronan. But let's just be thankful all's well again, hmm?'

'There will be an inquiry, of course.' Tony seemed reluctant to let the subject go. 'And you may be asked to give your findings about Ronan's injury, Dr Wakefield—will that be in order?'

'Of course.' Fliss tossed a quick look at Callum. 'If that's OK with my boss.'

'Oh, I think we'll be able to spare you for an hour.' Callum threw her a bone-dry look back and then glanced at his watch. 'You mentioned giving Fliss a quick tour of the place, Tony…'

'I'd be delighted.' Immediately, Tony was in his element. 'These are where the boys live with their house parents,' he said proudly, indicating the cottages Fliss had admired earlier. 'We try to make it a home from home but with a few more rules. Most of the boys experience an initial disquiet but once they settle in, they respond well.'

He took them further afield. 'This is our schoolroom and wood-working shop. We've a recreation room where the lads are able to play table tennis, watch videos—that kind of thing. And they're learning to use the computers someone donated recently. We try to equip the lads for some kind of productive future, even if they're only here for a short time.'

'I'm impressed,' Fliss said eagerly. 'And what's that building over there?'

'A gymnasium,' Colin said, responding to Fliss's enthusiasm with a wide smile. 'We haven't a lot of equipment yet but we're getting there. And we're in the process of having a swimming pool built. Getting the funds together takes a while. Oh—that's our playing field down there.' He pointed down the slope to what was not much more than a large paddock. But the grass was carefully mown and some attempt had been made to make a running track.

'We've horses so the boys can learn to ride and a small dairy herd as well,' Tony said as he began leading them back to where they'd begun the tour. 'Selling the milk generates some income and the lads are rostered to take care of the animals. That's where most of them are at the moment.'

Fliss tapped her finger to her chin, her gaze darting this way and that. 'How many boys are resident at the moment?'

'Twenty-five.'

'Then just enough for a couple of football teams and one or two to carry the oranges at half-time.'

'Good grief,' Callum said faintly.

Fliss shot him a loaded look before continuing, 'Do you have anyone on staff who'd be capable of coaching them?'

Tony looked dubious. 'Well…possibly. But we've not thought of taking on football. And physically, not all the boys would be suitable.'

'They don't have to be.' Fliss spread her palms expressively. 'It's being in a team that matters, especially for adolescent males, and more especially for the boys here who obviously crave a sense of belonging. But obviously…' she made a small face '…I don't want to be trying to teach you your job, Tony.'

'No, no,' Tony refuted quickly. 'Go on, Doc. We're always open to new ideas. And speaking of coaches, Jack Metcalf could possibly do it, I guess. He's a soccer nut—played a bit in his uni days and he follows the UK teams like a religion. I imagine it's worth thinking about, with winter approaching.'

'And it would give the lads an extra activity and there's nothing like a team sport to get a bit of camaraderie going. I'd help,' Fliss added, and saw Callum's raised eyebrows and faintly mocking smile. She turned to Tony. 'My background is in sports medicine. I'd be happy to set the lads an appropriate exercise programme so they're not straining muscles all over the place.'

Tony blinked. 'Well, that's more than generous of you, Fliss. But would you have time? I know staffing at the hospital is always critical.'

'We do manage time off, Tony.' A wry smile tugged at the corners of Callum's mouth. 'And, believe me, this lady's energy is boundless. If she says she'll do something, I've no doubt she'll find a way to do it.'

Fliss half smiled at his championing. But she knew he'd probably nag her all the way home about spreading herself too thinly. 'I'll work out what time I can give you,' she said to Tony. 'Perhaps initially we could have an early-evening session in the gym, get a fitness programme going. And I could give the lads a few clues about warming-up and warming-down exercises.'

'And we could get a competition going,' Tony added enthusiastically. 'Play a game on the weekends. Any of the parents or guardians who are planning a visit might like to watch.'

He stopped as they arrived back at the forecourt. 'I'll have a chat to Jack this evening and get back to you.'

* * *

As they drove back to town, Fliss cast several surreptitious glances in Callum's direction. When he remained quiet, she blurted out, 'Well, go on, then, tell me I'm spreading myself too thinly again.'

'Nothing was further from my mind.'

'Oh.' Fliss felt as though she'd been caught out in some way. But she couldn't let it go. 'What are you stewing about, then?'

He turned his head towards her for a second but it was long enough for her to register the wicked twinkle in his eyes. 'I don't know whether I'll tell you.'

She twitched a shoulder indifferently. 'Please yourself.'

Callum's mouth quirked. He could thrive on sparring with her like this. 'Oh, all right, then. I'll tell you. I was thinking I might approach one or two people I know in the Rotary club and see if they'd come up with some funds to buy the Trail Farm lads a strip for their footy teams. What do you think?'

'I think it's brilliant!' Fliss's eyes widened, shining with excitement. 'But it would be quite expensive, Callum. The boots alone cost a fortune.'

'Perhaps as a goodwill gesture the Rotary could get some of the local businesses interested in sponsoring them. It's worth a try.'

'So…' Fliss hesitated. 'You're on board, then?'

He laughed and sent her a comically rueful look. 'I suppose I must be.'

Her lips twitched. 'Thank you, Cal—lum.'

Cheeky monkey. Callum raised a dark brow but refrained from commenting further and both seemed content enough to let the silence hang gently between them until they were back in town and turning in at the hospital entrance.

'Are you going home now?' In an end-of-the-day gesture, Fliss raised her arms and stretched, dragging her fingers through her hair and shaking it out.

Callum brought his car to a stop in his usual parking spot and cut the engine. 'After I poke my head in and see if everything's OK. Like to come with me?'

'Don't think so.' Fliss blocked a yawn. 'I'm off duty.'

'I meant, come home with me. I'll make dinner.' Callum almost held his breath waiting for her answer.

'Oh.' Fliss looked across at him and her breath caught in her throat. 'I'd love to but I can't this evening.'

His mouth tightened and he asked thinly, 'Washing your hair?'

Oh, lord. He thought she was making excuses. She watched as he swallowed uncomfortably and rushed in to explain, 'I'm baby-sitting for my friends, Jo and Brady McNeal,' she explained. 'They're off to some State Emergency Rescue training night or something.'

He lifted a shoulder in dismissal. 'No worries. Some other time, maybe?'

'No, Callum, not *some other time*.' Fliss wasn't about to let him slink back into his hole and slam the trapdoor shut. 'We'll make a definite time now. What are you doing on Saturday?'

He looked taken aback. He blinked a bit before answering, 'Barring emergencies, working till midday.'

'If the invitation's still open, I'll come home with you after you come off duty on Saturday. And I'll expect lunch, Doctor.'

Callum felt as though he could hardly breathe, her proximity sending a wild rush of heat to every vital part of his body. 'You've got it,' he said.

'Will you bake me some bread?'

He nodded, his blue gaze stroking her like a physical caress. 'I'll bake you my special loaf.'

'I'll look forward to it.' Fliss's chuckle was spontaneous. 'It'll be the first time a chap's ever baked me a loaf of bread.'

'Good.' He dipped his head to hide a smile. 'I'll relish the thought of being the first for you at something, Felicity.'

'Cup of tea before you go?' Jo asked later that evening. She and Brady had just arrived home from their emergency rescue training session.

'Do you have decaf?' Fliss got to her feet and followed her friend through to the kitchen.

Jo rolled her eyes. 'Knowing you were coming over, of course I have decaf.'

'AJ behave himself?' Brady asked, referring to their little boy, Andrew James, now over a year old.

'Never stirred,' Fliss said. 'He's so like you, Brady.'

'Gorgeous, you mean?' Brady grinned and dodged the teatowel his wife threw at him.

Jo and Brady were so lucky, Fliss thought wistfully, watching their cosy interaction. So much in love, happily married, each with someone special to call their own…

Jo switched on the electric jug to boil and reached up to get mugs from the cupboard. 'Brady, you having tea?'

'Mmm, yes, thanks. But I'll take mine through to the lounge. I want to catch the late news.'

'That's my husband's subtle way of leaving us together for a girlie natter.' Jo grinned after Brady had made his exit. 'Not needed at work too early tomorrow, are you?'

'Not until eleven.' Fliss looked around the spacious kitchen. 'This is such a nice home, isn't it?'

'Well, it was Brady's when he first moved here.' Jo took a mouthful of her tea. 'It's larger and nicer than my place was so it made sense for me to move in here when we got married. We're still renting, though.'

'Will you buy eventually?'

'We'd like to. Or build. Brady's rather keen on moving to an acreage block. Angelo, our senior partner, and his wife, Penny, live on acreage.'

'So does Callum.' Fliss took an oatmeal cookie from the little plate Jo had placed between them and bit into it thoughtfully. 'He's invited me out there for lunch on Saturday.'

'Hmm.'

'What's that for?'

'You sly minx. You've only been in the place five minutes and you're getting off with the only serious talent in Mt Pryde.'

Fliss rolled her eyes. 'He's just being friendly to a new member of staff.' Then why was her heart pattering all over the place just at the thought of Saturday? she wondered. 'Um, how well do you know Callum?'

Jo lifted a shoulder. 'Brady knows him better than I do. They met through the SES. They're both volunteer personnel. And I know Brady was pretty impressed with Callum's all-round skills. And coming from my husband, that's not to be ignored. Brady was a member of the mountain rescue team when he worked in Canada. But all that aside, how are *you* getting along with Callum? And I mean, really.'

Jo's curiosity was obvious and Fliss toned down her response. 'We get on fine.'

'Oh, Flissy, don't give me that pathetic understatement. He's invited you to his home, for heaven's sake!'

Except she'd practically invited herself. 'Just because I'm

telling you this, Josephine, it's not an open invitation for you to try to set me up with blind dates.'

'I haven't and I won't.' Jo gave her friend's hand a little pat and then sat back in her chair. 'But if you feel like socialising, having lunch with Callum is a good start, isn't it?'

Fliss's heart hitched to a halt. 'Maybe.'

CHAPTER FIVE

IT HAD been a relatively quiet morning. Callum glanced at his watch. Eleven-thirty. At this rate, he'd make it on time to collect Fliss at noon. 'Should I meet you in the car park?' she'd asked.

'Why don't I swing by the doctors' quarters when I'm through?' he'd suggested instead. 'That way you won't be hanging about unnecessarily.'

Now, as he wandered back into his office, he looked around vaguely. He had a mountain of reports to tackle but he couldn't set his mind to anything. Half-heartedly, he sifted through some files and put them back and looked at his watch again. Eleven forty-five. To hell with this, he decided, springing up from his chair. He was out of the place.

He found Nick in the staffroom. The resident looked up as his boss stuck his head around the door and said, 'It's quiet, mate. I'm taking off. I'm on my mobile if you need me.'

'No worries.' Nick raised an eyebrow. 'Plans for the after-noon?' he ventured daringly.

'Possibly.' Callum gave a lopsided grin. 'See you.'

'Yeah, see you,' Nick responded faintly, and frowned. If he hadn't known better, he'd almost think the big man had a woman waiting for him.

The *woman* was indeed waiting for him. Fliss was perched on the verandah of the doctors' quarters, her nose buried in a glossy magazine, when Callum pulled neatly to a stop beside the steps.

Looking up with a start, she got to her feet swiftly. In one fluid movement she tossed her magazine onto the outdoor table. Then, gathering up her bag, she slid the strap over her shoulder and ran down the stairs to meet him.

Watching her approach, Callum felt his heart thump against his ribs. Just the sight of her revved his body into a swift burn of desire. And she looked so alive, so lovely in her jeans and skinny little T-shirt, a bright red jumper knotted around her shoulders.

'Hi,' she said, as she slid smoothly into the passenger seat and flashed him a grin. 'You gave yourself an early mark.'

'Yep,' Callum replied economically. 'I guess being the boss has to count for something.'

'You're learning.' Head slightly bent, she adjusted her seat belt and then, looking up, sent him another quick smile. 'I'm all buckled up.'

'Let's go, then.' Callum caught the drift of a flowery shampoo as she tossed a long strand of dark hair back over her shoulder. He realised he felt oddly pleased she'd left it hanging loose today. Idiot, he berated himself. Get a grip before you make an absolute pig's ear out of what was to be nothing more complicated than spending a few pleasant hours with a colleague.

Deep breath, then. *Deep* breath.

'I made ratatouille for lunch.'

'Did you?' Fliss gave a warm, rich chuckle. 'I'm impressed.'

Callum snorted. 'It's not too difficult to throw some vegetables into a dish and shove them in the oven.' He turned and flicked her a sheepish kind of grin. 'And I made bread this morning before I left for work.'

'Oh, good.' Fliss gave him her wide-eyed look. 'I like a man who keeps his promises.'

'It's a worthy concept,' he countered in a slightly bitter tone. 'But sometimes not always possible to carry out.'

'Perhaps not,' Fliss conceded, and decided she'd touched him on an obvious raw spot. More history obviously and she wasn't going there. Instead, she concentrated on the landscape around her as they sped along the narrow strip of bitumen. Small clumps of thistles ran along beside the road and through the windscreen she watched in awe as a flock of pink and grey cockatoos soared from nowhere, circling in the rising wind currents, turning and gliding against the bluest of blue skies.

So much space, Fliss marvelled, her gaze skimming over the autumn grasses, their brown tinge contrasting sharply with the green pockets of vegetable crops, which she took to be beans or perhaps peas. Tipping her head on one side, she smiled at her companion quizzically. 'What made you come to live in Mt Pryde, Callum?'

'I guess I wanted a change from everything I'd been doing,' he said a bit gruffly. 'And I wanted to breathe in some clean air, free my spirit—if that doesn't sound too off the wall.'

'If you'd been working for MSF, I think it would have been perfectly understandable.'

He gave a noncommittal grunt. A beat of silence. 'Am I allowed to ask why *you* came here?'

Well, he could ask but there was no way she was about to tell him. Suddenly she felt boxed in and vulnerable. 'Perhaps that's a story for another time,' she said in a carefully neutral voice. 'Oh, look!' She changed tack, contriving a lightness in her voice. 'Those bales of hay dotted over the paddocks look like enormous cotton reels. How quaint.'

In other words, back off! Callum got the message loud and clear. Perhaps they were two of a kind. He'd told her barely a modicum of the reasons he'd come here, so why should he have expected her own reasons to have come tumbling out uncensored? 'Not far now,' he said.

Fliss craned closer to the window. 'The country looks quite scrubby here.'

'Mmm. There's a small creek running across the back of my land. I actually have a platypus in residence there.'

'Really?'

He flashed her a mocking kind of look. 'Really.'

'Will I be able to see it?'

Callum shrugged a shoulder. 'Depends. They're shy creatures. They only show themselves if they think they're unobserved.'

Fliss put a finger to her lips. 'Then I'll be especially quiet.' Hearing Callum's disbelieving snort, she raised an expressive eyebrow at him. 'What?'

'I never said a word,' he said with a deadpan expression. 'Here we are. Welcome to my home,' he tacked on softly, as they crested a hill to reveal the simple outline of a green-roofed cottage.

'Oh! What a lovely setting.' Peering forward excitedly, Fliss took in the riot of flowering bougainvillea across the front of the property, along with a timber footbridge that led across what was some kind of gully to the grassed area beyond. 'Is this how it was when you bought it, Callum?'

'Pretty much.' He eased the car to a stop in the back yard. 'Well, here we are,' he said unnecessarily, as he released the locks and they got out.

Fliss looked interestedly around her. About a hundred yards away the land sloped down towards the little creek he'd mentioned. And then higher, where the land rose again, there were trees, many of them clothed in their burnished winter colours. She turned back and studied the rear view of the cottage. It looked like it had always been there, she marvelled. It was neat and pretty with a set of wide shallow stairs up to a back verandah that ran the entire length of the building. 'It's gorgeous!' Fliss reacted instinctively to the feeling of warmth and belonging that encompassed her.

His arms folded, Callum looked at her with an indulgent half-smile. 'What would you like to do first—a quick tour, early lunch, glass of wine and relax?'

Fliss raised expressive eyebrows. 'All three, I think.'

Callum clicked his tongue and shook his head in mock-resignation. 'Why am I not surprised?'

Fliss tossed him a speaking look, not willing to acknowledge that just being there with him, getting to know him away from hospital, was making her flesh tingle, every nerve end zing. And how odd was that when she'd thought her heart had been broken only weeks ago? 'What animals are you looking after at the moment?'

He looked enigmatically from under half-closed lids. 'A mother kangaroo and her joey. Mum was hit by road traffic and left for dead. Fortunately someone found her and took her to the wildlife sanctuary. They patched her up and she's here with me for the last phase of her recuperation. Providentially the youngster, a little female, was uninjured.'

'Oh, thank goodness.' Fliss's tender heart was touched. 'Could I see them?'

His mouth puckered briefly. 'If that's what you want.' He led her towards some outbuildings. 'This place used to be an old dairy,' he explained, 'before the farm was cut up into blocks. And this is where our girls are.' He veered away towards a large fenced enclosure with a shelter at one end. 'Ah, we're lucky. Mum's out and about.'

'If I go up to the fence, will I scare her?' Fliss asked.

'Shouldn't think so. She's getting used to being around humans. And there, see? Her joey is taking a look at us from her mother's pouch.'

Fliss's look became entranced when the joey, having satisfied herself that it was safe, tumbled from her mother's pouch. For a moment the little animal paused, head lifted as if listening, her little front paws in a quaint prayer-like pose.

'Isn't she adorable?' Fliss shot Callum a dimpled smile over her shoulder. 'Won't you be sorry to lose them?'

He lifted a shoulder dismissively. 'As wildlife carers we're cautioned about getting too attached so, no, I'll be glad for both their sakes when they're released back to the wild.'

'And when will that be? Soon?'

'The vet's due to check them over in the next couple of days. I believe he also wants to implant a microchip in each of them. It'll be particularly beneficial for the joey. We should be able to keep track of her as she grows.'

'It's all so worthwhile, isn't it?' Fliss mused softly.

'Yes, I think so.'

Fliss raised an expressive eyebrow at him. 'Are you allowed to name them, or is that against the rules as well?'

Callum smiled a little crookedly and confessed with an air of embarrassment, 'I haven't named the mum but I call the little one Missy.'

Heavens, he was just a big softy after all. She sent him a teasing smile and flapped a hand towards the enclosure. 'Look, Missy is returning to base again. Wow, that's some co-ordination.' She chuckled as the tiny animal sprung deftly off her rear legs and landed neatly in her mother's pouch.

Callum chuckled softly. 'Seen enough?'

'Mmm.' Fliss turned away from the enclosure and they began to walk back towards the house. 'That was lovely, Callum. Thank you.'

For a while they walked in silence, until Callum asked, 'Ready to eat now?'

Her mouth curved saucily. 'Probably a good idea, seeing that's why I invited myself.'

'No, I invited you,' he said.

'That was originally,' Fliss said. 'I had to turn your invitation down because I was babysitting.'

'Well, you're here now.' Callum's eyes gleamed as he held the kitchen door open for her. 'That's all that matters…' Out of nowhere, a gossamer-thin thread of awareness shimmered and began drawing them slowly, so slowly together and she was much closer than he'd realised. 'Mind the step,' he cautioned, but it was too late. Fliss wasn't prepared for the step down into the kitchen and fell against him as he reached out to steady her.

It was more than enough. The expectation of a kiss was tense, sizzling, and Fliss felt its impact slip right through her like a bolt of the brightest sunlight.

Sweet heaven—what now? Desire and need slammed into Callum like a great breath of scorching wind at the height of summer. So much was happening here. So much more than he'd dared to dream. With his hands at her waist he lifted her down onto the kitchen floor. He felt his breath jam as he eased her closer, aligning her body with his from her breasts to her thighs. 'Fliss...?'

Almost against her better judgment, Fliss forced herself to meet his eyes and what she saw there melted her inside. Her mouth began tingling, sensitised with just the expectation of his lips on hers. Yet when it happened, she felt almost dizzy with the suddenness of it. His body felt so warm against hers, so expectant, so right.

They tasted each other slowly. It was dreamlike, heady, drenched with unreality. Fliss closed her eyes, savouring the shape and feel of him as she pressed her hands against his muscular back and then walked her fingers up to the curve of his neck and into the soft strands of his hair.

And she didn't let herself think for one second whether any of what they were sharing had a future. She was just amazed that they should be kissing at all and that she'd so longed for it without even knowing why.

'You kiss so sweetly,' he murmured much later, moving his hands to her shoulders and then cupping her face in his hands.

'Do I?'

He pulled back a little, brushing the tips of his fingers across her mouth and smiled. 'Mmm.'

She laughed shakily. 'No one's ever told me that before.' And what their kisses meant she didn't know. She just knew she needed time to think, time for her heart to stop its frantic beating. She took a little step back from him. 'Are you going to feed me, then?'

'Sounds good to me,' he murmured, brushing her mouth with the words. 'Glass of wine to start?'

Her mouth fell into a soft pout. 'No champagne, Doctor?'

'Cheeky monkey.'

She tinkled a laugh. 'Next time, then.'

'Sounds hopeful.' His mouth brushed hers again. 'Could I ask you to do something so mundane as setting the table?'

'Oh, I think I can manage that. Just tell me where I can find things.' A few seconds later she asked, 'Shall we eat out on the verandah?'

Callum had gone to the fridge and extracted a bag of salad greens. 'Where else on a beautiful day like today? Can you find everything?'

'Easily.' Fliss tipped her head up, taking a quick inventory of the timber benches and the navy blue and white tiles. 'This is such a country kitchen. I love it.' Bundling cutlery and placemats onto a tray, she made her way outside and began to set the weathered wooden table. Then she returned to the kitchen to help Callum with the rest of the meal.

'Ah—perfect timing,' he said, as the microwave oven pinged. 'I'll carry the casserole to the table if you'd bring the salad, please?'

'And my loaf,' she reminded him.

'Did you think I'd forget that?' He sent her a smile that curled her toes. 'One wholemeal loaf coming up.'

'Oh, yum.' Fliss made a show of licking her lips in anticipation. 'I just love crusty brown bread.'

Callum chuckled, pretending to cast a discerning look at her figure. 'I'd never have guessed.'

The food was delicious and Fliss told him so. 'When did you learn to cook?'

'Years ago,' he said casually. 'My two brothers and I spent most of our school holidays on our grandparents' farm. Nana made sure we could all put some kind of meal together. I just got a bit more adventurous about food later in life. But I like to cook. It's creative and relaxing.'

'Well, you're very good at it.' Fliss forked up the last morsel of her ratatouille. 'You mentioned your brothers—where do you come in the family?'

Head slightly at an angle, Callum wrapped his fingers around the stem of his wine glass. 'I'm the eldest. Then there's Dominic and Sean is the baby.' He grinned. 'Sean wouldn't like me saying that, though. We're all only two years apart.'

'Are you close?'

'As much as we can be. My family is from the Armidale district in New South Wales, so I don't get home much these days. But we keep in touch pretty regularly. My brothers are both married with kids, both on the land.'

'You broke out of the mould, then?' Fliss's smile was warm and she hoped her questioning was gentle enough not to be thought intrusive. But she was determined to get to the real Callum O'Bryne.

'I guess I did.' Callum leaned back in his chair. He was eyeing her thoughtfully and his gaze had gone all smoky.

'What?' Fliss flicked him a startled look. 'Am I being nosy?'

'No.' He shook his head. 'I haven't felt this relaxed in a long time. And I guess it's good to talk about ordinary things sometimes. Not that I'm calling my family *ordinary*. But you know what I mean.'

She did. 'So, does your cottage have a name?'

He lifted his hand, making an arrowing motion behind her and Fliss turned her head sharply to register the nameplate MY PLACE in fancy gold lettering attached to the wall. She chuckled. 'Original. How come?'

'Apparently, I'd been rabbiting on non-stop about "my place" to my family after I'd bought it. So Dom's eldest, Bronte, came up with the cheeky idea of the nameplate. She presented it to me at Christmas. It's been on the wall ever since.'

'That's so cute.' Fliss lent forward, her chin in her upturned hand, her look expectant. 'So, tell me your story about becoming a doctor.'

He gave her an *Oh, lord, must I?* look and ran a hand through his rumpled hair. 'We all went away to a rural boarding school for our higher education. Dominic and Sean leaned towards farm management from the word go. But I was drawn to the humanities and I loved the discipline of science. It seemed a good option when my final marks were good enough to get me into medicine to go ahead. I trained at the Prince Alfred in Melbourne and then later went over to Perth for my surgical training. Had a couple of years in the UK to gain experience, then back to Sydney to St Vincent's before I joined MSF.'

Fliss digested all that. Judging from what he'd said, his whole career had been challenging, emotionally high-powered stuff. She had to wonder just what kind of professional satisfaction he was achieving by practising medicine in a tiny rural community like Mt Pryde. But she sensed now wasn't the time to pursue any of that.

Instead, she decided to approach things from a personal angle. 'You mentioned both your brothers are married. Did no one ever tempt you to make the walk down the aisle yourself?'

His look became shuttered. 'Someone did once. It didn't last.'

'Sometimes marriages don't,' Fliss responded quietly. 'No one's fault.'

'No.'

There was a tiny silence, as if both of them felt uncomfortable about the direction the conversation had taken. And then…

'Well, come on, Dr Wakefield.' Callum broke into her thoughts, shooting her a twisted smile. 'That's me done. Now it's your turn.'

She made a small face. 'There's not all that much to tell. I'm an only child. My dad's an ENT consultant. I trained at the Royal Brisbane then diversified later into sports medicine. I was nuts about sports at school. Or maybe I just loved the accolades when I'd won an event,' she added wryly.

Callum lifted an eyebrow. 'So, happy childhood?'

'Oh, definitely. When I was twelve, I went with my parents to live in France for a year. I've been back a few times since. Love the food.'

His mouth crimped at the corners. 'So you've travelled a fair bit then?'

'Mmm. But mostly only for holidays.'

'And your parents still live in Brisbane?'

She sent him a smile that didn't quite reach her eyes. 'These days it's just Dad. Mum died from breast cancer about two years ago.'

'Awful time for you, I imagine,' he commiserated quietly.

'Mmm.' Fliss expelled a hard breath. 'But Dad's met a new lady since. And before you ask, no, I don't mind. Debra's a nice person and I always hated the thought of Dad rattling around in the family home on his own.'

'You didn't consider moving back home when your mother died?'

'Dad wouldn't hear of it. I'd had my own apartment for years. My own life to live.' She almost blurted out that it had been a life she'd expected to be sharing with Daniel, but managed to bite the words back. It would be the last thing Callum needed, for her to become emotional… 'But now all that's changed,' she added with an air of bravado and too quickly and with a small down-turning of her mouth. 'And here I am, working in rural medicine.'

Callum thought perhaps he was supposed to say here that she was making a good job of it but he'd already told her that. And as far as conversation went, he thought they'd done pretty well. Dipped their toes in the water, so to speak, and disclosed a little of their personal lives to one another.

And they'd kissed almost like lovers. He couldn't forget that.

Almost by mutual silent agreement, they kept the rest of the afternoon light, deciding to go for a walk, crossing the tiny creek and making their way along the bush track up the hill to Callum's boundary fence at the rear of his block. 'Let's sit over here.' Callum touched her elbow, drawing her across to a huge gum tree and a grassy patch of dappled shade beneath.

For a long time they did little else than absorb their surroundings, their gazes following the beams of sunlight dipping deep into the little valley below and breathing in the pungent scent of eucalypts and wattle.

'No wonder you love living here,' Fliss said softly, pulling her knees up to her chin and letting her gaze drift across the multi-faceted winter landscape to where his cottage sat like a doll's house on the natural rise of the land. She turned to him and smiled. 'You probably inherited some of those farming genes after all.'

Callum scoffed a laugh, pulling off a blade of grass and beginning to shred it with his fingers. 'This is pocket-handkerchief stuff compared with Dominic's and Sean's properties. They farm over two thousand hectares between them.'

'Horses for courses,' Fliss countered practically. 'How could you possibly manage a huge property along with the hours you spend at the hospital?'

'Point taken.' Her sweet attempt at rationalising touched him and he got to his feet, holding out a hand towards her, drawing her upright. 'Come on. The afternoon's drawing in already. Want to race me home?'

Fliss made a face at him. 'Race down that hill and possibly break my ankle in the process? Don't think so.'

'I'd be on hand to patch you up,' he declared manfully.

She gave a soft huff of laughter. 'Then you'd have to carry me.'

Callum shrugged. 'You look like you don't weigh much. I think I could manage to hoist you over my shoulder in a fireman's lift.'

Her nerves tightened at the thought. 'The heck you could!' She tried to skip out of his way, only to see his hand move like lightning, feeling his fingers slide in a quick, feather-like caress from her shoulder to her wrist then complete their journey to link her fingers.

She shivered.

'You're cold,' he said. 'The wind's freshening. I should get you back.' He held up the thick mass of her hair and let it tumble over his hand and wrist. 'But I don't want to—not yet. I want to kiss you again, Flissy…'

He was doing it even before he finished speaking, nuzzling behind her ear, whispering his lips across her throat to her jawline, winding her hair loosely around his hand and using the impetus to draw her closer and find her mouth.

Fliss went to him willingly, craving his strength against her body, his touch and his heat, the whisper of his words, low and husky, filling her mouth as they kissed. And she drank the taste of his mouth like wine, with eager lips. And it felt so much more, kissing the second time around. So good. So perfectly, wonderfully right.

Callum pressed kiss after kiss on her mouth—kisses that became hotter and more hungry. Her response swept him clean away. Urging him on, teasing. Yet meltingly sweet.

But they had to stop.

'Things never happen quite the way you expect them to, do they?' His mouth was merely a breath away from hers as he spoke. 'You've knocked my socks right off. Shoes as well.'

'I'm glad…' She looked up into his face so close to hers. 'You needed them knocked off. But now you'll have to walk home barefoot.'

He smiled. Held her tighter and looked deeply into her eyes. 'Odd, the way things turn out sometimes.'

'Mmm,' she agreed. Odd and a little frightening as well.

On the journey back to town, Callum's thoughts were churning with indecision.

He hated the thought of literally dumping Fliss back at the doctors' quarters on a Saturday night, yet he hesitated about asking her out somewhere for dinner. And she'd given no indication she wanted an extension of the day they'd spent together.

But he would have loved to suggest they go dancing. The slow and smoochy kind so he could hold her again, draw her close to him, feeling their bodies moving as one…

The scenario beat into his brain, heightening his senses unbearably. What did it all mean? It was too soon to think of the L-word. But the possibility rocked him to the core. In his passion-dry existence of the past couple of years, he'd thought never to feel that way again. He couldn't push her though. Every instinct told him that wasn't the way to go. But what was the right way?

A huge knot of uncertainty tightened in his gut. He cast it away. He had to at least try. 'Got plans for this evening?' he asked, keeping his voice carefully neutral.

'Ah—yes.' Fliss had been miles away. Turning, she smiled at him a little drowsily, lifting up her hair, tunnelling her fingers through it and tossing it back over her shoulders with a little shake of her head. 'Nick and I are going to try out the karaoke at the pub. Should be fun. Nick's almost convinced me to get up and sing with him.' She chuckled irrepressibly. 'He does quite an impressive tenor in the shower.'

Callum's snort bordered on disdain as a bolt of jealousy ripped up his spine and left a pulse pounding in his neck and head. 'I understood, with the refurbishments, all the accommodation had *en suite* bathrooms these days.'

'They do. But Nick's and my rooms are next to each other. And the walls are pretty thin.' She turned, noticing Callum's tight expression. 'You OK?'

'Bit of a headache,' he lied.

'Come inside when we get back, then. I'll give you something for it.'

That possibility sent his heart thrashing around like a cement mixer. He took a deep breath and let it go. 'It's fine. I'll get something from the hospital dispensary.'

Fliss gave a click of annoyance. 'You're going back *there?*'

'Just poking my head in.'

'And if I believed that…' She wanted him to smile, expected him to make one of his droll remarks in return. But when he didn't, she felt suddenly disconnected from him. She felt bereft. Locked out. Which was silly, she told herself firmly.

Callum let her remarks go unanswered, because with the best will in the world he could think of nothing light-hearted to say. With a jagged sigh of relief he saw the turn-off to the hospital barely metres away and thought the sooner he got her out of the car, the sooner he could begin regrouping his defences. Before he made a complete ass of himself.

He pulled the car to a stop outside the doctors' quarters—more like jerked, he thought in self-disgust, cursing his lack of control. Leaving the engine running, he released the locks, dying a thousand small deaths as he waited for Fliss to gather up her gear. As well as her shoulder-bag, she had a huge bunch of wild flowers she'd found on their walk and had insisted on picking some for her room.

'Oh, hang on, I've dropped one.' She gave an embarrassed little laugh and reached down to the floor of the car.

Callum's jaw tightened as her hair fell forward in a shimmering curtain and it was all he could do not to reach out and draw it back and press slow, lingering kisses on every part of her face and throat...

'Got it now,' she said a little breathlessly, tucking the wayward bloom in with the others. She turned to him and said softly, 'Thank you for today, Callum. I had a lovely time.'

'Yes, it was a good day,' he answered shortly.

Fliss blinked a bit. His response had sounded almost as detached as if they'd had a good day at the races. She hesitated, catching the flicker of something in his eyes, and for a split second he swayed towards her. Not far enough to kiss her but...

'Enjoy your evening,' he said, and seconds later he was gone in a crunch of gravel, almost before she'd had time to close the passenger door and step away.

'Fool!' Callum berated himself between clenched teeth as he circled the doctors' quarters and then drove next door to the hospital car park. For a long minute he stared blindly through the windscreen, his jaw working. He had a good mind to pull rank and recall Rossi back on duty. That would put an end to his karaoke caper.

He thumped the steering-wheel with the heel of his hand. He couldn't believe Fliss would want to spend her evening like that. But then, perhaps she would. How well did he really know her? Not as well as he wanted to—craved to, if he was honest. Visions of them together exploded his mind—of her wild and willing under him, her long legs capturing him around his waist, her breasts crushed against his chest, while they drowned in each other...

On a muffled groan he snatched the keys out of the ignition and swung out of the car. He'd send Simon off and take the night shift himself. God knew, he had nothing better to do. Besides which, if he was at the hospital, he could look across at the doctors' mess now and again and watch for the lights to come on in Fliss's window. Then at least he'd know she was home safely.

As she dressed for her evening out with Nick, Fliss came to the cynical conclusion she would never understand what made men tick if she lived to be a hundred and six!

As she leaned down to push her feet into ridiculously high heels, she thought again of Callum's weird attitude when they'd got home. There'd been no little intimate words or actions to acknowledge the very special day they'd spent together. No further invitation either. Just—shut down. And 'Enjoy your evening.'

Well, she *would* enjoy her evening, she decided. She might even get up and sing.

With this decision firmly in place, she gathered up a gossamer-fine silk shawl and tossed it almost defiantly across her shoulders. She'd have a good time tonight if it killed her.

CHAPTER SIX

FLISS was back on duty on Sunday afternoon. She made her way to the nurses' station and found Troy had just begun his shift.

'It's been pretty quiet apparently,' he said. 'Let's hope it stays that way.'

Fliss shook her finger at him. 'You know it's asking for trouble to say things like that, Troy. But while it is quiet I'm off for a coffee. Staffroom if you need me.'

Barely fifteen minutes later Troy sought her out. 'I shouldn't have tempted fate.' He grimaced. 'We've had an emergency call from the ambulance base.'

Fiss got swiftly to her feet. 'Casualty on its way in?'

'Ah, no—not at this stage. The ambulance has requested a doctor at the scene.'

Fliss's stomach did an uncomfortable little dive. 'Fill me in.'

'A farmer is in trouble with his tractor. It all sounds a bit iffy.'

Fliss's hand went to her throat. Tractor accidents and their usual grisly results were the bane of the farming community all over the country. 'Has he rolled it?'

'Apparently not. But he's brought down power lines.'

'Oh, lord…' Fliss looked at the charge in disbelief. Electrocution. The word had a terrible finality about it. She swallowed the lump in her throat. Was she going to have to write out a death certificate when she got there? Well, she was the doctor on duty and if that's what was needed, that's what she'd have to do. She toughened her resolve. 'So—how do I get to this place, Troy? Do you have a map or something?'

'Actually, Callum's on his way in. He said for you to wait for him.'

Fliss didn't know whether to feel relief or resentment. She recognised the shaking in her knees and relief won. 'Who's the injured man? Do we know?'

'Errol Anderson. He's well known in the district—not exactly young, though.'

Fliss fought for and found professional detachment. 'So, we have an elderly man trapped on his tractor in the middle of live power lines. Just how are we going to get to him to ascertain his condition?'

'The power company will have to get a maintenance gang out there to make the area safe. But it's Sunday. The guys could be anywhere so it could take a while until they can get a team together.'

'So we hold a watching brief on the patient in the meantime?'

'But from a distance, obviously,' Troy conceded grimly.

'Right.' Fliss's thoughts leapt ahead. 'I'll dash home for a jacket. This caper could go on into the evening. Could you assemble what we'll need to take with us, please, Troy?'

'Will do. Callum should be here any time.' The charge hurried away.

By the time Fliss got back to the ED, Callum had arrived. He looked approvingly at her jeans and sturdy footwear and said brusquely, 'This emergency will need both of us. Besides which, you don't know the farm's location and there could be another complication. I'll explain on the way.'

'Fine.' Fliss pretended a calmness she was far from feeling. 'How could this have happened, Callum?'

'Don't know yet. I'm waiting on a call from the State Emergency guys. They'll know what's going on.'

'I've included a couple of waterproofs as well,' Troy said, as he returned with the trauma packs. 'The Anderson place is high up. If it's going to rain, you can be sure it'll fall there.' The phone rang and he leaned over the counter and snatched it up, listening for a second. 'SES for you.' He handed the receiver across to Callum.

Callum was grim-faced as he finished the call. 'OK, this is the situation. Apparently the paddock Errol was ploughing was rough going—the ground hadn't been cultivated for some time. He went too close to a dividing fence and struck a power pole that was white-anted at the base.'

'Has it fallen on him?' Fliss was almost too scared to ask the question.

'Not on him directly, but across the tractor's cabin where's he was sitting. But he's injured and stuck there until the power can be switched off.'

Fliss shook her head in disbelief. 'How come he's not been electrocuted?'

Callum's jaw tightened. 'By some miracle the rubber tyres are keeping him insulated.' He swung the trauma packs over his shoulder. 'Let's go. The sooner we can get out there, the better we'll be able to judge the situation.'

'We'll have to step on it.' Callum reversed his vehicle in a swift arc and within minutes they had left the hospital and the town proper behind. 'And heaven only knows what chaos we'll find out at the Andersons'.'

Fliss turned her face towards the ribbon of country road and thought of the marked contrast from their almost holiday mood of yesterday. 'I hate this part of being a doctor,' she said candidly.

'The not knowing…' Callum speared her a concerned sideways glance. 'It can be rough sometimes.'

'Do we know anything about Mr Anderson's actual injuries?'

'The SES guys think he's caught some of the weight of the power pole across his shoulder. Missed his head fortunately but no doubt he'll be suffering shock.' Callum's dark brows drew together. 'He's a great old boy but stubborn as a mule. He has some arthritis in his hands. Has trouble controlling machinery. Shouldn't be anywhere near a tractor.'

Fliss frowned a bit. 'Is that the complication you mentioned?'

'Not really—just adds to an already difficult situation. Errol's son, Brent, manages the farm now but Errol still insists on "helping".'

'Which this escapade proves he's *not*,' Fliss sighed.

'No. And right now Brent and his wife, Michelle, could have done without this drama. Michelle is expecting their first baby in a few weeks. When Errol didn't turn up for his lunch, she went looking for him…'

'Oh, no. She found him?'

'Yes. She'll be pretty shocked. May need a calming influence.'

Hers presumably. Fliss nibbled her bottom lip and wondered whether they were looking at a premature labour thrown into the equation as well? 'Where's the son—Brent?'

'Out all day with the pickers on the other side of the property, apparently. One of the SES team has gone to find him and bring him back.'

'Surely the family should be in touch with mobile phones, especially with Michelle about to deliver?'

Callum shrugged. 'I guess they will be from now on. Sometimes lessons have to be learned the hard way.'

Fliss glanced at her watch and thought starkly about the possible scenario they were facing. 'I'm on a steep learning curve here to some extent, Callum. What's the plan when we get there?'

'I guess much will depend on how soon the area can be made safe.' He gunned the motor and they began to climb higher.

Fliss felt the nerves in her stomach react. This wasn't the soft green countryside she'd become accustomed to. This was wild, all bony ridges, huge rocks and windblown tussocks.

'We may have to consider pain relief orally,' Callum said cautiously. 'That's if we can get close enough to Errol with safety.'

'That's a big "if", isn't it?' Fliss's reply was sceptical.

In answer, Callum's mouth pulled tighter. He swung the vehicle through the farm gates, the big tyres rattling over the metal grid. 'According to the directions I have, we head about two Ks northwest from here. That should bring us close to the accident scene.'

Thank heavens for his off-road vehicle, Fliss thought as they juddered and bumped over the rough terrain. But Callum seemed to know what he was doing and soon, he was nosing in beside the bright yellow vehicles belonging to the rescue team.

Fliss closed her eyes and swallowed as the enormity of what they were facing hit her.

Callum, sensing her unease, said quietly, 'It'll be OK. Just follow my lead.'

She shot him a wry look. 'And don't do anything stupid?'

'That'll help.' He managed a bark of grim laughter and reached out to cover her hand with his larger one and squeezed. 'They're waiting for us, Doctor. Let's go do what we do best.'

There wasn't a moment to lose. Fliss almost threw herself out of the car, looking around to get her bearings. She suppressed a shiver. The tension in the air was palpable.

And no wonder. She stood in stunned horror. Several hundred metres up the hill a grey tractor was skewed into the fence, imprisoned by a band of sparking wires.

'Heck of a situation, folks,' Jeff Curtis, the ambulance officer said in an undertone. 'I can't get any sense out of Michelle about how she's feeling. I offered to take her back to the house but she refused absolutely. Said she needs to know what's going on with Errol.'

'Well, that's understandable.' Shading her eyes, Fliss looked to where the obviously pregnant young woman stood halfway up the hill, arms folded protectively across her tummy. Oh, poor love… Fliss took off in a run.

'Felicity!' Callum's bark was like a whiplash. 'What do you think you're doing?'

'I'm seeing to Michelle, as you asked me to…'

'Not until we know where we can safely put our feet you're not!'

Fliss jerked to a stop. She'd done the unthinkable—plunged ahead without thinking of the consequences. Cheeks on fire, she made her way back to the assembled group of emergency workers. She mumbled an apology, preparing to be bawled out by Callum.

Instead, he drew her aside and said calmly, 'I realise your natural response is to help. But the last thing we need is another casualty. So let's wait until the SES chief briefs us before we do anything, all right?'

Fliss bit her lips together and nodded.

'Everyone, if I can have your attention, please?' Steve Conroy, the team leader from the State Emergency Service, looked measuredly at the company. 'The responsibility for a successful outcome for Errol depends entirely on everyone's co-operation. Understood?'

A murmur of agreement went around the ranks.

'I've had word from the electricity people. They're in the process of organising their flying gang. Hopefully, they'll be on their way to disconnect the power pretty soon.'

'Where's the actual transformer located, Steve?' Callum asked the question on everyone's minds.

'Up near the house, I reckon.' Steve rubbed a hand around his jaw. 'Someone will alert us the moment it's rendered inactive. Meanwhile we wait.'

Callum wasn't satisfied with that. 'Can I at least get close enough to Errol to ascertain how he's doing?'

Fliss felt a lurching sensation in her stomach. Hadn't he taken on board *anything* Steve Conroy had said?

The SES leader looked doubtful. 'It's a possibility…as long as you follow my instructions to the letter, Callum. No heroics. And I mean that.'

'Understood. Fliss?' With his hand on her arm, Callum drew them aside from the group. 'We'll need to wear special gear for this junket.'

Fliss sent him an uncertain look. But she presumed he meant the thick overalls and insulated boots the emergency people were wearing. She steadied herself for what lay ahead—a medical retrieval that was rapidly turning into the stuff of nightmares.

Nevertheless, Fliss's expression was clearly determined as she pulled on the orange-coloured overalls with the insignia on the back that indicated the wearer was a doctor. 'I need to check Michelle over, Callum.'

'I'm aware of that.' Callum dipped his head into the rear of the emergency vehicle and emerged with a pair of thick-soled boots. 'Here, these look about your size. You take care of Michelle and I'll do a wander and see what I can make of Errol's condition. Agreed?'

Fliss's mouth pressed down in disapproval. Even with the insulated clothing, Callum's safety couldn't be guaranteed. She had no real idea but surely the downed lines had to be generating enough volts to flatten a rhinoceros—let alone a man. 'Shouldn't you be waiting until the power is cut?'

'I'll be safe enough,' he said dismissively. 'I'm guessing Errol will be scared witless, which will be exacerbating his pain. I intend to get treatment to him whatever way I can.'

Fliss snorted rudely. 'Heroes have a limited lifespan, Callum.'

'Heroines, too, Felicity,' he countered, his eyes glinting. 'How the hell do you imagine I felt, seeing you taking off earlier?'

'OK, OK.' She held up her hands. 'I'm suitably chastened. Just let's get on with it.'

Callum swung up one of the trauma kits and handed her the other one. 'Try to get Michelle back down here to base. At least then you'll be able to keep an eye on her for post-trauma signs. There's no guarantee how long we'll be here, so there'll be food and hot drinks laid on for everyone.' He turned as Steve Conroy approached.

'If you're ready, Callum, we'll make tracks up to Errol.'

'Right. In the meantime, Fliss is going to check Michelle. I'd like an escort for her, please.'

'Jonno can go.' Steve beckoned to a young man who was

watching keenly from a short distance away. 'He's a local, one of
our more experienced members. He tells me he went to school with
Michelle. It might help her to see a friendly face.'

As they moved off in different directions, Fliss felt an odd dis-
connectedness with the unfamiliar situation. Fleetingly she
looked back at Callum, hoping to gain an added grain of reassurance in the form of a quick nod, a lift of his hand—even a bleak
smile would have done. But he was already on his way, accompanied by Steve, and moving painstakingly over the rough
ground towards the accident scene. A sudden anxiety for his
welfare claimed centre stage in her mind. If anything happened
to him… It didn't bear thinking about. Please, keep him safe, she
prayed silently.

'We should be OK if we go this way,' Jonno said. 'Let's hope it
doesn't start raining, eh, Doc? We'll be in big strife if a storm breaks.'

Fliss felt a prickle of unease. Water was a natural conductor of
electricity. The possible scenario Jonno was painting sent the
nerves of her stomach into a tight ball. Almost in defiance, she
hitched her trauma pack higher and followed in her guide's wake
as he led them through bracken and coarse ferns to where the
young mother-to-be stood like a small, silent statue.

'Michelle…?' Fliss was close enough to call gently. 'I'm Fliss
Wakefield. I'm a doctor at the hospital. Will you let me help you?'

Michelle turned and stared blankly. Then her eye lids flickered.
'I…need Brent to be here…'

'Take it easy, Shell,' Jonno said gently. 'One of the guys has
gone to get him. The Doc here just wants to make sure you're OK.'

Fliss lowered the trauma pack to the ground. 'Jonno, would you
get a space blanket out for me, please? Michelle looks frozen to
the bone.' Almost on reflex Fliss had taken Michelle's hands and
began rubbing heat into them, unobtrusively feeling for the
young's woman's pulse. So far, so good, she decided.

'Will Errol be all right?' Michelle turned stricken eyes back up
the hill towards the tractor.

No one could know that for sure. Fliss and Jonno exchanged
guarded looks. 'Dr O'Byrne's gone up there, Michelle.' Fliss
wrapped her arm around the girl's shoulders in a comforting
squeeze. 'He's very experienced. He'll do whatever it takes to
give medical help to your father-in-law.'

Michelle's hands fluttered to her tummy. 'This is his first grandchild. We know it's a boy and Errol's been so excited…' She paused and shook her head despairingly.

'Chill out, Shell,' Jonno said bracingly. 'Errol's a tough old coot. Bet your boots he'll come out of this with a stupid grin on his face.'

Michelle managed the ghost of a smile. 'You reckon?'

'Yep. For sure.'

Jonno's firm reassuring response won approval from Fliss. Perhaps now was the time to coax Michelle away from her lonely vigil and back down to the tent the SES had erected. At least she'd have more privacy there to examine her patient—that's if Michelle would allow her to, of course.

As if he'd read her thoughts, Jonno spoke again. 'Come on, Shell, it's freezing here. Let's get you back down to base and the doc can look you over, OK?'

With Michelle more or less settled, Fliss asked Jonno if he would accompany her up the hill to Callum.

Jonno looked uneasy. 'I don't think Callum would be too happy with that idea, Doc.'

'If we follow the path they took, we should be all right,' she insisted. 'I just can't hang about here, Jonno. And I might be of some help when they get Errol free.'

Callum was aware of their approach. He took a breath, its rough expulsion laced with frustration. The whole rescue business was dragging on far longer than he'd anticipated. Eyes narrowed, he watched Steve pocket his mobile phone. 'Any news?'

'They've had a few hiccups, Doc. Still can't give us an ETA.'

'Get that insulating device you mentioned, then, Steve.' Callum sounded very definite and full of authority. 'I'm not waiting any longer.'

'Callum—?'

Twisting his head, he gave Fliss and then Jonno a questioning look. 'What's this, a deputation?'

Fliss stood her ground. 'Michelle is fretting about Errol. I told her I'd find out what's happening.'

'Precious little, as you can see. How's Michelle doing?'

'She's still a bit shaky. No sign of contractions, thankfully. Brent's with her now but she's scared stiff for Errol.'

'Aren't we all?' Callum drew in a long breath and let it go.

'How does he seem?' Fliss's sharp look went to where the

elderly man's head was just a silver-grey blur through the splintered window of the tractor's cabin.

'I've managed a bit of sign language with him. Everything points to a dislocated shoulder. And he's feeling ill. At this point the last thing he needs in his exhausted state is a bout of vomiting.'

The scenario they were facing hit Fliss like a lead weight. 'You're going to try to give him pain relief orally, aren't you?'

Callum frowned. 'Is there a choice? I don't see one.'

Fliss sent him a stricken look. 'Surely the power people can't be much longer?'

'They're somewhere on the way to us, that's all we know.' Callum hunkered down and began selecting the drugs from the trauma kit.

Fliss felt her throat tighten. 'What are you giving him?'

'Morphine syrup, five milligrams. It's a relatively light dose but we can't risk upsetting his stomach any more than it is already.'

So, he'd add an anti-emetic and hope to heaven it kept the morphine down. Fliss watched as he prepared the medication, securing it in a plastic container small enough to pass through the jagged opening in the tractor's windshield yet simple enough for Errol to grasp and swallow the contents. As doctors, they both knew it was a gamble but, then, in the uncertainty of the conditions they were faced with, it was the only option available.

Fliss's eyes widened in disbelief when Steve handed Callum the insulating device—nothing more than a stick made of fibreglass. 'And that it?' She looked at the team leader, appalled.

'Should do the job,' Steve replied gruffly. 'And I don't like this any more than you do, Doc.' Slowly and carefully, Steve's broad fingers taped the little container of medication to one end of the stick. 'Now, you know what to do, Callum,' he reinforced, slicing the tape neatly.

'I know what to do. And thanks for your co-operation here, Steve.'

He was really going to do it. Fliss realised her heart was pounding and her breath tight, so tight. He was going to walk into that electrical minefield with minimum protection of his person and a *stick* to protect him from getting zapped. 'I don't think you should be doing this, Callum.'

He ground out a harsh expletive. 'I'm doing my job, Fliss. And if you can't watch, go back down and keep Michelle company.'

'Don't patronise me!' Her eyes sparked. 'I'll be here—in case *you* need rescuing.'

His mouth dipped into a lopsided grin. 'That thought's cheered me up no end.'

Stubborn man. Fliss's breath spun out on a tight little sigh. It was useless telling herself Callum had taken every precaution. Anyone who spent any time in an emergency department knew that accidents could and did still happen as swiftly as taking a breath. 'Just make sure you get back here in one piece,' she threatened softly.

Callum's jaw tightened but he turned away without further comment.

Fearing for him, praying for him, Fliss watched as Callum moved inch by careful inch closer to his target. And it seemed as if the world about her had shrunk, become muted, almost surreal.

'Stop there!' Steve's snapped command sent Fliss's hand to her mouth.

And then it was done. Callum had made the transfer and Errol had swallowed his painkiller and Callum was reversing his steps, backing away from the crackling power lines with studied slowness. Until he was well away, striding to safety.

Fliss's arms ached to reach out to him, to hold him, but professionalism kept her arms stiffly at her sides, her fingers bunched tightly. 'Well done,' she said quietly.

'Took guts, all right,' Steve agreed, his mouth compressing.

Now what? Emotions began clogging Fliss's throat. So much had gone on here today and was still going on. And there was such a quiet dignity about these bush people, an inbuilt instinct to do the best for one another that they possibly could. And Callum was the centre of it. They depended on him. She'd even go so far as to say that in medical matters his word was law.

A sudden warmth shot through her. Almost without her knowing, she'd become part of this community as well.

And it felt good.

She had no time to become too introspective. At Callum's request, she'd made her way back down to Michelle to reassure her about her father-in-law's condition. And then, satisfied there was nothing more she could do for the moment, she retraced her steps to Callum.

'What's the word?' He was carefully monitoring his watch, not looking up.

'Things are OK for now. Brent seems a steadying influence. But the waiting is getting to everyone.'

'Almost twenty minutes since Errol had his medication,' Callum said with quiet triumph.

'So far so good, then.' Fliss looked up at the sky. The day was already drawing in and huge black clouds were hugging the tops of the mountains. Surely the men would get there soon…

'The guys are here.' Steve materialised quietly beside them. 'They're at the transformer now.'

'So, any minute?' Fliss's voice rang with a kind of muted relief.

'Stay calm,' Callum said tightly.

But *calm* was hard to manage. And it seemed word had already travelled that the power was about to be switched off and the area made safe. There was an expectation in the air, the whole atmosphere bristling with suspense, straining towards a climax.

'There they go…' Fliss's hand went to her throat as the electrical sparks, bright and white, sputtered and died. 'Oh.' Out of the blue, she felt her mouth trembling uncontrollably, and tears of reaction spilled down her cheeks. Hastily, she blinked them away, holding her hands against her eyes, gathering her composure.

'Fliss? Hey…' Callum's arm came round her shoulders hugging her. 'No need for tears. We're safe now.'

'I— Yes, I know… It's great,' she said huskily, turning to meet his eyes briefly and then looking back at the scene before them.

'Things will start happening quickly now,' Callum said with quiet certainty.

And he was right, Fliss realised with something like amazement. It was as if the starter had fired his pistol. A huge cheer rang out, echoing up and down the hillside. Engines were gunned into life and emergency vehicles fanned out and began racing to the accident scene.

'Stand back.' Callum placed a guiding arm at Fliss's elbow as the crews thrust forward with wrecking bars. Within seconds the doors of the tractor's cabin were sliced through and Errol was being lifted gently out and laid on to a stretcher.

Callum's examination of his patient was swift and sure.

'What's…the damage, Doc?' Errol's words were strained.

'You'll live, old mate. No more messing with machinery, though.'

'Reckon not…'

'Fliss, I'll need you here, please.' Callum motioned her to the top of the stretcher.

'Now?' Her eyes widened in query.

'I don't want to dope him any more than is necessary. So let's give it one shot to pop that shoulder back in, shall we?'

They worked instinctively, Fliss steadying the injured man while Callum repositioned the shoulder.

'Ready?'

Fliss nodded and braced herself for Errol's pain-edged groan as the limb clicked back into place.

'I'll ride back in the ambulance with him,' Fliss said briskly. 'Michelle?' She looked around for her other patient.

'I'm here, Doctor…'

Fliss's heart contracted. The young mother-to-be looked pale again. The adrenaline rush that had come with the rescue of her father-in-law had subsided and she was beginning to exhibit all the signs of post-trauma exhaustion. 'I'd like you to come back to the hospital and be checked over thoroughly, Michelle. Could you come in with Brent?'

Michelle swallowed hard. 'What about Errol? Shouldn't one of us stay with him?'

'I'll travel back in the ambulance with him,' Fliss said. 'And I promise to take great care of him.'

'Everything OK from your end?' Callum asked. It was nearly two hours after the hillside rescue.

Fliss nodded. 'The midwife checked Michelle over. She seems fine but they've decided to keep her overnight. How's Errol?'

Callum gave a hollow laugh. 'Feeling pretty sorry for himself. I'm keeping him in. He needs to be perfectly stable before he goes home. Michelle doesn't need extra work.'

'Is there no Mrs Anderson, senior?'

'He's a widower,' Callum said shortly. 'He wanted to move out of the family home when the young people got married but they wouldn't hear of it. He's very fond of Michelle. Excited about the baby.'

'Mmm, she mentioned that.' Fliss's look was soft. 'Nice when families get on.'

And marriages worked, Callum thought bitterly, but kept his mouth firmly shut on the subject. 'What are you up to now?' he asked instead.

'I'm still on duty.'

'No, you're not. I worked for Simon last night. He's happy to come in early and cover the last of your shift.'

Fliss rolled her eyes. 'Callum, I don't need favours.'

'Who mentioned favours?' He lifted a broad shoulder dismissively. 'It's called being flexible.'

'And that applies to all of us, I presume.' Fliss fixed him with an innocent look. 'So, if Simon's on take, that means you and I are both off duty.'

'So?'

Fliss looked more keenly at him, taking in the lines of strain around his eyes, the almost grim set of his mouth and wondered how much of an ordeal the afternoon's medical retrieval had been for him. He needed to relax. But whether or not he'd let her help him do just that was another matter entirely.

But she had to try.

'*So* why don't you come over to my place and we'll send out for a pizza? I might even find a nice bottle of merlot to go with it. Interested?'

'Could be.' His smile felt crooked. But he could no more resist her invitation than fly like Superman over the treetops. 'But not without a shower.'

Fliss's sense of triumph faltered. Did that mean he'd have to go home and change? And if so, would he really want to come all the way back to town? She had to head him off at the pass. 'Shower and change into scrubs, then. I don't mind.'

'Are you that desperate for my company, Dr Wakefield?'

Oh, heck—had he read her mind? 'Must be,' she managed lightly, reaching out to touch his cheek, and her heart hiccupped. She reclaimed her hand quickly but not before the slight roughness of his stubble had shot her nerve endings to pieces, leaving them jangling and aware.

'Not to worry.' He reciprocated, stroking the back of his index finger gently over the curve of her cheek and across her chin. 'I keep a change of clothes here. I can be with you in ten minutes.'

'Fine,' she countered weakly. 'I'll, um, scoot home and order the pizza, then.'

'With all the toppings, please. I'm starving.'

And not just for pizza, she'd bet. His body was very close, his mouth closer still. And there was such a need inside her… She tried to laugh but the laughter caught in her throat and she swallowed hard. 'See you in ten,' she managed huskily, before she swung on her heel and hurried away.

Fliss showered hastily, the butterflies in her stomach having a grand old time as they fluttered non-stop, as if debating whether to make her feel sick with anticipation or merely sick! Oh, for heaven's sake, get a grip, she admonished herself. It was simply going to be an impromptu meal with a colleague and a glass of wine to wash down the pizza.

Who was she kidding? With shaking fingers, she towelled herself dry and slid her legs into her jeans and pulled on a khaki sweater with a deep V neckline. The evening wasn't about pizza or wine. It was about a man and a woman. And they both knew it!

She didn't bother with make-up and had just dragged a brush through her hair when the knock came softly on her door.

In the few seconds while he waited for Fliss to answer the door, the silence was absolute and Callum was more than a bit disturbed to find that through it he could hear the thudding of his own heart.

'Hi.' Fliss opened the door and again felt the swoop of butterflies in her tummy. 'Nice timing,' she said, opening the door to let him come in. In a nervous gesture she bit into the softness of her lower lip, her gaze flicking over him. He was dressed in well-worn jeans and a lightweight black jumper, the sleeves pushed back over his tanned forearms. 'Uh, glass of wine?'

'Sounds good.'

'Not much room in these places,' she apologised, moving across to the minuscule kitchen bench where she'd left the merlot to breathe.

'You've made it nice, though.' Callum's eyes did a quick inventory, taking in the scattering of photographs, the wildflowers from yesterday in their glass jug and the bright cloth she'd thrown over the little round table near the window. His mouth twitched into a wry smile. 'Is this the result of your feng shui make-over?'

'I just moved things around a bit,' she said casually. 'Borrowed that gorgeous screen from Jo to hide my bed and added my own bits and pieces.' She finished pouring the wine and replaced the bottle on the bench. Picking up one of the glasses, she turned to hand him his drink. He was much closer than she'd realised and as she turned she bumped into him and he reached out to steady her.

It was enough to reignite the tension that had been lashing the air between them since their hungry kisses yesterday.

'You seem to be making a habit of this.' Callum's voice was throatily soft. He took the glass from her nerveless fingers and put it down.

Her heartbeat revved as he turned back to her. 'What habit?'

'Falling into my arms.'

'As long as you're there to catch me.'

'Always…' For a brief intense moment their gazes locked. And fused.

'Callum…'

'Shh.' His lips came down and closed over her tiny sigh. She tasted more wonderful, if that were possible, her lips soft and warm, parting further to give him access, and she slid slender arms around him, drawing him closer. And it was back again, more urgent than ever, the simmering burn he had struggled to control yesterday, threatening to consume him. The feel of her ripe firm body pressed against him nearly drove him over the edge and all the suppressed need of the past months rose up to mock him.

Her little moan against his lips was almost his undoing and only an iron control kept him from taking the few steps to her bed behind the Chinese silk screen and making love with her there and then. Lifting his head, he took a breath that came up from his boots, staring down into her wide, confused eyes.

Fliss held his gaze for agonised seconds then, lowering her eyes, she broke free from his arms and took a step back, putting the barest distance between them. She wrapped her arms tightly around her middle. 'I…guess we expected that to happen, didn't we?'

His jaw tightened. He couldn't deny it. He'd have walked on glass to come to her tonight. 'I don't want to rush you, Fliss.'

Her throat constricted. 'You haven't.'

'I'm glad you feel that way.' He opened his arms and she went back into them and for long moments they stood there, his hand stroking the back of her head where it rested against his shoulder. 'You're the loveliest thing to have happened in my life for such a long time.'

Slowly, Fliss raised her head. 'You've been hurt, haven't you?'

He lifted a strand of her hair and wound it around his finger. 'One way or another, I think we both have.'

Slowly, she leaned forward and placed the softest kiss on his lips. 'Time to heal, then.'

CHAPTER SEVEN

THEIR pizza arrived and they settled down to eat it straight out of the box. Fliss watched amusedly as Callum set out his food as though he hadn't eaten in weeks, pulling out a long curl of melted cheese and eating it with exaggerated relish.

'What?' He caught her look, his grin a bit lopsided. 'Am I being a pig?'

Her mouth curved lazily and she nudged his foot under the table. 'Not so you'd notice.' In fact, she'd actually been turned on by the unfussy, masculine way he did everything.

'More wine?' Fliss waved away the last slice of pizza and got to her feet. As she did so, the sleeve of her sweater caught the open lid of the pizza box and upended it onto the floor. Her unladylike comment brought a howl of amusement from her dinner guest.

'Little bull in a china shop,' he teased, getting down and helping her gather up the tiny fragments of pepper and olives that had scattered onto the carpet.

At least he hadn't called her a cow. She forced a smile at her weak private joke and took the box from him. 'Finish your pizza. I'll dump this in the garbage. Which means I'll sit it on top of my little kitchen tidy and take it out to the trash tomorrow.'

'Is the lack of space getting to you?' Feet crossed at the ankles, Callum leaned against the wall beside her and finished off his slice of pizza.

Fliss turned to the sink to wash her hands. 'Only when I have large men to dinner.'

'Large?' Callum let out an offended squawk.

She turned her head and smiled sweetly at him. 'What about tall, rugged and athletic, then?'

'Better,' he agreed, mollified. With the last of his pizza consumed, he moved across to the sink and washed his own hands. 'Seriously, are you feeling cramped, Flissy?'

'Sometimes. But I'm not here all that much. And I can go along to the doctors' lounge when I want space and company.' She went to refill their glasses but he stopped her.

'No more wine for me, thanks. Do you have any decaf coffee, by any chance?'

'I do.' She smiled. 'I might even have some chocolate mints to go with it.'

Fliss set the electric jug to boil and then reached up into a top cupboard for the after-dinner mints. Taking down the box, she turned and handed it to Callum. 'Would you mind opening these, please? The Cellophane packaging drives me crazy.'

Callum obliged and Fliss made their coffee, adding milk to both and piling everything on a little tray.

'Where do you want this?' Callum asked, picking it up. 'Back on the table?'

'If you'd prefer more room, we could wander along to the communal lounge.'

'You are kidding?'

She suppressed a smile. 'We'd only be having coffee together, O'Byrne. Nothing to set the hospital grapevine whirring.'

Callum's huff of unbelief indicated his doubt about that conclusion.

'Well, that only leaves the bed,' Fliss said decidedly.

His heart thumped. 'Sorry?'

Fliss's gaze ran over the rangy, lean length of him. 'Callum, I saw how difficult it was for you, trying to ease your legs under that doll's table earlier. We could throw some big cushions at the top of the bed, put our coffees on the side tables, kick off our shoes and make ourselves comfy. Your decision.'

It wasn't a hard decision to make. But were they were inviting trouble? Callum wondered a bit later as Fliss relaxed like a boneless cat beside him and they began feeding each other chocolate mints.

'That was fun, wasn't it?' Fliss all but purred a little later. They'd finished their coffee and most of the mints and, replete, she snuggled in against him and Callum obligingly draped his arm around her shoulders.

'Quite comfortable?' he asked wryly, looking down at her.

'Mmm.'

They shared a smile, but somewhere in the middle of it something happened, something languid and profound that crept up on them.

'Tell me what it was like, working for Médecins Sans Frontières?' Fliss broke the mood quickly.

Callum's head jerked up as if she'd activated a string. 'It's ancient history,' he responded shortly. And bringing it all back would only remind him of Kirsty…

'In other words, you don't want to talk about it?' Fliss fixed him with a perceptive, clear gaze. 'If that's the case, just say,' she said gently. 'And I won't persist.'

Callum let out a long breath. 'It's a bit involved—intertwined with other stuff…'

'Your marriage.'

He averted his eyes quickly but not before she saw the pain in them.

Fliss held out her hand to him. 'Talk to me, Callum. Sometimes you have to go back before you can move forward properly, and I promise nothing you tell me will leave this room.'

He took the hand she offered, pressing her fingers tightly, as if to gain strength from the contact. Then he began to talk, very quietly, in an oddly impersonal voice that told Fliss more clearly than anything else just how much it was costing him to finally let go.

'All up, I was with MSF for three years.'

'That's a long time to be doing that knife-edge kind of medicine, isn't it?'

'I had leave between assignments. That's the only way to stay more or less sane.'

'That makes sense. Otherwise you'd burn out, wouldn't you?'

'I guess. And it wasn't all doom and heartache. And the patients were so stoic, patient, so damn grateful for the little we could do for them sometimes. But then you'd get a few days off and see the country a bit, watch the fantastic sunsets that you can only see in those far-flung parts of the earth. And you'd feel uplifted, as though you were making the very best use of your medical skills.'

Fliss asked the question she was almost afraid of asking. 'Was your ex-wife a doctor with MSF as well?'

'No. Kirsty is a photo journalist.' Callum's stomach did a somersault at the thought of resurrecting it all. He paused and went on, 'We met when she was working freelance, sending material worldwide. One day, she arrived at our field hospital and announced she had permission to spend two weeks with us to do a documentary about our work '

'Tall order,' Fliss said guardedly. 'And rather ambitious to think she could capture the essence of working for MSF in two short weeks.'

He hesitated infinitesimally. 'Kirsty was aware of that. That's why she chose to shadow only one of the medical team for the two weeks.'

'You?'

He nodded.

'You mean she got inside your head?'

'It wasn't like that.' Callum rubbed a hand across his forehead, feeling the familiar tightening in his throat. 'Kirsty was a professional. Most of the time she was unobtrusive.'

'I'll bet her camera got up close and personal, though,' Fliss huffed disdainfully.

'It had to, if her documentary was to be credible. We'd talked about it beforehand. I was prepared.'

Fliss didn't quite believe that. In her opinion, he'd have been absolutely vulnerable. 'I imagine in the circumstances, your relationship would have become intense very quickly.'

How on earth did he answer that objectively? Callum eased his head back onto one of the cushions, unaware his eyes had assumed a bleak look. Within days he and Kirsty had catapulted into a physical relationship, which, looking back, he guessed hadn't been the smartest move on either of their parts. 'Yes,' he said quietly.

Fliss gave a sharp glance at the sudden tight set of his shoulders. 'OK…' She took a steadying breath. 'Then what? You got married?'

His mouth moved into a twist of a grim smile. 'Not that quickly. Kirsty went back to the States to edit her work. I had leave due so I joined her. We had a month together. At the end of it we got married. Unfortunately, our respective jobs meant we were separated almost immediately.'

'That must have been difficult.'

'To say the least. And that was the state of things for the next two years. Less time together, more time apart. It was crazy to think we could make a marriage work under those circumstances. At least I thought so.'

The final words were said with a trace of bitterness and Fliss's thoughts ran riot. She wondered whether he meant that Kirsty had thought it *could* work. If so, it was no wonder she was now his ex-wife. 'So, what did you do about it?'

'I suggested we buy an apartment, somewhere central we could use as a base to come back to, even when the other wasn't there. Somewhere to call home. As it was, we were both living out of suitcases, flying to spend even a few hours together. Her work took her all around the world. She loved it. More than me, obviously,' he added broodingly.

'Was there no room for compromise?' Fliss asked guardedly.

He shrugged. 'You'd have thought so, wouldn't you? For my part, I was willing to resign from MSF, settle down in a teaching hospital somewhere, so that at least we could have some permanency for the future. Kirsty said that kind of lifestyle would bore her to tears, take the immediacy from her work as a photo journalist. She liked to break new ground,' he expanded. 'The first sniff of a trouble spot, she was on the next flight out.'

Fliss was unimpressed. 'Sounds like she got off on thrills and danger.'

'It certainly wasn't conducive to keeping a marriage intact,' Callum sighed, pressing the heels of his hands against his eyes, then stretching his face muscles in an attempt to focus and clear his head. 'I mean, we were both in our mid-thirties,' he said in a baffled kind of voice. 'We should have had the maturity to make things work. We *should* have.'

'But from what you've been telling me, it wasn't what Kirsty wanted,' Fliss pointed out gently. 'And it takes two, Callum. Did you not want children?' she added after a minute.

He snorted. 'I knew early on that wasn't an option. Kirsty lived for her work.'

She sounded like a right spoilt madam, Fliss decided uncharitably. 'Are you still sad about it, Callum?'

He thought for a second. 'Sometimes I feel…a sense of failure, I suppose. But I'm divorced now—signed the papers only last week.'

Fliss sat up straight. Oh, lord, the whole exercise was probably still a bit raw for him. And she'd jumped in boots and all and practically dragged the story out of him. 'I didn't mean to pry—really.'

'It's fine,' he answered, meaning it. 'And you know what, Dr Wakefield?'

'What?' She fluttered an innocent look at him.

'You're a very good listener.'

'Oh. But I—'

He kissed her into silence.

'You have the sexiest lips,' he said gruffly, looking down at her.

'Do I?' Her eyes widened and she saw the heat flare in his.

'You do,' he murmured, just before he claimed her mouth again.

She sighed and felt a sudden strange lightness, as if love and desire had rolled into one wild surge, sweeping through her body and out to the tips of her fingers and toes. And with a feeling of whatever would be, would be Fliss curled her body into his, each curve and hollow finding a home, a placement, as though they'd been carved out and had been waiting to be filled.

Callum's mouth devoured her, feasting hungrily on her lips, tracking over her throat and into the valley between her breasts. 'I want you...' he whispered tautly. 'Let me stay, Flissy. Make love with me...'

Fliss was shaken to her depths. Her whole body cried out for him to fill her, but from somewhere she found the strength to break the contact with him. She struggled to sit up, uncertainty and wariness clouding her eyes. 'I can't, Callum.'

'Why?' He pulled himself into a sitting position and took her shoulders. 'You want me as much as I want you.' He frowned a bit. 'Don't you...?'

She nodded, biting her lips together to stop them trembling.

'I won't hurt you, Flissy.'

Her eyes widened and she shook her head. Every detail of his hands was conveyed to her through the fine wool of her sweater. The long tapered fingers, curved over her shoulders, the angle of his thumbs pointing inwards, their tips teasing the hollow at the base of her throat. She took a shaken breath and said, 'On the other hand, we could end up hurting each other quite badly, Callum.'

'Are you saying there's no hope for us?' he asked tersely.

She lowered her gaze. 'Not that.' Then what was she saying? She turned the question back at herself. In the rawest sense, wouldn't they be just using each other? Both emotionally scarred by partners they'd given their entire trust to, both abominably let down by those same partners. 'You're vulnerable, Callum.' We both are, she added silently.

'That's rubbish!' His head went back on a dismissive growl. 'I haven't set eyes on Kirsty for two years. I've accepted she's never coming back. That's why I signed the divorce papers. So how am I susceptible to being hurt now?'

Fliss was shocked. 'Are you saying you're willing to just take what's on offer and to hell with the consequences?'

Callum didn't move for a moment, uttering a short expletive under his breath, before swinging his legs to the floor and standing up. Stuffing his feet back into his boots, he crossed to the window and stood rigidly with his back to her, resentment in every line of his body.

There was a sickening kind of silence, suddenly broken by a rap on the door that had them both turning sharply towards the sound. They heard Nick's voice.

'Fliss, are you decent? I'll be in the lounge. Don't make me come and hunt you down like last time.' A chuckle and then he added, 'See you, babe.'

Callum stiffened and went very still, his eyes never leaving Fliss's startled gaze. 'You should have told me,' he said grittily.

'Told you what?' Fliss scrambled off the bed and stood beside it, her arms wrapped defensively around her middle.

Callum's mouth moved into a grim twist, the grooves of tension spiking his lean cheeks like slashes from a sharp-edged sword. 'That you're in deep with Rossi.'

Shocked, sick to her stomach, Fliss could only stare at him. Did he believe she was playing one man off against the other? If that was his low opinion of her, he could go to blazes. She wasn't about to explain her relationship with Nick or anyone else. 'I think you should go, Callum.'

'Don't worry. I'm going.' His face was carefully expressionless, but his eyes were unable to disguise the baffled disillusionment that stalked him. With his hand on the door knob, he turned and stared at her. 'You're a fast worker. I'll give you that.'

And you've ruined everything between us, Fliss wanted to yell at him. Instead, she held her head high and countered flatly, 'You believe what you want to believe, Callum. But, sadly, you wouldn't recognise *trust* if it sat up and bit you.'

'In your world maybe.' His mouth snapped shut, his tightly clamped lips a harsh line across his face. 'And don't think you can sleep in, tomorrow, Doctor,' he warned. 'You're covering for me, remember?'

'I'm well aware of my professional obligations.' Fliss sent him a glare that should have scorched him from the socks up.

He lifted a shoulder dismissively. 'Hadn't you better join your boyfriend?' he said thinly, before he turned and left quietly.

Wasn't it just typical of her life lately? Fliss sat at the window and watched Callum's tail lights disappear around the side of the building. She dragged in a shallow breath, feeling hurt and anger in equal parts clogging her throat.

She'd fallen flat on her face again but she'd learned yet another painful lesson. She would never, *never* bare her heart and feelings so freely again. And she'd call on every strength she possessed to get through the rest of her contracted time. She owed the people of Mt Pryde that much.

But Callum O'Byrne had better keep his distance.

Callum slammed his car into gear and drove home, just missing several species of wildlife by mere centimetres. He cut back on his speed. Hells bells, what was the matter with him? He was supposed to be preserving native animals, not destroying them.

He took his foul mood to bed with him and lay for ages staring at the ceiling. But all he saw was Fliss's hurt little face staring back at him, twisting the blade of shame inside him.

How could he have reacted like that? Said all those hurtful things to her? He rolled over, burying his face in the pillow. He felt so alone. Lonely. He needed her beside him. He needed her.

Sweet heaven, what did all it mean?

'Fool,' he muttered, his voice clogged with emotion. 'You've hurt her irrevocably, stuffed up any chance you may have had with her. Because you couldn't wait to jump to stupid conclusions about her and Rossi. Couldn't wait to feel the martyr.'

Had Kirsty destroyed his trust in women so thoroughly? Fliss had suggested as much. And he'd scoffed at that. Well, *she* was lost to him now, and he deserved it. He rolled to his back again, staring at the ceiling, his eyes raw with pain.

And he didn't want to have to attend that damn stupid conference in Brisbane tomorrow. The board had insisted so he'd had no choice. But Fliss shouldn't have been dragged back on duty to cover for him—not after the rough kind of day she'd already had.

But on the other hand, perhaps a day away from the place

would help him put the unmitigated mess he made of things into some kind of perspective. And when he came back, he could eat crow and try to claw back some of the respect he'd lost with Fliss.

Of course, it might take the whole of her six months' contract to do it.

In the staffroom, Fliss sat over her mug of coffee and thought what a relief it was to know that Callum would be absent for the entire day. She would have found it very difficult to face him. More like impossible, she reflected bitterly.

She'd been awake for most of the night, trying to sort out things in her mind. Obviously she'd been not much more than a diversion to Callum. Shame, she'd read so much more into things. But he need never know that. In fact, she'd make darned sure he never did.

Never by any looks or actions from her would he ever know how he'd made her feel. Weak at the knees one minute, walking on air the next. Feeling her heart leap just at the sight of him...

She suppressed a shiver and cuddled more firmly into her long cardigan. Surely it was colder than usual this morning? But maybe the cold was only in her heart—

'Morning, Fliss.' Nick breezed into the staffroom.

'Morning.' Fliss made a weak attempt at a smile. 'How was your day off? Did you manage to get to Brisbane?'

'I did. Managed a bit of quality time with my two favourite people as well.' Giving her a quick, all-encompassing look, Nick went across to the bench and made himself a cup of tea. Dangling the teabag in his mug, he turned and said, 'The boss is in Brisbane all day, isn't he?'

'Conference,' Fliss rejoined shortly. 'We're *it* today.'

Nick snorted. '*You're* it. You've got years more experience than I.'

'Not that many,' she said, a little more tartly than she'd intended.

Nick frowned. 'I missed you last night.'

'Sorry.' Fliss lifted her coffee and took a mouthful. 'Bit tired, that's all.'

But Nick still looked puzzled. 'You OK?'

'Of course.' Fliss gave him her wide-eyed look. 'Why? Don't I look OK?'

Nick sent her a dark-eyed stare and moved a bit uneasily in his chair. 'You seem...'

'What?' Fliss's mouth pulled down at the corners. 'Dull, boring or both?'

Nick shrugged. 'I was about to say, unhappy.'

'Oh,' she said lamely, and then managed a passable smile. 'It just a bit of Monday-itis. Nothing that a hard day in Emergency won't cure.'

Nick cradled the teamug. 'I heard you and Callum had a rough time yesterday. Tractor accident, wasn't it?'

'Mmm. I got a really good taste of rural medicine.' She broke off and turned as Anita popped her head in the door.

'We've an MVA coming in, guys,' the charge said. 'Collision between a car and a farm utility. Woman driving out of her gateway into the main road, guy in the ute didn't see her.'

'Ouch!' Nick grimaced. 'The fog's thick as your arm this morning. It was already coming down when I drove back last night.'

Fliss asked calmly, 'Do you have any details of injuries, Anita?'

'Jeff said the woman's pregnant, ten or so weeks. She's a bit shaken but nothing broken. The other driver said he blacked out for a few seconds and Jeff thinks maybe seat-belt injuries. Ribs, probably. It happened just out of town a bit so they'll be here directly.'

'Do we have names?' Nick asked as they hurried from the room.

'Beth Knightly and Harry Zahnow.'

'Right.' Fliss began issuing orders swiftly. 'Anita, would you make sure the resus room is ready, please? And check the radiographer's on hand. At some stage we'll need to do an ultrasound on the pregnant woman.' She turned to Nick in query, 'Which patient do you want?'

'I'll take the ribs,' he said emphatically. 'I've a bit to learn yet about pregnant ladies.'

'Better start, then, if you're aiming to be a rural generalist,' Fliss told him, her tone dry.

'I know, I know.' Nick held up his hands in self-defence. 'I'm working up to it, that's all.'

As they sped towards the ambulance bay, Fliss felt her nerves begin to tauten. In such a short time she'd become almost attuned to the adrenaline rush that came with emergency medicine.

Fliss's patient was taken quickly into Resus. 'Hi, Beth.' She took the young woman's hand. 'I'm Fliss Wakefield. I'll be the doctor treating you today. How are you feeling?'

'Scared…' Beth was shivering, her eyes wide in trepidation.

'Have you felt any bleeding?'

'Don't think so.' Beth took a shaky break. 'I'd know—wouldn't I?'

'You would.' Fliss projected calm. 'But we'll make sure anyway. Anita, would you check Beth, please?'

A few moments later Anita was able to report, 'So far, so good. But we'll pop a pad on you, Beth so we'll be able to monitor you.'

'I don't want to lose this baby.'

'We'll do everything we can to stop that happening,' Fliss interposed gently. 'Now, I want to check your tummy for any injury from your seat belt.'

Beth gave a ragged little breath. 'The impact from the farm utility wasn't all that bad. Harry really stood on the brakes. Poor man—he didn't see me. The fog was so thick and I didn't have my headlights on—I know I should have.'

Fliss's hands worked their way methodically across her patient's stomach, palpating, checking, rechecking. Finally, she lifted her head and smiled. 'You seem to have escaped any spleen damage, Beth. Now, let's see what the rest of you is doing, shall we?'

Fliss turned to Anita, her brows raised in silent query.

'BP and pulse within normal range.'

Fliss sent up a silent prayer of thanks. Turning back to her patient, she shone a torch into her eyes to check her pupils were normal and reacting. 'OK, that's fine. Beth, I want you to squeeze my hand as hard as you can. Excellent. Now, I'll just check your legs and feet. You're doing great,' she added with a reassuring little pat to the other's arm.

'Are you ready for the Doppler now?' Anita asked quietly, from beside Fliss's shoulder.

'She seems stable enough,' Fliss agreed and, waited while Anita spread a film of gel on Beth's abdomen.

Beth lifted her head slightly off the pillow. 'Are you going to check the baby's heartbeat now?'

'We certainly are,' Fliss said, running the special obstetric stethoscope over Beth's slight bump. For several seconds Fliss concentrated, listening. Shifting the stethoscope slightly, she listened again.

'Is s-something wrong?' Beth's voice was wrung with fear.

'Nothing at all.' Fliss took the stethoscope away from her ears and smiled at her patient. 'Nice regular heartbeat.'

'Oh, thank God.' Tears spilled from Beth's eyes and down her cheeks. 'Thank you so much, Doctor…'

'I don't think you've anything to worry about.' Fliss patted her patient's forearm. 'But to make absolutely sure, we'll do an ultrasound as well. Now, is there someone we should notify—your husband?'

'Jason—No.' Beth bit her lip. 'He'll want to turn around and come back, and he has an important meeting at work this morning. If you think everything's all right with the baby, I'll wait and call him later on.'

Anita spread a blanket over the pregnant young woman. 'But wouldn't he want to be here with you?'

Beth sighed and looked from doctor to nurse. 'We're living a bit of a complicated life at the moment. Jason works in Brisbane, only gets home for weekends. I work here at the council offices.'

'I see,' Fliss said, although she didn't.

Anita caught Fliss's eye and said brightly, 'I'll arrange a cup of tea for Beth, shall I?'

Fliss nodded. 'Thanks, Anita.'

'I guess I should explain things,' Beth said quietly. 'My mother had a stroke a while ago. I came home to look after her. Jason can't leave his job in Brisbane so that's why he gets home only at weekends.'

Fliss lowered herself on to a corner at the end of the bed. 'That must be very difficult for you both. How long does it look like continuing?'

'Mum's improving,' Beth said with a little shrug of her shoulder. 'But she needs help with certain things and someone there at night. I'm the only child so I have to—no, I mean I want to be there for her. And Jason's been great. We're managing.'

What a nice, unselfish man, Fliss thought. Lifting a hand, she rubbed a small ache across her temple. 'Is it not possible for you to take your mum to live with you in Brisbane so you could all be together?'

Beth shook her head. 'We've only a one-bedroom inner-city apartment. Besides the lack of space and privacy for Mum, she'd never be comfortable away from her own home. Dad died last year. They were married thirty years,' she added with something like wonder and gave a funny little grimace. 'Jase and I have been married barely three.'

'Well, I'm sure there's no reason to think you and Jason won't make it to thirty,' Fliss suggested with a smile, and got to her feet. 'I'm going to keep you here for a couple of hours, Beth, just to make sure everything's fine with you and the baby. We'll pop you on a saline drip and a little later we'll take some blood to check your haemoglobin levels are where they should be. Now, should we try to get a message to your work and your mum?'

'Yes, please. I've all the numbers in my diary. It's in my bag. If someone could call Mum's neighbour, Jane Ferris, and explain what's happened, I'd be grateful. Jane's unflappable. She pops in and gets Mum her lunch each day when I'm at work.' Beth glanced at her watch. 'I'll give Jason another half-hour or so before I call him. He should be at work by then.'

'I'll speak to him as well, if you like,' Fliss offered. 'Just to reassure him.'

'Thanks, Dr Wakefield…' Beth gave a watery smile '…for looking after me and the baby and everything.'

'That's what we're here for.' Fliss scribbled quickly on her patient's chart. 'Now, who's your GP here in Mt Pryde?'

'Dr Jo McNeal. She's Mum's doctor, too.'

'Good.' Fliss looked up and smiled. 'I'll see she gets your notes.'

Fliss was thoughtful as she walked back to the nurses' station. What an inspirational young couple. Supporting each other, going to extraordinary lengths to keep their marriage together. But, then, if it was what both of them wanted… For a fleeting second she thought of Callum's heartache when his marriage had failed because his partner hadn't felt able or had refused to go the extra mile to save their marriage.

But she wouldn't go there.

It was late afternoon when Nick came to find Fliss. 'Shouldn't you be going off?' she asked.

'Presently. You?'

She shrugged. 'Have to wait until Callum gets back. Did you need me for something?'

Nick fisted his hands into the pockets of his white coat. 'I'm a bit stumped for a diagnosis. Could I run it past you?'

'Of course.' Fliss raised fine brows at him. 'Is it urgent or could we do it over a quick coffee?'

'Oh, coffee, please,' Nick said gratefully. 'It's not life-threatening—just a bit iffy. And I don't want to make a stuff-up.'

'Been there,' Fliss empathised, steering him towards the staffroom. 'Talk while I get the coffees, Nick, in case we get sidetracked by a real emergency.'

'The patient is Vanessa Grant, age twenty-five, six-months-old baby.' Nick sat sideways at the table and stretched his legs out in front of him. 'She's presenting with aches and pains in her limbs, feeling tired all the time, no get up and go when normally she's a pretty energetic person. And she's overweight for her frame. I'll do bloods, of course, but what should I test for—RA?'

Rheumatoid arthritis. Fliss looked doubtful. 'Possibly, but if she's recently had a baby, it could be something else entirely.'

Nick made a face. 'Vanessa said her mother-in-law keeps banging on about her having postnatal depression.'

'Not likely?'

'She insists she and her husband are nuts about their little boy. She's managing to look after him and wants to be well. She just can't seem to get there.'

'Mmm.' Fliss handed Nick his coffee and took a mouthful of her own. 'Shouldn't this be a matter for a referral from her GP?'

'She doesn't have one. They're carnival people. Here in Mt Pryde for a couple of days before they move on. She said she was driving past the hospital and decided on the spur of the moment to come in.'

Fliss grimaced. 'Lucky old us, then.' She began looking out the window and sipping her coffee slowly.

Nick cleared his throat affectedly. 'I don't want to rush you, Dr Wakefield, but I've a patient waiting.'

'I know.' Fliss turned and gave him a dry look. 'I'm thinking.'

'Come up with anything?'

'Maybe. I had a patient when I was in sports medicine, young mum, progolfer. She was desperate to get back into training for the summer circuit. Couldn't find the energy to go to the gym, let alone anything more. In her case her baby was nine months old. I had a few hunches, ruled a few things out. Turned out she had an underactive thyroid.'

Nick whistled. 'That would make sense. She get OK again?'

'In time.'

'And no one thought to test for it?' Nick was appalled.

'She'd slipped through the cracks. Her physician kept insisting her iron stores were low.'

Nick snorted. 'Well, they would've been, wouldn't they?' He drew his feet in and stood up purposefully. 'So, would you talk to Vanessa?'

'If you want me to.' Fliss collected both their mugs and rinsed them. 'But you'd be quite capable of handling this yourself, Nick.'

'I'd feel better if you did it, but I'd like to sit in, if that's all right.' He gave a cracked laugh. 'Don't think I'm being a wimp, do you?'

'A terrible wimp,' Fliss told him sternly, and then mock-punched him on his pec muscle. 'It's called getting a second opinion, Dr Rossi. Never be afraid to call for one.'

Nick grinned sheepishly. 'Thanks. Vanessa's in cube one.'

A few minutes later Fliss was speed-reading Nick's notes on their patient. 'Mind if I ask you a few questions now, Vanessa?' she asked, placing the chart aside.

'Do you think you can help me?'

'Let's hope so.' Fliss smiled guardedly. 'How overweight would you say you are?'

The young mother dipped her blonde head. 'I used to be a size ten. Now I'm up to a fourteen in some things.'

'That's quite a jump.'

'I've been careful with my diet and I've tried getting up early and doing a power walk, but I'm just so exhausted when I get home I start to feel sick. And it never ends—this tired feeling.' She blinked back tears, hunching forward and tearing a tissue to shreds on her lap. 'My mother-in-law is nagging me to death. Says I'm disorganised and l-lazy.'

'But of course you're not,' Fliss commiserated. 'Dr Rossi tells me you travel with a carnival. Must be an interesting life.'

'It used to be. Not so much now with bubby. But I know if I could just get my energy back…' Vanessa stopped and bit her lips together.

'I see from your notes that you've been experiencing some muscular aches and pains. What about in your feet especially?' Fliss questioned gently. 'More pain there?'

'Oh, yes.' Vanessa's gaze was agonised. 'When I get out of bed in the mornings it's so bad I want to cry out.'

'Hair falling out?'

'Heaps. That's not right, is it?'

'No,' Fliss agreed. 'But there's usually an underlying cause for it. Where are you off to after you leave Mt Pryde?'

'Brisbane for the royal show. But we take a few weeks off to get everything set up and relax a bit before the show starts. Wayne says we might even get to the coast for a break.'

Fliss began thinking ahead. 'Would you mind giving up some of your holiday to see a specialist while you're in Brisbane, Vanessa?'

'No. What kind of specialist?'

An endocrinologist. All your symptoms point to an underactive thyroid function.'

Vanessa shook her head. 'What does that mean exactly?'

'Simply put, it means you may have a low thyroid hormone concentration in your blood and I stress may. The only way we can find out for certain is from a blood test. But you need to be seen by a specialist so I'll give you a referral to Dr Mitchell Jarvis. If you're able to give me the dates you'll be in Brisbane, I'll call his office and make an appointment for you to be seen urgently. And we'll ask for the results of the bloods to be sent directly to Dr Jarvis. That way he'll be up to speed and able to make a diagnosis and get you on to the appropriate medication so you'll begin feeling better and your weight will begin coming down as well.'

'Oh, thank you so much. ' Vanessa looked as though she'd been thrown a lifeline. 'And if I have an underactive thyroid, will the treatment be complicated? I mean, I'll be travelling. I won't have a regular doctor.'

'No, it won't be complicated,' Fliss reassured her. 'Usually, it's in the form of tablets. You should be able to get your script filled at any chemist along the way. And Dr Jarvis will discuss whether he'll need to see you periodically, but I'm sure when he makes his diagnosis he'll work in with whatever suits you.'

Vanessa's lashes flickered. 'I'm so glad I decided to stop in at the hospital today.'

'We are, too,' Fliss said kindly. 'Now, stay put for a few more minutes and I'll send someone to take some blood from you.'

'And someone will get you a cup of tea before you leave,' Nick added with a wink. 'Stay cool, hmm?'

'Yeah, I'll try.' Vanessa smiled shyly. 'Thanks.'

'Nice one, Doc,' Nick said with satisfaction as they walked back through Casualty towards the nurses' station. 'You were pretty sure of your diagnosis, weren't you?'

'Only because Vanessa's symptoms are so acute. And because of the similarities with my other patient. In many instances, hypothroydism is difficult to detect because the symptoms are relatively nondescript.'

'That figures.' Nick's grin was wry. 'So it's always wise to dig a little deeper and not dismiss anything as unrelated.'

'By George, he's got it! Nick, you're a good doctor,' Fliss said earnestly. 'You're caring and you listen well. I'd say you'll make an excellent GP. And there's Simon right on time.' She fluttered a wave. 'So off you go now. See you tomorrow.'

'What about you?' Nick's jaw worked for a second. 'It doesn't seem fair you have to hang about waiting for Callum when you've worked such a long day already.'

'It's called the pecking order.' Fliss lifted her shoulders in a helpless little gesture. 'Now, scoot, Dr Rossi, before I reassign you.'

CHAPTER EIGHT

OH, LORD, he was back!

Something in Fliss's heart scrunched tight as she looked at Callum. He was parked at the nurses' station, his dark head bent over the day's patient charts.

She flattened against the wall, gaining time, her gaze almost hungrily fixed on him. The dark grey suit made him look unfamiliar, increased her unease. And he didn't appear all that composed either, she decided, suddenly aware of his restless body language, his fingers drumming on the counter top then reaching to rub at the nape of his neck.

Fliss felt her nerve ends tingle with powerful awareness. If he had a point of tension in his spine she could massage it away in a second. But, of course, she couldn't possibly suggest it. From now on, touching Callum O'Byrne was strictly off her agenda.

She took a calming breath. She had to be professional here. She had to approach him, resume a working relationship with him. Perhaps it mightn't be as awkward as she dreaded. But, of course, it would be. They'd come so close to making love last night—so close. How could she face him and pretend nothing had changed between them?

Well, she'd just have to if she was going to stick to the letter of her contract with the hospital. And she was determined to do that. Lifting her head higher in a little gesture of bravado, she instructed her legs to move.

'Hi.' She paused by the desk.

'Fliss.' Callum's head jerked up, two frown lines jumping into sharp relief between his eyes. 'What are you still doing here?'

Fliss all but rolled her eyes. What did he think she was doing there? 'Covering for you, as requested.'

He made a click of annoyance. 'Didn't Angus Charlton show?'

'I'm not with you,' she said evenly.

'I arranged for one of the senior doctors from the after-hours clinic to be on call for any emergencies after your shift finished.'

'Well, as there have been no emergencies so far this evening, I guess he wouldn't have needed to show, would he? And for the record,' she emphasised, her gaze widening and sharpening in sudden accusation, 'no one told me anything about the arrangement.'

His mouth drew in. 'Communication breakdown on my part. Entirely my mistake. I should have told you. I wouldn't have wanted you to continue working into the night like this.'

'*You* do it all the time,' she reminded him coolly. 'And anyway, it's not that late.'

'No, I suppose not. Have you eaten?'

'I had a piece of toast earlier.'

'That hardly constitutes dinner.' He glanced at his watch. 'There's still time to grab a meal somewhere. Join me?' As he spoke, he loosened his tie as if it was choking him, at the same time releasing the top buttons on his plain blue shirt, the whole action emphasising everything about his uncomprising masculinity and revealing a smooth expanse of olive skin at the top of his chest.

Fliss felt her mouth dry and took a step backwards as if to regain her space. Her breathing immediately felt tight and her stomach went into free fall. Physically, she was intensely attracted to him but she had to put the brakes on her feelings. Feelings didn't count any more. He didn't trust her. And what made him think she'd want to share a meal with him anyway? She caught back a little huff of annoyance. 'I'll heat something in the microwave, thanks.'

He blew out a controlled sigh and then shrugged. 'I guess I'll have to do it here, then.'

Fliss's felt her heart skitter. She licked her lips. 'Do what?'

'Apologise for my juvenile behaviour last night.' The suggestion of a twisted smile flickered briefly against his lips. 'What else did you think I had in mind?'

'After last night nothing would surprise me, Callum?'

A nerve in his jaw twitched for a second. 'We need to talk.'

'No.' She shook her head. 'I've done all the listening I intend to. But I imagine if we both put our minds to it, we can manage a civil working relationship.'

Callum opened his mouth to speak but what he was about to say was lost when Troy came bearing down on them, ready to take over the night shift.

'Hey, guys,' the charge greeted them cheerfully. 'How was the conference, Callum?'

'Uh, quite good actually. Better than I anticipated.' Callum handed the charts back over the counter. 'You're OK for cover, then?'

'I believe so. Simon's here and Angus Charlton's on call for back-up?'

'That's the plan.' Callum lifted a hand and rubbed the back of his neck again. 'Long day,' he said, and his mouth tightened. 'Fliss and I are just off to grab some food.'

'Get out of here, then, the pair of you.' Troy flapped a hand in dismissal. 'The Gettalong should still be serving counter meals.'

With his hand firmly at her elbow and Troy watching interestedly, Fliss had no option other than to allow Callum to guide her out through the foyer. But once outside in the subdued lighting of the car park, she jerked to a stop and stood her ground. 'What do you think you're doing, hijacking me like this, Callum?'

'We both need to eat,' he said reasonably. 'In fact, I can hear your tummy grumbling from here.'

Which was partly true. Fliss tossed her head. 'You're not giving me a choice here, are you?'

'Nope.' Callum continued propelling her towards his car.

'Where are we going?' Fliss demanded. 'And what in heaven's name is the Gettalong?'

'It's a pub,' he informed her. 'You wouldn't have come across it yet. It's about a K out of town. Named after a local racehorse that did rather well for the townsfolk some years back.'

Fliss made a sound of disbelief in her throat. 'They don't serve horse meat, do they?'

'They do a pretty good steak, but I'm almost certain it's prime beef,' he said with a deadpan voice. They stopped by his vehicle and he activated the remote on his keypad to open the doors. 'Hop in,' he said. 'It's cold.'

But, arms wrapped tightly around her middle, Fliss refused to move, reluctantly watching as Callum hauled off his jacket and tie and tossed them onto the back seat. He pulled out a bulky black jumper and dragged it on.

'What now?' he asked, barely controlled impatience in his voice.

Fliss licked her lips and edged from one foot to the other. 'I…don't want to do this, Callum…'

A beat of silence.

'What *do* you want, Flissy?' Almost without her realising it, Callum had pulled her gently into his arms and held her. Turning his head, he bent and nuzzled a kiss to the side of her throat. 'Tell me.'

Fliss fought for control of her wildly see-sawing heart. 'You can't think the barest of apologies can let you off the hook. You practically accused me of being a—'

'Don't!' He cut her off, his voice anguished. 'I acted like a clod. It's none of my business if you're seeing Nick.'

'I'm not *seeing* him!' Fliss felt like thumping his chest. 'He has a fiancée in Brisbane. And *you* don't trust my word.'

'OK…' Callum gave a sharp sigh. 'I admit to a streak of juvenile jealousy a mile wide.' He leaned away from her then and took her face between his hands. 'I messed things up last night.'

'We both did, I suppose,' Fliss admitted grudgingly. 'But you should have waited and let me explain.'

'I know. I acted like a lunatic. But all that granted, we still could have something wonderful together, couldn't we?'

In the semi-darkness, her eyes flashed with bitterness. 'You mean a stop-gap kind of relationship while you get over Kirsty?'

'I *am* over her, dammit!'

'Your voice changes when you mention her name.'

He snorted. 'You're imagining things. And what about you? Who is it in your past you're trying so hard to forget?'

Her heart quickened and her throat felt dry. And Callum's heavy-lidded gaze was trained directly on her face. 'I can't talk about it.'

'So it's OK to drag my innermost secrets out to air and not yours. How is that fair, Felicity?'

It wasn't fair at all, she had to admit. But she'd been left so hurt, so broken. Feeling such a fool. She dragged in air and expelled it in a shuddering sigh. 'This is a ridiculous place to be having this conversation.'

'The place doesn't matter.' His voice was soft, intense. 'The telling does.' As if he sensed her confusion, he bent, his mouth pressing a series of feather-light kisses on her mouth. 'Start with his name,' he coaxed. 'And go from there.'

'Daniel,' she faltered after the longest pause. 'He was an airline pilot, mostly flying the Pacific run between Australia and New Zealand, Fiji and so on.'

'So he was in and out of the country a bit then?'

And in and out of her life, Fliss thought wretchedly. 'I met him when he came to the sports clinic complaining of sore neck and shoulder muscles, said it was from the constant hours of flying.'

'Hell, Fliss, you didn't start dating one of your patients, did you?'

'Of course not,' she refuted crossly. 'He went to one of the male physios for a massage and then began to come in regularly.'

'And began chatting you up?'

'Yes, I suppose,' she admitted reluctantly. 'We became involved pretty quickly. He was fun to be with, generous, always bringing me presents from wherever he'd been. I thought he was special. I began to think we might have had a future together…'

'So it was serious.'

'On my part, yes. Until the day I found out he was leading a double life.'

Callum heard the pain in her voice and a soft oath left his mouth. 'You must have been gutted.'

Fliss dragged in air and released it in a shuddering sigh. 'It might have been funny if it hadn't been so terrible. He had a flight to Fiji with a two-day stopover. He asked me to go with him, made sure I was spoilt rotten by the cabin crew on the flight over and we had a luxury hotel. Everything was perfect…'

She stopped as if the memory was still too raw to be faced.

'And the worst part is you had no warning of what was to come,' Callum assumed quietly.

Fliss sent a wide-eyed look up at him. How could he have known so well?

'Finish your story,' he said, his gaze, dark and caressing, locking with hers.

'We'd been for an early swim and Daniel had gone directly into the shower while I ordered breakfast. His mobile rang and because our phones were practically identical, I thought it was mine and I answered it.' Fliss hesitated and then went on, ' It was a woman's voice and she asked for Daniel. I didn't have an inkling anything was untoward. I said he was in the shower and asked if I could give him a message. She said, "Tell him his *wife* called to thank him for the flowers he sent for my birthday today."'

Callum swore darkly, feeling anger and outrage on her behalf rise and pound at his skull. 'I won't ask what happened next.'

'Please, don't.' Fliss laughed, a harsh tight sound that echoed eerily around the almost empty car park. She couldn't bear to recount it even now.

She buried her face in his chest and clung to him.

'OK?' he asked eventually.

After a minute, she nodded. 'OK.'

He put his arm around her waist and eased her into the passenger seat of his car. When she was safely belted in, he leaned over and traced the outline of her cheek with the backs of his fingers. 'We'll work this out,' he promised softly, before he closed her door and went round to the driver's side of the car, leaving Fliss knee-deep in confusion.

'This is really different,' Fliss's interested gaze took in the pub's exposed beams, old wooden furniture and the soft glow from the antique coach lamps. 'Rustic,' she reconsidered with a faint smile. 'But nice.'

'The beer garden's great as well.' Callum chose a table and held out her chair. 'But in winter they have it open only on a Friday and Saturday night.'

Fliss pulled her cardigan more closely around her. 'Must be a bit cold out there surely?'

'Not so you'd notice.' Callum sent her an amused look. 'They've actually heard of heating. Installed braziers all over the place. It's cosy. I'll bring you some time.'

He was assuming a lot. But Fliss didn't have the energy to disagree. Instead, she lifted her gaze, noting the place was almost empty. Well, it was a Monday after all. Anyone who had any sense would be tucked up at home. She gave a fractured sigh. 'Shouldn't we order, Callum? It's getting very late.'

'Ah, yes.' He glanced at his watch. 'But it's OK. A lot of the hospital staff come here. The chef's usually happy to rustle up something no matter what the hour. But a grill won't take long so we'll have the steak and a salad, if that's all right?'

'It's fine.'

'Something to drink?' Callum drew her attention back to the menu.

'A glass of merlot, thanks,' Fliss said, hoping the red wine would warm her up. And perhaps even cheer her up, she thought, watching Callum's broad back as he went across to the bar to order their food.

They made desultory conversation until their steaks arrived, grilled to perfection and accompanied by a huge mixed salad on the side. Fliss's mouth watered at the lushness of three kinds of lettuce, locally grown tomatoes, chopped black olives with chunks of avocado and red pepper thrown in for good measure. 'This looks fantastic.' She shot him a wry smile. 'And I've just realised I haven't had anything substantial to eat since our pizza last night.'

His mouth compressed for a second. 'All things considered, perhaps we'd better forget about that.'

On the other hand, perhaps it was only the bit that had come afterwards, that they should forget about, Fliss thought painfully.

Halfway through their meal, Callum commented, 'You said Nick has a fiancée in Brisbane?'

'That's right.' Fliss looked up, her forehead creasing in a tiny frown. 'She's a nurse at St David's.'

'Why haven't we seen her down here, then? Simon's friends are here all the time, visiting.'

'Perhaps with both Nick and Julie working shifts, it's difficult to coincide their days off.'

'But not all the time, surely?'

'It obviously suits them for Nick to go to her,' Fliss said dismissively.

But Callum was like a dog with a bone. 'Driving mile after mile to Brisbane and back today, it suddenly occurred to me how physically tired I was at the end of it. It can't be helping Nick's ability to do his job if he's covering that distance every time he has a day off.'

'What point are you making?' Fliss countered.

'The point I'm making...' Callum placed his cutlery neatly together on his plate and wiped his mouth with his serviette '...is that I could probably review the duty rosters and Nick could take his days off in a block instead of in dribs and drabs, like he's obliged to now.'

Fliss's downcast lashes fanned darkly across her cheekbones. 'He'd probably appreciate that. Well, I guess he might.'

Callum thought she sounded cautious and asked bluntly, 'Is there something you're not telling me, Fliss?'

She raised her eyes in query. 'About Nick?'

'You talk together,' Callum said gruffly. 'And I don't imagine it's all about medicine. If there's anything I should know about, tell me. I promise I won't break your confidence.'

When Fliss remained hesitant, Callum went on. 'Amongst the topics at the conference today was a discussion about the long hours presently being worked by junior doctors in hospitals. I've been under the impression we're fairly reasonable here at Mt Pryde but on the way home tonight it occurred to me that perhaps more streamlining could benefit us all—not just the juniors.'

Fliss took up her wineglass, her expression faintly disbelieving as she looked at him over its rim. 'You mean you'd actually consider taking more time off yourself?'

He shrugged. 'If it turns out to be feasible, I don't see why not.'

Fliss put her glass back on the table. Nick did have a lot on his plate and, whatever else she felt about Callum, she knew instinctively, as far as keeping a confidence, she could trust him. She took a mouthful of her wine and swallowed it carefully. 'Julie has a five-year-old child to look after, a little boy, Matthew. What with school and shift work, I gather it's just too difficult for her to visit here.'

'But not insurmountable,' Callum considered.

'Well, in this case, it is.'

Something in her voice caught his full attention and Callum frowned. 'Explain,' he said tersely.

'Matthew has Down's syndrome. He's not severely impaired but he needs to go to a special school and he's doing well because the teachers are properly trained to deal with differently abled children. But he becomes very unsettled if Julie has to leave him with anyone else for any length of time or if he's out of his own environment. That's why Julie can't travel very far from home and why Nick goes to her.'

Callum looked stunned. 'And why did Nick think he couldn't tell me any of this?'

'For heaven's sake, Callum, would you have gone to your boss when you were a junior and asked for special treatment because you had a difficult personal life?'

'Depends on the boss.'

'Rubbish! We all got our heads down and prepared to work until we dropped just to come out at the end of our training as remotely qualified.'

'I'm not an ogre.'

Fliss struggled for diplomacy. 'No, you're not—but you set such high standards for yourself that the rest of us feel we have to keep doing high jumps to meet them.'

Callum was silent, dropping his head back and staring at the ceiling. He needed to take stock, that was evident. Funny how you jumped to conclusions. He'd had Nick taped as bright enough but emotionally a lightweight. Too easily distracted by a pretty face. When in reality it was a front—well, it had certainly fooled him. Rocking forward in his chair, he said quietly, 'It seems mature of Nick to have accepted that the child comes with the relationship.'

'Well, of course he would.' Fliss's voice was slightly strained. 'Matthew is his son. Look…' she flapped a hand '…it's a long story but, put simply, Julie doesn't want to get married until Nick is fully qualified and done his GP training. Then, as you probably know, he's aiming for a rural practice, the reason being that he and Julie can put down roots in a caring community, raise Matthew together and perhaps have another child.' She broke off, bit her lip and blinked uncertainly. 'What?'

'Good grief,' Callum said faintly, and shook his head. 'You've found out all this in just over a week in the place. I'm terrified.'

Fliss balled her paper serviette and lobbed it at him. 'I can't help it if people choose to confide in me.'

'Even me.'

Fliss's mouth dried. She couldn't miss the irony in his voice. 'You won't let on to Nick even by the tiniest hint that I've told you any of his background, will you?'

He shot her a reproving look. 'Do you think I'd have got to where I am by blabbing all over the place, Felicity? It's obvious I need to review all the duty hours of the entire A and E staff. It's time it was done anyway and I intend to start with you, Dr Wakefield.'

She huffed a cracked laugh. 'What've I done?'

'Worked too many hours.' Callum's eyes narrowed over her. 'As of this moment you're off duty. I don't want to see you until the late shift on Thursday.'

Fliss's hand went to her throat. 'But that's nearly three days off!'

'And that's my business.' Callum was unequivocal. 'Go and have some fun. You've more than earned it.'

She blushed. 'Thanks, then. I'll, um, drive to Brisbane and stay

with Dad, link up with a couple of friends, do some shopping…
Do you really mean this, Callum?'

'Of course I mean it.' His jaw tightened for a moment. 'But
there's one condition.'

Overcome with the thought of such a long break, Fliss dimpled
a smile at him. 'Bring you back a present?'

Sweet heaven, she was lovely! Callum felt his mouth tip up at
the corners but was powerless to prevent it. The need to hold her
and kiss her senseless was so urgent he almost jumped up from
his chair to make it happen. But, of course, that would be complete
madness. Instead, he exchanged the half-smile for a frown and let
the avalanche of emotion wash over him. 'No, I don't need a
present from you, Felicity,' he murmured gruffly. 'I just need you
to come back, that's all.'

CHAPTER NINE

FLISS was back on duty. She called at the nurses' station first and brought herself up to date. 'Anyone hanging about for tests or sutures?' she asked Anita.

The charge shook her head. 'We've cleared everyone out so you can sit down, twiddle your thumbs and wait for the next emergency.'

Fliss chuckled. 'Not too good at thumb twiddling. But I'll go and check with Callum. I imagine he'll have plenty of paperwork for me to do.' She could hardly wait to see him.

Callum made himself concentrate. But the endless paperwork drove him to distraction. Some of it he could pass on to Fliss. She seemed to fly through it. He looked at his watch again. She'd be on duty now. He took in a hard breath and let it go slowly. He knew he was back because earlier he'd made a point of checking her sporty little hatchback was in its usual spot in the communal garages.

He'd missed her. Oh, boy, how he'd missed her. He brought his head up at the soft tap on his door. Fliss. He knew it would be her. Schooling his expression and forcing himself to focus and try to ignore the searing ache of want that permeated the whole of his body, he called more sharply than he'd intended, 'Come in!'

Fliss popped her head in and then the rest of herself. Turning, she closed the door and looked across at him. 'Hi.' She smiled, a warm, pretty, sexy smile that lit up her face and made his breath jam in his throat. 'I'm back.'

'So you are.' Callum got to his feet slowly, meeting her where she'd stopped at the front of his desk. 'It's good to see you,' he murmured.

'You, too.'

They smiled at each other, careful not to touch. Callum parked himself against the edge of the desk, folding his arms and crossing his feet at the ankles. His gaze narrowed down on her. 'Feeling refreshed, then?'

'Yes, thanks. Went wild with shopping. And some friends took me to a long lunch at the latest up-market eatery. Being in the city always gives me a tremendous buzz.'

At her carefree, throw-away words, Callum felt as though she'd slammed a door in his face and the cloudburst of anticipation that had drenched him at the thought of her return fizzled to a trickle. Oh, hell, was he already fighting a losing battle here? She was positively glowing, hyped, no doubt, from the adrenaline rush of her time back in the fast lane. Suddenly in his mind was a queue of questions he daren't ask, let alone expect answers to.

Fliss brought her gaze higher and sent him a faintly puzzled look. He'd gone quiet, jumped right back into his shell. Was it something she'd said—or not said? 'How have things been here?' she asked, her bright interest genuine.

He stayed silent for a moment and straightened carefully from leaning against the desk, watching her. 'Uh, quite busy,' he said neutrally. 'But I've had time to revamp the duty hours for the team. Simon and Nick have had input but I thought I'd wait and discuss your preferences with you.'

'You haven't forgotten my commitment to implement the fitness programme for the boys at the high school and Trail Farm?' she reminded him. 'I'll need to make a definite time for that.'

'We could do that now, if you like.' Half-turning, he snapped a manila folder from the corner of his desk. 'Here or in the canteen over a coffee?'

Disconcerted at his businesslike tone but unable to quell the warm, bubbly feeling she got from just being around him, Fliss decided it would be much safer in the canteen. 'What about your own hours?' she asked as they left his office and made their way along the corridor.

He shrugged. 'I've cut back a bit.'

'I managed to speak to the head teacher at the high school and Tony Buchan as well when I got back today,' Fliss said over their coffee. 'Thursdays would appear to suit them both so if I could manage to have a part of that day off, I could begin setting up a regular training and exercise programme for the boys.'

'Barring emergencies, you could take the whole day off.' Callum spread out the paperwork he'd prepared and passed it across to her.

'This looks very fair for everyone,' she said, perusing the times on the roster carefully. 'And I quite like what I'm seeing here.' She stopped, her teeth biting into the softness of her lower lip reflectively.

'Oh, that.' Callum gave a rough laugh.

'Mmm.' She shook her head in mock disbelief. 'You're actually cutting down on your own duty hours—not much,' she allowed, a tiny dimple flowering in her cheek as she smiled. 'But some.'

Callum didn't return her smile. Instead, he stuffed the paperwork back into the folder and said stiffly, 'I'll pencil you in for Thursdays off, then.'

'But I expect to work in lieu,' Fliss made clear. 'I'm not asking for an extra day off here.'

'Understood.' Callum drained his coffee and got to his feet. 'I'll fix it and give everyone a revised copy of the duty roster.' And then his bleep sounded. He pulled it out of his pocket and checked the message. 'Apparently, there's a phone call for me at the station.'

'I'll walk with you.' Fliss leapt to her feet.

'Maddie for you, Callum,' Anita said, handing the handset across the counter.

'She's not at work today?' Fliss raised a questioning brow at the charge.

Anita shook her head. 'She's begun her new revised hours, working Monday to Wednesday only.'

'Oh, of course.' Fliss remembered the grievance she'd felt on Maddie's behalf with the secretary's hours being cut back so drastically. 'Did she say what the problem is?'

Anita shrugged. 'One of the twins seems poorly. She wanted to check with Callum—'

'I'll have to get round there,' Callum broke in, replacing the receiver on its cradle. 'It's young Sam. Tummy ache, vomiting and temp.'

'Couldn't we call an ambulance for her? Or perhaps she could bring Sam in?' Fliss suggested.

'No chance.' Callum dismissed. 'Jeff's away at a regional meeting and taken the car. The ambulance he normally drives is in for a service and the other one's on duty at the Ibis Plains race meeting.'

Fliss looked appalled. 'What if we suddenly had a road trauma?'

Callum's shrug was so slight she hardly saw it. 'This is rural medicine, Dr Wakefield. We'd manage. Like we always do.'

Feeling slightly rebuffed, Fliss stood silently as Callum took off towards the exit. Watching him, she shook her head mutely, feeling as though she was suddenly floundering around in deep, unknown waters with nowhere safe to place her feet.

Callum took only a few minutes to get to the Curtis home. Swinging out of the car, he collected his bag from the boot. He knew Maddie was not one to panic but she'd sounded close to it when she'd spoken to him. Obviously she'd been watching out for him. The door was flung open before he was even through the front gate.

'Thanks for coming so quickly, Callum.' Maddie ushered him through to the bedroom, her fingers pulling agitatedly at the edge of her shirt collar. 'Why do these things always happen when Jeff's away?'

Callum put his hand briefly on her shoulder. 'Just let's have a look at Sam, shall we?'

He sat carefully on the edge of Sam's bed, noticing at once, that the child was sweaty and very pale. 'Hi, Sam,' he said gently. 'Mum tells me you're not feeling so well.'

Sam shook his fair head and closed his eyes, a little moan like that from a small animal escaping from his lips.

Callum wasn't surprised to find the child's pulse rapid and thready. He looked up at Maddie. 'How long has he been like this?'

'Yesterday, when he got home from school, he said he'd felt sick all day. I put him to bed and he vomited during the night. He said he had a stomachache. I gave him a hot-water bottle and he seemed to doze off. Then this morning he was sick again and he's just got worse as the day's gone on.'

Callum nodded, turning back the covers and gently easing Sam's pyjamas down to expose his abdomen. Even the gentlest palpation revealed a telltale rigidity. Callum's mouth drew in. Poor little kid. They were going to have to move fast. 'I'll need to get him straight into hospital, Maddie.'

'What's wrong with him?' Maddie lifted a trembling hand to her mouth.

Callum stood to his feet, motioning her out of earshot. 'I'll give this to you straight, Maddie. Sam has acute appendicitis.'

'Oh, my God!' Maddie's eyes flew wide. 'I should have called you earlier. Instead, I dithered—'

'Don't worry about that now,' Callum cut in gently. 'But there's no time to lose. Sam will need surgery. So round up Jacob and I'll take the three of you to the hospital.'

When Maddie had gone running down the hallway, calling to Sam's twin, Callum pulled his mobile out of his back pocket and hit a logged-in number. 'Anita? Callum. Could you alert Theatre, please? I'm bringing young Sam Curtis in, suspected burst appendix. He'll need an emergency laparotomy. I'll do it. Penny there to gas him?'

'Yes, I just saw her,' Anita confirmed. 'I'll fill her in. She'll be waiting for you.'

'Thanks. See you in a bit.'

Fliss ripped off her gloves and moved to the basin to wash her hands. Lord, that woman's carping voice was still in her head.

'You OK?' Anita stuck her head in.

Fliss made a small face. 'Kids! Who'd have them?'

'And mothers like that one,' Anita added with dry humour. 'Now, why don't you take a break while you can? I'll get this lot cleared up.'

'Thanks, Anita. I might just do that. Any sign of Callum? It's been ages since he took Sam to Theatre.'

'Just saw him heading for the station.'

'Oh, good.' Fliss finished drying her hands and tossed the length of paper towel into the disposal bin. 'I'll catch up with him there.'

Callum sensed her presence when she was still six feet away. Hell, he was even getting psychic about her.

'How did it go with Sam?' she asked quietly, coming to a stop beside him.

He looked up and she saw at once she'd interrupted a focused train of thought. He blinked a bit. 'Bit of a mess when I got in there. But I tidied him up. He should spring back fairly quickly and we'll hit him with antibiotics for the next little while.'

Fliss didn't believe for a minute that the surgery had been as straightforward as he'd made out. 'You looked whacked,' she said bluntly.

'I am a bit,' he admitted, adding his signature to Sam's notes and placing the file to one side. He looked at her through half-closed eyes. 'Any coffee going?'

'I can do better than that.' Fliss's breath caught and she found herself in a kind of holding pattern beneath his moody blue appraisal. 'What about some home-made soup?'

'Sounds good.' He glanced at his watch. 'Ten minutes? I promised Maddie I'd call Jeff and give him an update on Sam.'

'He's not on his way back, then?'

Callum lifted a hand and rubbed the back of his neck. 'He wanted to drop everything and head back but he's enrolled to do some advanced paramedic training tomorrow and if he misses out, heaven knows when he'll get a place again. Maddie insisted he stay put. She'll cope and Sam's out of danger now.'

'Thanks to you.'

He raised his eyebrows. 'It's what I do.'

'Added to what you do already in A and E. Where was Max Birrell?'

He gave a controlled sigh. 'He'd already left for the day. He hasn't been able to spend much time with his wife lately. Anyway, I wanted to do Sam's surgery for Maddie's sake.'

Of course he did. And he certainly didn't need *her* going to bat for him about his workload. Her smile was wry and repentant. 'OK, point taken. See you in the staffroom in ten, then. I'll heat the soup.'

It was nearer fifteen minutes later when Callum joined her in the staff room. He came up behind her and peered over her shoulder at the jug of soup she was stirring. The aroma of home-style cooking reached his nostrils. 'What kind is it?' he asked. 'Vegetable?'

'Mmm.' Fliss turned abruptly, her mouth almost colliding with his collar-bone. 'I threw in everything I could lay my hands on, plus a can of kidney beans.'

'And you really did make it yourself?'

'Don't sound so surprised.' Fliss showed him the tip of her tongue. 'I made it last night. Dad and Deb had tickets to a concert. So I stayed home and did my laundry and made the soup.'

Callum felt the unease in his gut begin to unravel. It didn't sound as though she'd spent her entire time away partying. A smile nipped his mouth. 'My nana used to make a huge pot of soup when we stayed with her in the school holidays. She'd always maintain it would *stick* to us.'

Fliss gurgled a laugh. 'Mum used to say that, too, about porridge in the winter. Gruesome thought, isn't it? Food sticking to you.'

'I don't think they meant it in the literal sense.' There was a sheen of softness in Callum's eyes as he watched her neat co-ordinated movements. In a couple of minutes she'd set a bowl of the steaming soup in front of him and a small basket of bread rolls on the table between them.

His brows shot up. 'We are dining in style.'

'Elaine from the canteen gave them to me,' Fliss explained casually. 'They're leftovers from this morning's bake so they'd have only been thrown out, or Elaine sometimes takes them home for her chickens.'

A bemused expression came over Callum's face and he picked up his spoon. After more than a year in the place, he hardly knew who worked in the canteen, let alone intimate details like who took bread home for their chickens! 'You like to get to know *everyone,* don't you?'

'I've never thought about it.' Fliss reached out and took a roll and broke it open. 'It's not a bad trait, is it?'

'No.' Callum shook his head. 'Not at all.' In fact, her sassy, outgoing personality was one of the things he loved about her. Hell, had he connected her with the L-word? Suddenly, his heart began trampolining. He'd almost forgotten what it felt like to have these gut-wrenching feelings about a woman. When you didn't know whether you were on your head or your heels. He bit back a derisive laugh. Or perhaps the answer to his uncertainties lay in the simple fact he'd never met a woman like Fliss Wakefield. He set about his meal with a relaxed kind of enjoyment. 'Every bit as good as Nana's,' he approved a little later chasing the last spoonful of soup around his bowl.

'I'm flattered,' Fliss responded laughingly. 'Could you go a second helping?'

He looked a bit sheepish. 'If there's enough…'

'I made plenty, knowing I'd have to feed you.' She got to her feet and zapped the remainder of the soup in the microwave. 'I've seen you demolish a giant-sized pizza, remember?'

He laughed, then asked, 'I guess your father was pleased to see you?'

'Mmm.' Her look was soft. 'But it wasn't as though I hadn't seen him recently. What about your parents? When did you last see them?'

His face settled into soft, reflective lines. 'I got down to Armidale for Christmas last year.'

'And do your parents keep in good health?'

'Exceptionally. Dad's coming up to sixty-two but he still works as a surveyor with the city council there. Mum's now retired from her office job and loving the extra time to devote to the grandkids and golf. She heads up a couple of committees fundraising for various charities as well.'

Fliss poured the reheated soup into his bowl. 'That must be where you get your organisational ability from.'

'Must be.' His look was droll. 'My folks have been married nearly forty years.'

'What a marvellous achievement!' Fliss took her seat once more, cupping her chin on her upturned hand and looking across at him. 'That's practically a lifetime, isn't it? Can you imagine being with someone so long?'

He swallowed a raw laugh. 'Hell, I couldn't even make it to *four* years in my marriage, let alone forty.'

'But surely you haven't given up hope of giving it another shot?'

His jaw worked for a second. 'It takes some coming back after you've been dumped.'

Fliss dropped her gaze. She could empathise with that. Although she hadn't actually been dumped. Still her relationship with Daniel had ended as disastrously as Callum's appeared to have done. She swallowed. 'It would be awful to give up hope of it happening, though, wouldn't it?'

For a long moment Callum looked at her, his gaze unwavering. 'Yes, it would be awful to give up hope,' he agreed quietly.

'Oh, help.' Fliss gave a jagged laugh and flew up from her chair. 'This is way too deep a conversation to be having over a snatched meal in a casualty department.'

'Speaking of Casualty,' Callum said. 'How's it been since you came on?'

'Not too bad.' Fliss ran water into the sink and shot in detergent. 'A trickle of walking wounded who could probably have been patched up at home. An elderly lady from the caravan park who thought she was having a stroke. Felt giddy when she'd got out of bed this morning and kept getting little flurries of imbalance all day. I could find no evidence of stroke and diagnosed her condition as being vertigo related. I told her it was probably self-limiting but advised her if she's still unwell in a few days to come back. She may need referral.'

'Was she experiencing nausea?' Callum asked.

'Some. I prescribed accordingly.'

'Anything else?' He took his dishes across to the sink.

'A fourteen-year-old boy who'd been skateboarding along the main street and wrapped himself around a lamp post. Egg on his forehead and great gash on one knee, needing sutures.'

Callum made a click of impatience. 'When will these kids learn to wear protective knee and elbow pads when they're skateboarding?'

'Probably when they're too old or too crippled, whichever comes first,' Fliss joked. 'His mother brought him in and harangued the life out of him. It was a wonder you didn't hear her in the theatre suite.'

'You should have chucked her out of the treatment room.'

'Believe me, I thought about it. But then the father showed up and things calmed down a bit. They went off playing happy families—well, kind of,' she ended with a grin. 'I think they were going to the pub.'

Callum raised his gaze to the ceiling. 'That'll help.' He rolled back his shoulders and stretched. 'Thanks for dinner. I'm just going to pop up and check on Sam, before I head home.'

'OK.' Fliss rinsed the last plate and placed it in the rack to dry. 'I'll check him later as well and let Nick know when he comes on at eleven. Off you go.' She flapped a soapy hand at him. 'The place won't fall apart because you go home and get a decent night's sleep for a change.'

'I guess it won't.' His mouth folded in on a dry smile. 'Not when I have a bossy woman in charge. Hey!' With a quick twist of his body he dodged the wet sponge she threw at him. 'OK—hold your fire! I'm going!' Backing away and holding up his hands in self-defence, he left, laughing.

It was two weeks later and a Monday at mid-afternoon. Fliss had taken a break and wandered outside the casualty department to sit on the garden seat. Lifting her head, she caught the now familiar country smells, her gaze stretching to the fields beyond, drinking in the scenery: the patchwork of the winter crops and stands of eucalypts that dotted the paddocks.

Glancing at her watch, she stifled a sigh. Another hour before she went off duty. Over the past days she'd seen Callum only briefly at the hospital and it seemed he was giving her much more autonomy. Apparently he was taking his decision to stop working such long hours quite seriously.

And she should have been glad for him. And she was, really. But she'd got used to seeing him at all hours, couldn't stop the rush of pleasure when she heard his deep voice greeting her.

Almost without her knowing, he'd become an integral part of her life.

But now it seemed he'd taken a step back, almost distancing himself from the closeness that had crept up on them so quickly, and the intimate moments they'd shared may as well have been consigned to the history books. Would he ever say to her again, 'You kiss so sweetly…'

'Ah, there you are, Dr Wakefield.' Callum's voice cut into her dreaming like scissors through silk and to her dismay Fliss felt herself flush guiltily.

'Just taking a break,' she said, trying to ignore the wild thumping of her heart. 'Did you need me for something?'

'Just felt like a chat.' He glinted a blue gaze at her, before sitting down next to her and stretching out his arm along the back of the seat behind her. 'We don't seem to have caught up properly for a while.'

'No. Uh, how was your weekend?' she asked in a rush of words.

Callum rocked his hand. 'A bit mixed, actually.'

A tiny frown creased her forehead. He looked rather serious. 'Something wrong?'

'We've several cases of animal cruelty happening in the district. I've a young wallaby recouperating at My Place. It had been injured and left to hop through the bush with an arrow protruding from its shoulder.'

'That's sickening.' Fliss put a hand to her throat. 'How was it found?'

'A couple of young lads roaming through the bush with their dog stumbled across it. Because of the arrow it had been caught up in bushes and couldn't release itself.'

'Oh, poor thing.' Fliss's tender heart was touched. 'It must have been petrified.'

Callum's mouth compressed. 'The vet had to tranquillise it. And now the police have become involved. It seems some lunatic is out there taking random shots with a longbow.'

Fliss suppressed a shiver. 'Lord, Callum—it could be a child next!'

'Yes.' He looked grimly into the distance. 'I understand the police have been up to the school, warning the kids but also asking them to keep their ears open for anyone bragging about their prowess with a bow and arrow.'

'What's the world coming to?' Fliss stared ahead to the distant shape of the mountains. She couldn't believe the anguish she felt. Poor unsuspecting creatures cut down in their natural habitat where they had every reason to feel safe. 'What other wildlife have been hurt? Do you know?'

'Two Eastern Grey kangaroos. One was so badly injured, it had to be euthanised and the other was killed outright. She had a joey but it later died from pneumonia.'

Fliss shook her head silently, then asked, 'How is your wallaby doing? Will it survive?'

'The vet's pretty hopeful. Fortunately, the wound was new so the chance of infection has been lessened.' There was a short silence and then he asked softly, 'Want to come out and see her after your shift?'

'Could I?' Fliss jumped to her feet excitedly. 'I'm off in an hour. Do I have time to shower and change?'

'Of course.' Callum drew in his feet and uncurled slowly upright. 'I have to catch up on some paperwork but I should be able to get away about four.'

Callum ploughed on through his paperwork and then threw his pen aside. Funny, he couldn't seem to concentrate at all. Thoughts of Fliss kept intruding. Thoughts like the softness of her breast under his hand, and the sweetness of her mouth. And the ache she was going to leave him with when she returned to the city.

As she surely would.

Although he knew she was making the very best of things in Mt Pryde, he guessed she was missing her life in the city. She'd looked as though her thoughts had been far away when he'd found her in the garden earlier. He sighed. He couldn't ask her to stay on for his sake, no matter how much he was beginning to realise he might want to. He'd be asking her to compromise. And he'd been down that road before with Kirsty and look at how that had turned out.

Suddenly, none of it bore thinking about.

* * *

'Fliss?'

She looked up from her magazine, her heart leapfrogging all over again at the sight of Callum. 'Hi.' She couldn't help the smile that curved her lips. 'You're early.'

'I've jacked it in for the day. Paperwork gives me a king-sized pain in the head. And it's worse now with Maddie's hours cut back.'

Fliss made a sympathetic click with her tongue. 'I've told you to pass it along to me.'

'You're already doing enough.'

'By your estimation.' She stood to her feet and tossed her magazine aside. 'Sock it to me. I find all those forms we have to fill out a challenge.'

'You would.' He chuckled. 'OK, I'll delegate.' His gaze lingered over her. She looked good enough to eat in her close-fitting jeans and toffee-coloured fleecy top, her hair loose and tumbling free and her eyes like deep, dark pools with the sun glinting around the edges. 'Ready to go, then?' Callum struggled to find a neutral tone among the chaos of his thoughts.

'I'm quite ready. I was just killing time until you showed up. Any more word from the police?' she asked, as they made their way down the stairs from the verandah to his car.

Callum shook his head. 'Nothing. It's a big call. There's only the sergeant and two constables to cover the whole of the district. Perhaps they're going to have to rely on help from the public.'

'Or get a couple of detectives up from the city,' Fliss supplied helpfully.

'Could I run something past you?' Fliss asked a bit later as they drove towards Callum's acreage.

He swung his head towards her and lifted an eyebrow. 'Sure. Fire away.'

'It's about the football teams,' she said carefully.

'Getting too much for you?'

Fliss made an impatient tsk. 'Not at all. The high-school lads are going great, really tuned in but that's because they're already sports fit, whereas the lads at Trail Farm have a way to go. I mean, they're all shapes and sizes and I'll have to get their fitness levels up before they can really enjoy their game, otherwise they're going to be falling in a heap and that won't help anyone's confidence.'

'So, how can I help?'

Fliss locked her hands together across her chest. 'Well, I've spoken at length to Tony and he's managed to find some extra funds to hire some exercise bikes. They should be delivered to Trail Farm by the end of the week. I wondered if you'd mind coming with me to help set up the programme?'

'I can do that.' Callum lifted a shoulder. He'd have tried to walk on water if she'd asked him to. 'But crikey, Flissy—exercise bikes? You'll never get the kids on those!'

She rolled her eyes. 'They're not those boring contraptions you're likely to find gathering dust in people's garages. These bikes are slick, state of the art. A whole new concept in training. It's called spinning.'

'I see,' Callum said, although clearly, he didn't. 'So, what does *spinning* entail, exactly?'

'Every class is a little different,' she went on to explain, 'but the great thing about it is that each person can go at their own pace. And it's low impact,' she emphasised. 'So it's especially suitable for the lads at Trail Farm. We'll get some great music going and project a virtual ride on to a screen so the guys will have the impression they're out on the open road with all its hills and bends. It'll be wonderfully motivating and most of all it'll be fun.'

Callum glanced at her narrowly. 'So, for my efforts, do I get to do the fun stuff as well?'

She chuckled. 'We'll have a race, if you like.'

'A virtual race,' he corrected. 'Saturday all right?'

'I'll look forward to it,' she murmured, snuggling into the bubble of happiness that surrounded her.

'It feels nice to be here again.' Feeling absurdly light-hearted, Fliss swung out of the four by four and looked around. 'Oh, look!' She raised an arm, pointing to the trees, which were covered in pink blossoms. 'The peaches have all come out since I was here. Aren't they pretty, Callum?'

'Mmm.' But not as pretty as you, he wanted to add, but didn't. Instead, a soft smile played about his lips and he casually draped an arm across her shoulders. 'Let's go over to the pens and see how our wallaby is doing, shall we? She'll probably be up and about by now.'

Fliss frowned a bit. ' Even with her injury?'

'It's to her shoulder,' Callum pointed out patiently. 'Not her hind legs. She's able to hop about. Although not as freely as she normally would. And if we go this way, we can look in on her without her seeing us. We don't want to add more stress to what she's already been through.'

Callum led her towards an opening high up on the back wall of the enclosure. 'Can you see?' he asked, drawing her closely in beside him.

'Just—if I stand on tiptoe.'

'Hang on, then.' Callum looked around him, spotting a sawn-off small log. Rolling it with his boot, he toed it across to the pen. 'Stand on this.'

'Thanks.' She smiled, putting her hand on his shoulder and hoisting herself up.

'Can you see now?'

'Yes. Oh, Callum…' she sighed in a stage whisper. 'Isn't she adorable?'

'I wouldn't go that far,' he responded dryly. 'But she's looking better. Her eyes are bright and she seems to be compensating physically with regard to the injury. She's eaten as well,' he added, pleased the dish of green shoots and grains he'd left were almost gone.

'That's a really good sign, isn't it, Callum?'

'Yes.' He sent her a tender look and after several more minutes asked, 'Seen enough?'

Fiss made a moue of regret. 'I could watch her all day and never get tired of it. Are we going to name her?'

Callum gave a strangled laugh and helped her down from the log. 'If we must. What did you have in mind?'

She smiled. 'I'm thinking.'

It seemed entirely natural to link hands as they strolled back towards the house, their footsteps taking them under the fringe of a lacy pepperina tree and for a moment they stood and watched a bee buzzing in and out of honeysuckle climbing rampantly over the back fence.

'I know!' Fliss broke the quiet of the moment with a little gasp of delight and turned to him. 'We'll name her Nutmeg.'

'Nutmeg?' Callum's eyebrows soared. And then he laughed and hugged her . 'Translate.'

'Well, she's brown,' Fliss justified, her hands on his forearms as she looked up at him. 'And sweet. And we could call her Meggie for short.'

'Or Nutty—which I have to be, going along with this. She'll

be released back to the wild soon, Flissy. It's not like she's going to become a pet about the place.'

'I know.' She tilted her head, regarding him serenely. 'But that's no reason *not* to give her a name, is it?'

'I guess not.' His mouth twisted. 'And it's kind of what I expected when I asked if you'd like to see her,' he added teasingly.

'You're getting to know me too well…' In a burst of emotion Fliss raised her arms, her fingers curling into the strong silk of his hair as she snuggled closer, loving the feeling of being close to him after what seemed like weeks of him holding her away. 'Why have you been avoiding me?'

'I've been around…' His mouth was so dry he could hardly speak.

'But not properly.'

'As properly as I dared be…' His mouth lowered to her throat to kiss the pulse that beat frantically beneath her skin.

She titlted her head back, her mouth opening with delight at his touch. And when his hand slid to cup her breast, a scattering of pinpricks showered over her skin. 'Callum…'

'Oh, sweet…' he said softly, and then his lips found hers.

Fliss's response was electric, desire sharp and shocking rocketing through her. She was powerless to end it, to pull away, making a little sound in her throat when his hands shifted and curled around her backside to urge her closer to him.

'Ah, Flissy.' Callum broke the kiss, burying his face in her throat again, his hands sliding beneath her top to roam restlessly across her back. 'You tempt me to distraction.'

'Mmm… I think I want to.' She drew his face back to hers, kissing him, opening her mouth on his, tasting him. 'Shall we go to bed?'

Callum stilled and then a low rumble erupted from his throat. 'I should have known you'd be the one to spell it out.'

She blinked uncertainly. 'It's what you want too, isn't it?'

'Are you crazy?'

'That's a *yes,* then?'

He hugged her hard so there could be no doubt about his answer. Then, pressing her closely to his side, he hurried her through the back gate and up the verandah steps and along the hall to his bedroom. He closed the door softly and for a long moment they looked at each other. Callum put his hands on her hips, his chest lifting in a deep breath. 'I…guess this is where it all begins for us, Flissy.'

And ends? But, no, she wouldn't let it end. Suddenly she felt filled with a life-giving force, wanting him more than she'd ever wanted anything in her life. 'Undress me,' she breathed, hearing her own heartbeat, already feeling the imprint of him on her body.

When it came to the undressing part, they helped each other, laughing like children as they threw their clothes to the four winds. 'All done.' Fliss couldn't wait a moment longer to burrow in against him. To hold him and be held in return.

'I was never quite sure we were going to get here.' After the longest time Callum stepped back and looked at her. 'You're quite beautiful,' he said, his voice rough-edged and husky.

'And your timing's exquisite.' The softest smile edged her mouth and she reached out to carry his hand to her breast, standing full and proud as she straightened back. 'See? My heart's going wild.'

'Do you think it's been easy for me?' His hand curved over the swell of her breast and tightened. 'I close my eyes and you're there and I want you. I can barely think straight.'

'Can't you? Really?' Fliss had never been so aware of her own sensuality. She gave a husky, feminine laugh that made his body clench.

They paused just long enough for him to protect her.

Then there were no more words, no need for words. Callum reached for her, rolling her with him on to the bed, his body hard and warm against hers. It was as though they crossed into another world, Fliss thought, trembling as his hands, gentle yet knowing, sought responses from her, touching her deepest senses, sculpting her body from head to toe.

'Let me now,' she whispered, dazed with emotion, aching to discover him. She heard his groan of pleasure and in seconds they were lost in the taste and texture of one another, moving in perfect rhythm, climbing ever higher to the place where they met in a wild storm of their shared release, drenched in a million stars.

As her breathing steadied, she found Callum leaning over her, his hand protectively over her quivering ribcage, raw emotion carved into his features. 'Do you feel anything like I feel?' he murmured huskily.

'Shattered?' Her face crumpled. 'Oh, Callum…' Overcome, she turned her face into his shoulder. How had Kirsty ever let him go?

'Oh, Flissy. Sweetheart…' He rocked her gently and kissed her hair, before spreading it like a dark river of silk across the pillow.

* * *

Later, as they lay drowsily replete, Callum turned on his side so they were facing each other. Lifting a lazy hand, he combed his fingers back through her hair. 'It'll be dark soon.'

'Mmm.'

'Shower and an early dinner, then?'

'Lovely.'

He sent her a look from under half-closed lids. 'By coincidence I put some champagne in the fridge this morning.'

She gave a slight shaky laugh. 'Decided today was the day, did you?'

'No. But I thought I may as well start living in hope.'

Freeing a hand, Fliss ran a finger along his jaw and across his bottom lip. 'Hopes fulfilled, then.'

He bent, brushing her lips once and again. 'You've turned me inside out, Flissy... You're incredible.' His voice held the slightest wonder. 'In every way.'

Fliss blinked rapidly, feeling tears of reaction spring into her eyes. Was this Callum's way of telling her he loved her? Filled with the joy at the discovery, yet terribly uncertain, she responded throatily. 'That makes two of us, then.'

CHAPTER TEN

'I'D FORGOTTEN life could be so good,' Callum declared, as they showered together.

'My hair's all wet,' Fliss complained, pouting at him.

'Sorry.' He ran a trickle of shower gel down her between her breasts and smoothed it over her skin. 'This establishment doesn't run to ladies' shower caps.'

'Hairdryers?'

'Nope.'

You're enjoying this, aren't you?' she said, her look somewhat indulgent and half-amused.

'Aren't you?'

Of course she was.

A few minutes later, he closed off the taps and insisted on towelling her dry. 'There you are, all pretty and pink.' He looped the towel around her and drew her close. Suddenly he looked uncertain. 'Tell me I'm not dreaming, Fliss.'

'You're not dreaming, Callum.' She reached up to bracket his face, her heart in her gaze. 'And I have a feeling all this was meant to happen.'

'We're lovers now, aren't we?' he said, almost reverently, his arms making two nurturing bands of warmth across her back. And then they kissed, sweetly and completely.

What a perfect, perfect end to the day, Fliss decided a bit later as she stood at the verandah railings and looked out at the gathering dusk. Lifting her glass, she took another mouthful of ice-cold champagne and smiled softly. No one had ever told her it could be like this. But now she knew for herself. She was truly, deeply in love for the first time in her life.

'Hey, what happened to a fair division of labour, Felicity?' Callum's exaggeratedly long-suffering tone came from the kitchen.

Fliss made a face at the back fence. 'Just coming…' And then she called shrilly, 'Callum! Here! Quickly!'

'What is it?' He bounded from the kitchen and crossed to the railings to stand beside her.

'I saw something move—over there, near the shed. See?'

Callum screwed up his eyes, adjusting to the semi-darkness. 'I don't see—'

'Yes—over there,' she said again, tugging at his sleeve. 'Oh, my God, Callum…' Her voice froze and then trembled. 'It might be the bow man.' Her eyes flew wide. 'What if he's come back to finish off Meggie?'

Callum frowned. He couldn't see anything. But on the other hand… 'Get inside, Flissy,' he rapped. 'I'll go out and check.'

'Be careful.' Fliss's heart began beating like a small fist inside her chest. But despite Callum's warning, she wasn't going anywhere. Watching his dark shape slip quietly along the fence-line, she felt the nerves of her stomach gather and clench. What if it *was* the bow man? Callum had no weapon to defend himself. Oh, lord…

Her throat closed in panic as a muffled kind of shout came from the direction of Meggie's enclosure. Should she call the police? Clamping her teeth on her bottom lip, she stood frozen, head tilted, listening. And then it came. Callum's voice, his message clear and actually containing a thread of laughter.

'It's OK. Don't panic. I'm coming back.'

In a few seconds Fliss saw him jogging across the yard towards her. 'Well?' she demanded, before he was even halfway up the steps.

'It was another wallaby.' He grinned. 'Probably Meggie's mate.'

'Really?' Fliss's shoulder slumped in relief. 'But isn't that sweet, Callum? He's come looking for her. Oh.' She sent him a look of dismay. 'What if Meggie gets upset, though? She could try to break out.'

'Stop fretting.' Soft humour glinted in his eyes. 'She can't get out. They'll just have to wait a bit longer to be reunited, that's all. And judging by her progress, it might be as soon as a couple of days.'

'Oh…right.' She gave a shaky laugh. 'Being a wildlife carer is a terrible responsibility, isn't it?'

Callum rolled his eyes.

'Well, it is,' she defended. 'It might be all right for you, you're used to it. But my tummy feels like I've just got off a roller-coaster.'

'Need a hug, then?' he asked softly, drawing her to him. Sweet heaven, it felt so good to have her in his life like this, he marvelled. So damn wonderful. He pulled in a shaken breath, still almost poleaxed with the newness of it. 'OK now?' he asked after a bit, leaning back to look at her.

'Just about.' A tiny frown marked her forehead. 'What if it had been the bow man, Callum? What would you have done?'

His mouth pulled down comically. 'Brought him down with a rugby tackle?'

'But what if he was bigger than you?'

He gave a mocking lift to his eyebrows. 'I'd have still tackled him.'

'Oh…' She pouted. Then, turning her face up to his, she placed the sweetest kiss on his mouth. 'My hero.'

'I'd ask you to stay but I've to be at the hospital very early in the morning,' Callum said, as they sat over a second cup of coffee.

'Big op?' Fliss asked, helping herself to another chocolate-coated digestive biscuit.

'Pretty big but hopefully straightforward. I'm assisting Max with an elective Caesar. The mum's delivering twins.'

Fliss looked thoughtful. 'You get a real variety of medicine here, don't you?'

'Mmm. That's what I like about it. No chance of getting into a comfortable rut.'

She flashed him her brightest smile. 'Challenges every day. I'm beginning to like that, too.'

Callum felt his hopes soar. But he wouldn't take anything for granted. What they'd found together was perfect. Enough to be going on with. When they'd finished their coffee, he drove her back to town.

'Don't come up,' she said softly, as he released the locks on the car. A teasing smile played around her lips. 'I know how you feel about hospital gossip.'

Nevertheless, they managed one fierce kiss before she slipped out of the car and ran lightly up the stairs to her room.

* * *

It was almost noon the next day when Fliss walked into A and E for her shift. She'd arrived early hoping to have a private word with Callum before she went on duty. She hoped with everything in her he wasn't having doubts about what they'd done. The *morning after* was tailor-made for regrets. Was he even now agonising that they'd travelled a bridge too far? But she trusted him and that was the whole reason she'd handed her heart to him on a platter, believing he would keep it safe. For ever. But had she been a fool again? Too trusting? But it wasn't as though he'd held back. A tiny smile nipped her mouth. Quite the contrary.

Her heart revved and she looked up and down the department, wondering if he'd be in his office, but then she heard his voice and her heart fluttered. She hurried to find him.

Callum couldn't believe how energised he felt. And he couldn't stop smiling. Hell, he felt like an adolescent in love. That thought brought him up short, all but brought him out in a cold sweat. Suddenly the weight of what he and Fliss had done tumbled down on him. Had he done the wise thing in letting her get so close? But what they'd had had been entirely special. Mind-blowingly so. But now perhaps he should be practising caution, take nothing for granted. Taking a step back was probably a good option—

'Callum!'

He swung round and saw her coming towards him, her beam of expectancy sending his feelings of uncertainty into orbit. He pulled air into his lungs and let it go. 'Morning.' He sent her a contained little smile. 'Or is it afternoon?'

'Just, I think. How are you?' she tacked on very softly.

'Fine,' he responded, a little too heartily. 'My office for a minute?' He led the way.

Closing the door quietly, he turned to her and Fliss would have gone straight into his arms but something in his face held her immobile.

Her confidence dropped to the floor. 'What's the matter, Callum?'

'Nothing.'

'Don't treat me like me like I'm less than bright.' She brought her gaze up sharply. 'You're acting as though we've just met.'

Callum felt his throat thicken. And standing so close to her wasn't helping. The faint drift of her distinctive floral shampoo was already escalating into the reality of her head on the pillow beside him. And the completeness of their loving. With great effort he forced himself to ignore the searing ache of want that enveloped him. 'Flissy—'

'Don't shut me out, Callum.'

Her earnest little plea shattered his reserve. 'I'm not—I don't want to.' His jaw tightened. 'I…just think we should take stock.'

'Of what?' Fliss felt a hard core of disbelief in her chest. 'Didn't you mean the things you said to me last night when we made love?'

'Of course I did!' His reply was harshly muted.

'Then what's changed this morning?

He expelled a rough sigh. *Nothing. Everything. I think I'm in love with you. And that makes me terrified for you.* He couldn't voice any of them.

When he didn't respond, Fliss spread her hands entreatingly. 'Look, this has kind of crept up on us. We're both feeling vulnerable. It's understandable. Both of us have been hurt by other partners.'

'Fliss, I was *married*. It's hardly the same thing as—'

'My hole-in-the-corner affair?' She gave a bitter laugh.

'That's not what I meant.' He twisted on his heel, took several swift steps to the window and looked out. Finally he turned back, shaking his head as though trying to rid himself of some unwanted burden. 'It's taken me a long time to get my life back together after watching my marriage go down the chute.'

'Don't you think I know all that, Callum? But I also recall you said it would be awful not to try again. And I'm not talking about marriage, for goodness' sake! I'm talking about turning your back on a relationship between us—one that's good and true.'

His throat moved convulsively as he swallowed. 'We don't know that for sure, though, do we, Flissy?'

'Can't we spare the time to find out?' she countered, spreading her hands in appeal. And wondered why she was fighting so hard to keep this man when he was riddled with enough doubts to topple an elephant. Because she loved him and because, although he probably didn't realise it yet, he loved her. She had to believe that. She just had to. Otherwise what had last night been about?

Her words went straight to Callum's heart, but before he could frame an answer two things happened simultaneously. The phone on his desk rang and Anita knocked and popped her head in. Callum waved the charge in and snatched up his phone. 'OK, thanks,' he said, replacing the receiver with a snap a minute later. 'That was Maddie, reminding me I have a lunch meeting with the

Rotary club,' he informed the two women tersely. His eyes went to Fliss. 'We might have some joy about that project for the Trail Farm lads.'

Fliss held his gaze—just. 'Crossed fingers, then.'

'Yes. Anita, sorry.' Callum responded to the charge's calm presence with an apologetic little nod. 'Can we help you with something?'

Anita's puzzled gaze flicked between them. Suddenly her antennae were twitching. Heavens, she must have been going around with her eyes shut. The chemistry between these two was not too far short of combustible. She pulled her thoughts up quickly. 'We're being sent a suspected whooping cough. Five-year-old boy. Referral from Dr Jo McNeal. As you probably know, Jo's had some experience in paeds. She's quite concerned about this little chap.'

'Do we take it he's not immunised?' Fliss enquired.

'Apparently not.'

Callum snorted. 'Parents need their backsides kicked for neglecting this basic part of their child's health care.'

Anita made a shrugging movement with her hand. 'According to Jo, they don't believe in it—or didn't. Perhaps now they're wishing they'd had him done. Whooping cough can be so debilating for children.'

'And contagious as all hell,' Callum growled. 'We'll have to set up a bed in isolation, Anita.'

'That's what I wanted to organise with you. We could use that four-bed verandah ward.'

'Fine.' Callum looked at his watch. 'I'd better get going in case the Rotarians change their minds.' He swung to Fliss, his lean jaw at an angle as he looked down at her. 'I'll leave you to admit our pertussis when he arrives. And involve Nick,' he instructed. 'It's quite possible he's never seen a case of whooping cough.'

'Let's get through the red tape as fast as we can,' Fliss said to Anita as they hurried back to the station. 'The sooner we can get this little lad admitted and receiving some kind of treatment, the better. By the way, do we have a name?'

'William Fielding. Parents, Hunter and Rosemary.'

'Bit of an epidemic starting, is there?' Nick said when he joined them at the station.

'Heavens, I hope not,' Anita sighed.

'According to Julie, they've had three admissions in as many weeks at St David's,' Nick informed them.

Fliss ran the tips of her fingers across her forehead, dragging her thoughts from personal to professional. 'Have you seen a case of whooping cough, Nick?'

He shook his head.

'Might be good for you to be involved, then,' she said shortly. 'Anita, is Jo sending some notes with our patient?'

'Yes.' The charge nodded. 'But the family are new patients so not much history available. But to save us time Jo said to tell you she's scribbled out the latest recommendations for what drugs they're prescribing in paeds for the treatment of pertussis.'

'Great.' Fliss felt the tension slip from her shoulders. Thank heaven for Jo's proactive approach to medicine.

'Ah.' Nick swung round, hearing the approach of trolley wheels through the ambulance entrance. 'Must be our people now.'

Jeff was escorting the trolley containing the child, with two people, obviously the parents, following closely behind. 'Where do you want him, Doc?' the ambulance officer asked quietly.

'Cube one, please, Jeff. And, Tammy.' Fliss addressed the young assistant in nursing. 'Would you help with the transfer, please?'

'Yes, Doctor.'

Taking one look at the parents' faces, Fliss bit down on her bottom lip. It was obvious they were almost falling apart. She went forward to greet them. 'Mr and Mrs Fielding? I'm Felicity Wakefield. I'll be the senior doctor treating William.'

The mother's eyes dissolved in a shimmer of tears. 'We never thought this would happen to our little boy…'

'Rosie, don't…' Hunter Fielding placed his arm awkwardly around his wife's shoulders. He sent the group an apologetic grimace. 'We had definite views on immunisation when William was born. Decided against it. Now…poor little kid…'

At her husband's words Rosemary gave a strangled cry and turned, sobbing, into her husband's chest.

Fliss began delegating quickly. 'Anita, if you wouldn't mind? We'll need some history.'

Anita got the message. Tea and sympathy and get a history as best as she could. She placed a guiding arm around Rosemary. 'If you'll just come this way?'

'W-what about William?' the mother asked piteously.

'The doctors will look after him now and you can see him when he's all settled in.'

'Crikey,' Nick muttered, as they watched the couple follow Anita, Rosemary dabbing at her eyes with a large handkerchief her husband had handed to her. 'I'm glad we got Matty done.'

'Wouldn't have been much of a health professional if you hadn't,' Fliss responded, her mouth faintly set. 'But now let's see what we can do for this little lad, shall we?'

'How are you feeling, sweetheart?' Fliss's face was set in concentration as she flicked her stethoscope over the child's chest.

'My tummy hurts…' the little boy whispered. His fair head went back on the pillow and he began a paroxysm of coughing.

Fliss pocketed her stethoscope. 'Let's get him onto a nebuliser, please, Nick.'

'Got it.' Nick gently tipped William's head back and settled the nebuliser into place. 'Breathe away now.' He flicked a query at Fliss. 'Usual bronchodilators?'

'Yes, please. And we'll run saline IV as a precaution.'

Fliss's mind flew ahead as she watched Nick prepare the IV. They were going to have to keep a careful watch on this little one. With his continual coughing, ending more likely than not in vomiting, the child would rapidly become dehydrated. She hooked up the bag of normal saline. 'We'll order some chest physio as well, Nick.'

'Right.' He scribbled on the card. 'What drugs will you treat him with?

Fliss hastily referred to Jo's explicit notes. 'According to Dr McNeal, erythromycin seems our best shot. And she's noted William's weight and suggested dose so, if you'll watch him, I'll get the drugs.'

'You did well in there, Nick,' she said when their small patient had been transferred upstairs to the ward. 'You were extremely gentle with William.'

'Second nature.' Nick grinned, obviously pleased. 'Comes of having a little guy of my own, I guess.'

Fliss's feet hardly touched the floor for the rest of the afternoon. It seemed the residents of Mt Pryde had picked Tuesday as the best day to have minor or messy accidents and at least for one of them a suspected heart attack. She sighed as she left the treatment room. Thank heavens they had a full staff on duty today and she was spared from the inevitable clearing up. As she made her way back to the station, she saw a familiar figure approaching. Her eyes lit up. 'Josephine McNeal, by all that's wonderful!'

The two hugged briefly. 'How's everything?' Jo's eyes ran discerningly over her friend's face.

Mixed up, crazy—take your pick. Fliss gave a jagged little laugh. 'Busy. You?'

'The same. Uh, I'm just here to see William, Flissy. OK if I go up?'

'Of course. He's in isolation on the verandah ward. And if you're uncertain about your own immunology status, gown and mask, please.'

Jo stuck out her tongue. 'I've been done.'

'I should hope so.' A teasing smile curved Fliss's mouth. 'Coffee when you come down?'

'Please.' Jo flapped a hand. 'See you shortly.'

Later, as they entered the canteen, Fliss said, 'Find a table, Jo, and I'll grab the grub. I missed lunch,' she explained a bit later, setting a plate piled with cinnamon toast on the table between them.

'Oh, yum.' Jo rubbed her hands together in anticipation. 'I'm starving as well.'

Fliss sent her friend an arch look. 'Not pregnant, are you?'

'No.' Jo chuckled. 'I'm more than fulfilled taking care of our little Andrew for the present.'

'You're really happy with Brady, aren't you, Jo?'

'He's my soul-mate,' Jo answered with a misty kind of smile.

Oh, help. Fliss tried to swallow past the lump in her throat. Why had she asked such a damn-fool question when her own love life was in tatters? She blinked a bit and took a hurried sip of her coffee. 'How did you find William?'

'Oh, by running up the stairs and asking Sister if I could see him,' Jo quipped facetiously. She wasn't fooled by her friend's quick change of subject. Fliss was down in the mouth about something. Perhaps, if she pushed gently, the lady might open up. And perhaps not. 'He's seems to have settled quite nicely,' she said seriously. 'Thanks for looking after him.'

Fliss lifted a dismissive shoulder. 'Thanks for the paeds update. Saved us heaps. The parents were a bit of a mess.'

Jo rolled her eyes. 'I was a bit direct with them, I'm afraid. But, lord, I hate to see kids suffer so unnecessarily. I know you do as well. So…' Jo took a bite of her toast '…you've had a while. How are you finding Mt Pryde?'

'Oh, by opening my eyes and looking around.'

'Oh, ha, ha. Seriously, Fliss, have you made some new friends?'

'Here and there. And mainly among the hospital staff.'

'I see…'

Fliss sent her gaze upwards. 'Jo, you've got your worried face on. I'm a survivor, remember?'

'Of course you are.' Jo leaned over and pressed the other's hand. 'Can you come to a party at our place on Saturday night? Brady and I want to return some hospitality. We're going to have it outdoors. We'll organise some braziers to keep warm and fairy-lights in the trees to make it romantic and lots of lovely food.'

'Like old times.' Fliss grinned. 'And I'm just in the mood to party. What time?'

'Sevenish. And feel free to bring someone.'

Fliss sent her friend a dry look. 'A date.'

'Perhaps you'd like to invite Callum?' Jo suggested innocently.

And perhaps she wouldn't. 'We'll see.' Fliss lifted her coffee-mug and took a careful mouthful.

Jo drained her own coffee and got to her feet. 'Thanks for the snack, honey. My treat next time. I'll pop back and see William tomorrow. And if I don't connect with you then, I'll expect to see you on Saturday.'

'Saturday,' Fliss repeated.

Jo slung her bag over her shoulder 'Gotta run. Take care.'

'You, too. Give my best to Brady and a kiss for Andrew.'

'Shall do.' Jo fluttered a finger wave and departed quickly.

Fliss went back to the ED. It was almost time for her to go off duty. She hadn't seen Callum since he'd left for a working lunch. Perhaps he'd had other hospital business to attend to. It seemed obvious he wasn't in any hurry to attend to the *personal* business hanging unfinished between them.

Well, she could wait it out just as well as he could. He couldn't avoid her for ever.

Callum's vehicle was in its parking space when Fliss crossed to the hospital for her early shift next morning. Her tummy dived. Would he hang about long enough for them to at least finish the conversation they'd started yesterday? Or perhaps he'd disappeared into his hidey-hole and intended to stay there? Whatever time it took, she'd wait until he came out. Her decision firmed as she made her way to the staffroom. Pushing open the door, she came to a swift halt.

Callum was sitting at the table, a cup of tea at his elbow and the local newspaper spread out in front of him. He didn't look up.

Bad sign, Fliss decided, going across to the fridge to store the salad she'd made for lunch. 'Morning.' She turned and looked at him, a rush of physical desire, urgent and totally unexpected, threatening to overwhelm her.

'The kettle's just boiled, if you want tea.'

'Thanks.' She didn't but she'd have drunk a dozen cups of the stuff if it meant reclaiming a shred of normal conversation with him.

'Have you seen the paper?' He pointed to an article on the front page. 'They've caught the bow man.'

'Really?' Fliss's hand went to her heart. 'That's brilliant! How did they get him?'

'It's all here in the paper.' Callum tapped the page. 'Apparently, an alert bar attendant at the Gettalong noticed this guy drinking on his own. Thought he looked a bit rough, smelt to high heaven. Then she noticed the odd-shaped canvas bag he'd propped up on the seat beside him. She waited until this customer took off towards the men's and then she acted. Had a quick gander in the bag and found the evidence—one bow and several lethal-looking arrows.'

'Oh, my stars…' Fliss's eyes were out on stalks. 'What did she do next?'

Callum lifted his head, sharp lines cutting into his cheeks as he smiled. 'Put the stuff back where she'd found it, got the cretin another beer on the house and called the police.'

'Wow! What a story. He's not a local, I take it?'

'Seems not. Drifter with a grudge against animals apparently.'

'That's sick.' Fliss shook her head. 'But it means Meggie and all her family are safe now, doesn't it?'

'Seems so.' He gestured towards the kettle. 'Are you having that tea?'

'I don't really feel like it, thanks. Were you called in early?' She crossed to the table and placed her hands on the back of a chair, facing him.

'No.' He rattled the pages of the paper together and threw it aside. 'Just wanted to let you know the Rotary have decided to sponsor the Trail Farm football team.'

'Oh—good.' Fliss's fingers tightened on the back of the chair. It *was* good news but it wasn't the kind of conversation she'd hoped to be having with him at all.

'I took several of the committee up there yesterday afternoon.'

'They hadn't been there?'

'No. They were pretty impressed. They want to get the lads kitted out a.s.a.p.'

Fliss raised her eyebrows. 'Boots and all?'

'Yep. They're even letting the guys decide on the colour strip they'd like.'

'That'll make them feel so special, Callum.' She paused. 'We did a good job there, didn't we?'

Callum's look was quick and speculative. 'It was mainly down to you. I just tagged along.'

'It was more than that,' she disagreed. 'You lent your support and that gave me the impetus to keep going.'

They exchanged a wary look that was almost a smile and Fliss thought that if she didn't bite the bullet and ask him now, she never would. 'The McNeals are having a party next Saturday night. Jo was in yesterday, visiting our little pertussis patient. She invited me and a friend. Would you like to go with me?'

He blinked for a second and then his mouth lifted in a dry twist. 'It seems I'm already going. Brady's invited me—and a friend.'

'Oh…' Fliss fought for control of her wildly see-sawing heart. 'Are they trying to set us up?'

'Probably. But we've beaten them at their own game, haven't we?'

'Have we?'

The two words hung like thunder in the air. Callum's heart was beating like a tom-tom. Just one night away from her and he'd missed her like crazy. And now here she was barely centimetres away from him, her faint delicate fragrance teasing his senses and making a mockery of his control. Damn! There was so much he wanted to say to her but for the life of him he couldn't seem to get his tongue to co-operate.

Scooting his chair back, he got to his feet, shifting awkwardly as he pushed in his chair. 'Flissy, I know we have to talk, but this is not the time or place.'

'Maybe not. But I need to know where we stand, Callum.' Her gaze faltered. 'I'm through with chasing shadows.'

There was a breathless silence, and Fliss felt sure if a pin had dropped she would have heard it. So much depended on what he told her now. So much. Probably what she ultimately did with the rest of her life.

'Flissy—' He began to speak and then broke off as his bleep gave its summons.

She turned away, feeling an unkind fate had stepped in again, the result leaving her feeling more vulnerable than ever.

Frowning, Callum checked the message and then shoved his pager back in his pocket. 'We'll talk, Fliss. I promise,' he said hurriedly.

'And what about your promise to come with me to Trail Farm on Saturday, Callum?' she asked, her voice cracking. 'Are you going to keep that as well?'

'Of course I am...' His voice roughened. 'And we'll go the party together on Saturday night. And afterwards I'll take you home to My Place for what's left of the weekend. Enough?'

Fliss swallowed the razor-sharp emotion clogging her throat. 'For now,' she said. But she couldn't stop the burst of happiness that bubbled up inside her, swamping all the worry and uncertainty. They'd have plenty of time to talk at the party. And if Jo kept her promise of a romantic setting...

CHAPTER ELEVEN

FLISS ploughed on through the week. Despite her frustration about a certain matter and with a certain man, she decided the only way she'd cope was to compartmentalise her emotions and put everything on hold until she and Callum could talk properly.

And now Friday had come round at last.

Almost impatiently Callum heaved himself to his feet, pacing across to the window and looking out. Frustration was killing him and he couldn't settle to anything. But worst of all, he still had no clear answers for Fliss. But, then, maybe there *were* no clear-cut answers. Perhaps, as she kept telling him, it was time for him to trust a little—a lot. At a tap on his door he turned sharply as the door opened. 'Fliss.' His mind emptied. 'Everything all right?'

'Just confirming about tomorrow—Trail Farm?' Fliss felt a flutter of unease as she moved across and joined him at the window. Had he forgotten his promise already?

But it seemed he hadn't. 'Are we driving up together?'

She shook her head. 'I'm going up quite early. I want to give the lads a verbal orientation before we begin the practical stuff, and Jack Metcalf's keen to join in. He'll eventually take over the training so he needs to be involved from the beginning.'

'So what time do you want me there?'

Her mouth pursed for a thoughtful second. 'Ninish should be OK. We've ten bikes so I'll have to take several classes. By the way, did you read up on that stuff I gave you?'

'About the fundamentals of the programme? Yes, I did.' He angled his back against the window-ledge and folded his arms. 'So, what do I have to wear for this spinning lark, then?'

She managed a small smile. 'Strictly speaking you should be attired correctly in cycle wear.'

'What?' he squawked. 'You'll never get me into that Lycra stuff that looks more at home at the ballet!'

She sent him a weighted look. 'Footy shorts and a T-shirt are fine. But I'll be wearing Lycra.'

'On you, Felicity, that's a different proposition altogether.' Callum's eyes flickered over her and the warmth in them made her own breath jerk in response.

The gym at Trail Farm was a hive of activity when Callum arrived on Saturday morning. His gaze went straight to Fliss and stayed there. Dressed in her black Lycra bike shorts and bright green top, she looked professional and in total control of things. Although he had to admit, with her stormcloud of hair caught up in a jaunty ponytail, she looked about sixteen.

Heat shot through him, and he was glad of the diversion when Tony hailed him from across the room and made his way over.

'She's great, isn't she?' Tony said, his line of vision following Fliss's movements as she went through a simple warm-up programme with the youths. 'Having Fliss involved has been a real turn-around for us. I hope we'll be able to keep up some kind of fitness regime going when she leaves Mt Pryde.'

Callum felt his stomach drop, as if he'd fallen over a cliff into a wide yawning space. 'Her contract still has a way to run,' he countered gruffly. And maybe she won't want to leave when her time is up, he willed silently. And then again, maybe it would be all down to him, whether he could convince her to stay...

Almost on cue, Fliss chose that moment to skip across to them. She was beaming. 'The guys are looking good, aren't they?'

'More enthusiastic than I've seen them about anything,' Tony agreed. 'Congratulations, Fliss.'

'Hey, not yet, Tony.' Laughingly, she held up a stalling hand. 'We've a way to go still.' She flicked a very direct look to Callum. 'You ready?'

Callum's mouth tightened for a second. 'Just tell me what you want me to do.'

'OK. I've split the lads into three groups. They're all beginners at this, so my job and Jack's will be to make sure they're all positioned correctly and stay that way throughout the class. And what

I'd like you to do is to keep an eye on how they're coping physically. Naturally, if you see anyone in distress, feel free to act.'

'I think I can manage that.'

'Thanks.' Her mouth curved in a quick smile. 'I don't expect any problems but, with adolescent males, you never know.'

Not even with fully grown ones, Callum decided moodily, watching her move quickly back to her charges.

In a few minutes Fliss had the boys for the first class seated on their bikes. 'OK, guys,' she instructed, 'get yourselves into position. Remember what I've told you. Place your foot over the centre of the pedal and make sure your shoelaces are tucked in and your feet attached securely attached to the pedals.'

'What if we fall off, miss?' someone asked.

'You get back on again. And this is not a competition, OK? Go at the pace that feels right for you.'

'Please, miss?' A skinny-looking redheaded fifteen-year-old stuck his hand up.

'Yes, Nathan?' Fliss replied patiently.

The lad hung his head a bit. 'Uh, will this help my legs bulk up?'

Youthful sniggers echoed around the gym.

'Actually, that's a very good question,' Fliss responded. 'As you know, we're going to be simulating a bike ride on the screen, which means there'll be hills involved. Climbing those hills is an excellent way to build strength, so of course you'll be acquiring firm muscles in your legs as a result.'

'Now, Jack and I will be moving among you during the ride to make sure you all get a great workout. So, hit the music, please, Tony. And have fun, everyone!'

She was amazing, Callum thought, watching Fliss as she slipped between the bikes, offering each lad advice or encouragement or repositioning them. And her pupils responded with enthusiasm.

Clearly, she was enjoying herself, her face alight with the process of empowering this very mixed bunch of troubled youths. She was in her element, on a natural high. His gut wrenched. He could only guess what the decision to come to Mt Pryde had cost her in terms of work satisfaction. Accident and emergency medicine was light years away from the adrenaline-pumping world of sports medicine.

Was she longing to get back? And if she was, what could he do to keep her here?

Some two hours later the last of the youths shuffled out of the gym, mock-punching one another and boasting about their prowess on the bikes. Fliss watched them go, then grabbed a bottle of water and drank thirstily. 'Oh, boy,' she said when Callum joined her, 'that was some workout.' She looked up at him. 'How did you think it went?'

'It was brilliant,' he said quietly. 'You've given those kids something real to strive for. Congratulations.'

She went pink. 'Thanks. I feel a real sense of accomplishment, if that doesn't sound too boastful. And they did seem to enjoy it, didn't they?'

He nodded. 'I rescued a couple of the lads, did you notice?'

'Yes. Thanks for that. What was the problem?'

'Dizziness. They recovered quite well but they may need a bit of private tuition before they feel comfortable with the concept of spinning.'

'Possibly. I'll have a chat to them later. Now, what about you, Doctor?' Her mouth kicked up in a teasing smile. 'Ready to go spinning with me?'

Callum's heart did a tumble-turn. He took a breath that expanded the whole of his diaphragm. 'I thought you'd never ask.'

Fliss dressed carefully for Jo's party. She wanted to look special for Callum. Heart fluttering, she stood in front of the mirror. The jeans, camisole top and figure-fitting suede jacket looked understated but smart. But something was missing to tie it all together. She thought for a second, clicking her fingers as the answer came in the form of the leather belt with a rather elaborate buckle she'd bought on her recent trip to Brisbane. Hitching it low on her hips, she looked in the mirror again and decided she'd got it just right.

It had been ages since he'd gone to a party. Callum's mouth turned down as he dragged on a bulky-knit jumper in an earthy brown colour. He wasn't antisocial but parties inevitably bored him rigid. But tonight he'd have Fliss by his side, and that fact banished any thoughts of boredom to the four winds.

He hauled in a long controlling breath and squared his shoulders. He couldn't hang about any longer. He had a certain lady to collect and a party to go to. Fifteen minutes later he knocked on Fliss's door and waited, his heart pounding like a herd of elephants on a rampage.

Fliss opened the door, her look expectant. 'Hi. I'm just ready. Come in for a second.'

Callum followed her inside, his throat so dry he could hardly speak. Memories of the first and only time he'd been there rising up to mock him. But surely emotionally they'd moved on a thousand miles since then. To what, though? The answers still evaded him.

Fliss picked up the small overnight case and held it out to him.

Callum's heart kicked and he swallowed. 'Still coming home with me, then?'

Her eyes clouded briefly. 'I'm still invited, aren't I?'

'Lord, yes.' He jerked a shoulder self-deprecatingly. 'I'm not taking anything for granted these days, that's all.'

Nettled, she said bluntly, 'Perhaps I should get "Trust me" tattooed across my forehead, then.'

Callum's emotions began to show. 'Flissy, I only meant—'

'Don't.'

His eyes narrowed on her flushed face, the angry tilt of her small chin. Damn! There was so much he *wanted* to say to her.

Almost as if she'd read his thoughts, Fliss softened. 'Look, let's enjoy the rest of the weekend, shall we?'

'Yes…' A gravelly sigh dragged itself up from the depths of his chest. 'Let's do that.'

She spun away, collecting a tiny beaded shoulder-bag from the end of the bed. 'This party is going to be such a treat after the long hours we've been working.'

'Looking at you is quite a treat in itself,' Callum said throatily. His gaze flickered all the way down her body and back again. 'You look stunning, Flissy.'

'Oh, thanks…' she said breathlessly, her hand flying to her chest to cover the peep of cleavage. 'You look stunning, too.'

His mouth kicked up in a crooked smile. 'If we've finished admiring each other, we should get going. We're already a bit late.'

'Oh, don't worry about that.' She tossed her head back, the action sending highlights bouncing off her dark hair. 'Jo will make sure we're fed.'

'Music's not too loud, is it, Brady?' Jo began gathering dessert plates to take outside to the supper table.

'Wouldn't think so.' Brady was peering out into the party scene beyond the kitchen window. He turned to his wife. 'Would you say Callum and Fliss are an item?'

Jo rolled her eyes. 'Of course they are. Callum hasn't taken his eyes off her all night and Flissy's stayed glued to his side. And that's remarkable for her. She's usually darting around like a butterfly at anything resembling a party.'

Brady slipped his arm around his wife's shoulders and grinned. 'Think we've given them a bit of nudge, then?'

Jo leaned forward and kissed him sweetly on the lips. 'No question.'

'You're looking very pensive,' Callum observed. They were up to the coffee stage and had taken themselves off to a love-seat under the hanging branches of a mulberry tree.

Fliss sent him a quick smile. 'I was just wondering if we'd been thoughtful guests and mingled enough.'

'You bet we have.' Callum was emphatic. 'Besides, I want you to myself for a while.'

She rested a hand on his shoulder and looked around her, breathing in the crisp night air. The tea-lights were sending out shards of diffused colour from within their glass containers and the fairy-lights Jo and Brady had strung in the trees had conjured up a misty, magical ambience. 'It's been a really lovely evening, hasn't it?'

'Mmm. The McNeals certainly know how to stage a party.'

'Jo, Sophie and I gave some memorable parties when we all lived together in our resident years,' Fliss reminisced softly. 'Seems ages ago now.'

'It must seem so from the great age of—what?' Callum turned to her, soft amusement in his eyes.

Fiss wrinkled her nose at him. 'Thirty-one.'

'We'd better dance, then.' Unceremoniously, Callum pulled her upright. 'Before we both qualify for aged care.'

In the shelter of the trees they could have been the only two people in the world. Her hands went up around his neck and they moved gently to the rhythm. 'Nice jumper.' She smoothed her palm over his soft cable-knit.'

'Alpaca wool. My nana knitted it.'

'I can't knit,' she confessed dreamily.' She felt his smile on her skin as he touched his mouth to her throat.

'Neither can I.' After a minute he asked, 'Shall we leave

soon?' His shuddering breath licked across her temple. 'I need
you so much…'

Her breathing faltered. It was what she ached for, wasn't it? To
be part of his life? Yet something pulled her back to sanity. She
loved him. He *needed* her. Was she being a fool to dream it would
ever change?

'What is it?' As if he sensed her confusion, he frowned and then
he was cupping her chin in his strong, clever hands. 'Have you
changed your mind?'

A couple of heartbeats.

Fliss's hand found its way under his jumper and T-shirt, loving
the feeling of the smooth sweep of his skin against her palm.
Loving him. She was just being silly. Pining for happy ever-after
and in danger of losing what she could have now with Callum.
Emotion welled in her and she raised her head and found him
staring down at her. 'I haven't changed my mind.'

'Then let's get out of here,' he whispered raggedly, wrapping
her in his arms and cradling her against his chest.

They slipped quietly away.

His bedroom looked the same, yet everything felt different.

Fliss's mouth seemed suddenly dry and her heart, with a mind
of its own, had gravitated to her throat. It had been ages since he'd
held her properly—nearly a week since they'd become lovers.
Could they possibly recapture what they'd found together?

'Flissy?'

The catch in his voice told her everything she needed to hear.
With a little cry she flew into his arms.

'Morning.'

Fliss opened her eyes and found Callum propped up on one
elbow, looking down at her. 'Hi…' She reached up a hand and
teased a little circle on his chest with her fingernail. 'Happy?'

'Mmm.' He smiled, a lazy, almost possessive smile and, leaning
closer, lowered his mouth to hers.

They ate breakfast out on the back deck.

'Everything looks so pretty from here, doesn't it?' Fliss's gaze
took in the flowering peach trees and the winter wattles ablaze with
gold along the edge of the little creek.

'Hardly believe it's winter, would you?' Already the rich bold colours of sunrise had faded, giving way to a clear blue sky. 'Fancy a picnic today?'

'Could we?' Fliss's face was alive with anticipation.

'I don't see why not.' Callum's smile was indulgent. 'I've arranged cover at the hospital. And we deserve a day off.'

'You're such a nice boss.' She smiled until her face felt it might crack. I could die at this moment, she thought, and know I'd never been so happy.

A couple of bliss-filled weeks later, Fliss finished an early shift and on the spur of the moment drove out to see Callum. He was taking a rare day off, to catch up on maintenance around the acreage, he'd told her.

When she arrived, he'd almost finished mowing a strip of lawn in front of the house. She got out of her car and waved, waggling the cake box she'd brought out from town. He lifted a hand in casual acknowledgment and pointed for her to go inside.

Ten minutes later he pounded up the back steps. Fliss went to meet him. 'Hello,' she said almost shyly. 'I've brought afternoon tea.'

'Have you just?' His hands slid down her arms, then shackled her wrists. 'Can you stay the night?' he asked softly.

'If I'm invited.' Her throat suddenly dried. What they'd found together was still all so new and wonderful.

His gaze locked with hers, his meaning clear. 'You're invited.'

She licked her lips. 'I'll stay, then.'

He drew back, smiling a little and brushing a tiny curl off her forehead. 'What did you bring for afternoon tea?'

'How was your shift?' Callum asked when they sat over their second cup of tea.

Her mouth turned down. 'Busy. Several cases of food poisoning. Turns out all the patients had been at the pub for dinner last night.'

'Not the Gettalong?'

'No—the other one. They had an all-you-can-eat buffet night.'

He made a sound of disapproval. 'They probably ate that hot-box food. Beats me how it can be guaranteed safe. The temperatures have got to be fluctuating the whole time.'

'I've notified the health department,' Fliss said. 'Are they normally responsive?'

Callum shrugged. 'Depends how busy they are. But in cases where the health of the public is concerned, they usually act quite swiftly.'

'Good.' She leaned across to stroke his jaw, loving the slight rasp of his beard. 'Can we leave the shop talk now? There's something I want to tell you.'

'And I've something to *show* you.'

'Oh, OK.' She reached up and pushed her hair back from her face, tucking it behind her ears. 'Do you want to go first?'

Callum felt a glitch in his heartbeat. He'd been storing up his surprise for the last few days, waiting for the right opportunity to spring it on her, anxious as a cat on a high wire for her reaction. Hoping with everything in him it would lead to the kind of future he could only dream about.. But Fliss seemed to be bursting with something so he forced himself to say steadily, 'Mine can wait a few minutes. Fire away.'

'I had a phone call from Daniel last night.'

Callum went still, almost rigid, his mouth tightening into a straight line. 'I can't believe you'd have wanted to give him the time of day.'

Immediately, Fliss felt wrong-footed. 'Are you saying I should have hung up on him?'

Callum shrugged a shoulder dismissively. 'What did he want?'

'To explain things,' she said defensively. 'The way things ended, he never had a chance to. I decided I could at least give him that.'

Callum merely moved his lips in a cynical little twist.

'He's getting a divorce,' Fliss ploughed on resolutely. 'He said he and his wife had married because she was pregnant. They'd tried hard but it hadn't worked.'

Callum snorted. 'So he decided to play the field.'

'No,' Fliss countered sharply. 'He didn't. He stayed faithful—until he met me. Then everything changed for him.'

Callum gave a derogatory growl in his throat. 'How touching! And you believed him?'

'Why would he lie? He has no future with me.'

'Does he know that?'

Fliss ignored the barbed question. 'He just wanted to let me know that he valued what we'd had and that it hadn't been some kind of casual fling…'

Callum stared at her in silence for a moment, his jaw clenched, a tiny muscle jumping. 'And why did *you* feel it was necessary to tell me any of this, Felicity?'

A flood of colour washed over her cheeks and her teeth worked her lower lip. 'Because…I thought you just might have cared enough to empathise with my feelings of relief that I hadn't been merely another affair for Daniel and that he hadn't deliberately set out to *use* me,' she ended brutally.

'Of course I care. And if you believe your former lover, fine. That's entirely up to you. I just wish you hadn't involved me in any of it.'

She flinched as if he had struck her. 'I don't think I'll stay after all.' She leapt to her feet, twisting out of his grasp when he would have contained her.

'Fliss—don't leave.' He spread his hands in appeal.

'Give me one good reason why I shouldn't?' she spat at him.

He swore—a couple of short pithy words. 'You can't hit me with something like this and expect me to just rationalise everything and relegate it to the past.'

Fliss stared at him, her heart aching. Funny, that was exactly what she'd hoped to achieve.

He didn't try to stop her leaving.

Tears blurred her vision as she drove back to town. It was only when she'd garaged her car and opened the door on her little bedsit that she realised Callum hadn't shown her his surprise. Well, she'd never know what it was now. They were history. A case of another attempt at finding her true love biting the dust. Throwing herself down on the bed, she howled as though her heart would break.

Callum wanted to throw things. Nothing he'd said to Fliss had come out right. He'd felt sick to his stomach as he'd watched her little hatchback head off down the road. Away from him. His heart lurched painfully. His response had been pathetic. Immature and thoughtless. No wonder she couldn't wait to get shot of him.

He buried his face in his hands. It had taken him under a minute to completely destroy everything precious between them. *Everything*.

Fliss dragged herself across to the hospital next morning. Callum was there already but he barely looked at her, wishing her a curt good morning before shutting himself in his office.

Fliss felt the sharp pain of rejection all over again. Why on earth

had she gone on hoping against hope he would have re-thought
things overnight and at least agreed to talk to her without anger
clouding the issue?

By ten o'clock she felt she was going crazy. The department
was unusually quiet and what casualties had come in she had con-
fidently handed over to Nick. Time hung heavily, like an invisible
yoke across her shoulders. Even the never-ending paperwork failed
to challenge her. She managed to fill in another half-hour, and then
a flurry of excited squeals sent her, a bit tight-lipped, towards the
nurses' station. What on earth was going on?

'Oh, Fliss—look!' Anita, Jess and Tammy were all crowded
around the most magnificent trailing bouquet Fliss had ever seen
in her life.

'They're for you!' Jess was wide-eyed and wearing a water-
melon grin.

'For me?' Could they be a peace offering from Callum? Fliss
felt her spirits soar and then plummet. This kind of wildly exotic
floral arrangement had never come from the local florist's shop.
Her throat went dry. And that only left Daniel. It was just like him
to do something so flamboyant. The hollow feeling in her
stomach intensified. But surely he wouldn't want to embarrass
her like this...

'A courier van delivered them from Brisbane,' Anita enlightened her with an arch smile.

'Oh.' Fliss smiled weakly.

'Crikey.' Nick appeared at her elbow, shaking his head in disbelief at the floral carpet taking up most of the countertop.
'Somebody dic?'

Tammy swallowed a giggle. 'Dr Rossi, you're awful!'

'Awful funny,' he shot back. 'Who are they for?'

'Dr Wakefield,' Tammy supplied helpfully.

'Wow! Who loves you, babe?' Suddenly his face lost its teasing
humour. Fliss looked in shock. He picked up the shiny gold
envelope accompanying the flowers and handed it to her. 'Why
don't you read the card, hmm?'

Oh, lord, why hadn't she thought of that? A bit dazedly, she
slipped the card from its envelope and blinked. Oh, thank heavens.

'Well?' Three female voices rose in unison.

A relieved smile curved Fliss's mouth as she satisfied their curiosity.

'Isn't that just the sweetest thing?' Jess's eyes turned soft.

'What will you do with them?' Anita asked practically. 'I mean, there are dozens of blooms there.'

Fliss shook her head. Anita was right. There were miles too many of them to take back to her room. 'I guess we could split them into vases and brighten the wards, couldn't we?'

Tammy stepped forward eagerly. 'Like me to do that for you, Dr Wakefield?'

'It's OK, thanks, Tammy,' Fliss rejected the youngster's offer gently. 'I'm not busy at the moment. I'll do it.' Needing both arms to carry the enormous sheaf of blooms, Fliss took them through to the utility room.

It was there Callum found her several minutes later. 'What was all the racket earlier?' he asked, censure in the coolness of his tone.

'I got a delivery of flowers,' she said inadequately.

His eyes went to the assortment of blooms she'd spread across the worktop. 'More likely an entire florist shop.' He huffed a bark of bitter laughter. 'Hoping to soften you up, is he?'

Fliss met his eyes, startled. Oh, lord, he'd jumped to the same conclusion as she had, that the flowers had come from Daniel. She took a shaken breath. What a muddle. 'Callum, there's a very simple explanation.'

His mouth grew taut. 'If you decide you want to go back to him…'

'What?'

'If you do,' he went on quite deliberately, 'I can ease the way for you to get out of your contract with the hospital.'

Fliss was appalled. She stared blindly at him. 'Callum…' she choked, but got no further. He'd turned and gone.

Fliss couldn't believe how things between her and Callum had broken down so quickly and completely. She'd dispensed with the flowers in record time, sending several big vases to the wards and keeping a mixed bunch back for herself.

When lunchtime came, she avoided the canteen. Instead, she collected her flowers and went across to her room. She made a sandwich she couldn't swallow, walking aimlessly around the small space until it was time to return to the ED. Anita was just putting the emergency phone down when Fliss arrived at the station.

'Are you OK?' The charge looked shaky.

'There's been an explosion in the science room at the high

school,' Anita relayed starkly. 'Two boys. Thirteen-year-olds. Burns. For a moment I thought one of them could have been my Joshua…'

'Oh, Anita.' Fiss squeezed her eyes shut for a second. 'What a scare for you. Is the ambulance there?'

'Both out on other calls.'

'OK…' Fliss took a moment to think the situation through, scraping up her professionalism. 'In that case we'd better get over there.'

'What's up?' Callum had come up light-footedly behind her.

Anita filled him in briefly.

'Right. I'll call Cliff Enright at the high school and tell him we're on our way.' He directed a sharp glance at Fliss. 'You up for this?'

Her heart beat an odd tattoo. Was he calling her a wimp now? 'Of course.'

His mouth pulled tight. 'Then, would you and Anita gather up what we'll need, please? Better prepare for the worst scenario,' he added, and Fliss knew he was referring to the possibility of full-thickness burns where the whole of the underlying tissues would be critically at risk.

She bit down on her bottom lip. Poor kids! Whatever way you looked at it, their injuries almost certainly meant pain.

'Dr Rossi!' Callum bellowed, and Nick came running. 'Fliss and I have an emergency over at the high school. You're in charge. Don't take any flak from anyone.'

Nick visibly grew. 'I won't let you down, Callum.'

'Should I include an IV cut-down tray?' Anita asked as she organised the emergency drug box and dressing packs.

Fliss's heart began beating with uncomfortable swiftness. 'Better, I suppose,' she said, praying fervently they wouldn't need it. With burns, however, nothing could be left to chance and if the skin on the kids' bodies had been badly damaged, it would be almost impossible to access a vein the usual way. Callum would have to execute a surgical procedure to get an IV inserted. 'And space blankets as well, please, Anita.'

Despite the reasons for it, Fliss felt a dizzying feeling of *déjà vu*, sitting beside Callum in his car.

'What's the situation with the ambulance?' he asked gruffly. 'Do we know?'

Fliss's stomach lurched and then settled. 'According to Anita, one has gone to an outlying farm to collect a midwifery patient.

The other is at the strip, waiting for the air ambulance to arrive from Brisbane.'

'Ferrying chemo patients home?'

'I believe so.' Fliss looked at him quickly. The atmosphere between them was so thick they could have sliced it into tangible strips. Her shoulders rose in a deep steadying breath. Whatever personal animosity lay between them, they had to remain professional. Two young lives could depend on their medical skills.

'I imagine the base will redirect that ambulance to the school and ask the air crew to hang on until we see what condition the kids are in,' Callum said bluntly. 'Anything like serious, they'll need the burns unit at the Royal. We have no facilities here to treat them indefinitely.'

Biting her lips together, Fliss could only silently agree.

Cliff Enright, the head teacher at the high school, was looking out for them. 'Shocking thing to happen,' he said, leading them swiftly along the wide verandah. 'We've put the lads into sick bay for the moment. They're both from outlying farms. Parents have been notified. They'll get here as soon as they can.'

'Was there a teacher present when the accident happened?' Fliss asked quietly.

'Claudia Mason. But none of this is her fault.' Mr Enright's voice roughened. 'She's an excellent teacher. Takes the welfare of her students very much to heart.' He opened the door to the sick bay and ushered them in.

'Thank heavens you've come.' Claudia's voice was full of muted relief but it was obvious she was deeply shocked. 'I've followed what I was taught in my first-aid course.'

Callum's face was like granite as he took in the scene. One boy was sitting hunched over at a sink, his injured hand dangling under a stream of water. 'That's good, Claudia,' he reassured the teacher briefly. 'What about the other boy?'

'He's not so good.' Claudia's composure began crumpling. 'The flame caught him as he bent over the Bunsen burner—ran up the side of his throat and into his hair. He's…lying down. We were making a very straightforward formula for epoxy resin. Without checking with me, they added a double dose of hardener…'

So, spontaneous combustion. Callum expelled a muted expletive and shook his head. Foolhardy kids with no idea of the consequences of their disobedience.

Claudia took a shuddering breath. 'It's not like I haven't warned them before every lesson—'

'You've done all you possibly could, Claudia,' Fliss came in gently. 'Could we have their names, please? Just first names will do for now.'

Claudia's teeth began chattering but she managed to get the names out. 'The boy at the sink is Tim.' She gestured towards the bed where the other boy lay. 'That's—that's Lucas…'

'Cliff.' Callum spun his head towards the head teacher. 'If you wouldn't mind…'

'Yes, of course.' He began to guide the young teacher outside. 'Might be best if we leave the doctors to it, Claudia. You need some looking after yourself.' He linked the doctors with a worried look. 'Yell if you need me for anything. I'll have someone keep a lookout for the ambulance.'

Callum lifted a hand in acknowledgment. 'Thanks, mate.'

Callum hated burns. He'd treated far too many during his time with MSF and the feelings of dread didn't lessen no matter how case hardened you'd become. He darted a concerned glance at Fliss. 'This might be a bit rough.'

'Bound to be,' she replied thinly, tossing him a sterile pack of gloves and snapping open her own.

With one accord they moved to Lucas, who was lying frighteningly still, his face towards the wall. Fliss had steeled herself against the sight of the burn but it was taking all her self-control not to gag at the shiny, marble-like mass that only minutes ago had been youthful, healthy skin.

The burn had taken all before it right up into the boy's scalp. Silently, she thanked heaven for Callum's all-round medical experience. It was going to be down to him to try to get Lucas stable enough to be airlifted to the burns unit in Brisbane. That's if they didn't lose him before that. That thought magnified a crippling fear that knotted her stomach.

It took Callum barely seconds to make his assessment as he flicked his stethoscope across the boy's chest, his face registering his grim findings. 'The kid's borderline. Very shocky. He needs saline as fast as we can get it into him.'

Her expression tight, Fliss was already swapping a site to get the IV in. Lucas whimpered and groaned.

'You're OK, son. We're doctors. We're going to help you.' Callum hunkered down beside the bed, his words of reassurance gentle. Privately, he doubted the child was registering anything at all.

'I'm drawing up some pain relief for him as well, Callum,' Fliss said urgently. 'What weight would you guess?'

He glanced up at her. Her mouth was tight and she looked pale. Damn! She hadn't needed this on top of all the soul-destroying personal stuff that was going on between them at the moment. He worked his face muscles in concentration. 'I'd say he's around forty to fifty kilos but we don't want to overdose. Make it twenty-five of pethidine and add Maxolon ten. His stomach's got to be in revolt. We'll need to keep monitoring him and if the ambulance isn't here directly, we'll consider a top-up.'

'Right.' Fliss began willing her own strength into the boy as she prepared the drugs.

Burns were such cruel injuries. Her heart was fearful. Lucas had been so close to crashing but miraculously they'd got to him in time. But this was only the first step. Medical skill and an extraordinary dose of luck was needed now to pull him through.

'OK, then?' Callum's query was muted and he stood by with a sterile dressing.

She nodded, her face tight, aching.

'Just let me fix this and then we'll look at the other lad.'

At a glance Fliss could see Tim's injury was barely of partial thickness. The skin was an amazing healer of itself and with scrupulous hygiene his hand should be well on its way to recovery in a couple of weeks. She looked across at Callum to judge his reaction, seeing his jaw tighten before he said brusquely, 'You've been lucky, sunshine. Much more so than your mate over there. What the hell were you thinking of?'

'Wanted to make a bang.' The boy sniffed, dragging in a huge uneven breath.

'You young idiots…'

'Callum.' Fliss's voice held faint censure. She appreciated his frustration and anger over such an avoidable injury but now wasn't the time to heap more blame on the already traumatised child. 'Your mum and dad are on their way in, Tim,' she said gently, as she prepared the boy's arm to receive the saline drip and painkiller.

'Yeah…' The youngster scraped the back of his uninjured hand across his eyes. 'Mr Enright told me.'

'Try to relax now, sport,' Callum relented gruffly, as he gently wrapped the injured boy in a space blanket. 'We'll need you in hospital for a short while but you'll be as fit as a flea again in no time.' Turning, he drew Fliss out of earshot. 'Would you go and see what's keeping the ambulance, please?'

Fliss drew in a jagged breath. 'The situation with Lucas is critical, isn't it?'

'It will be if we don't get him into Theatre in the next half-hour.' Callum was grim-faced. 'Tissue death is imminent.'

Fliss swallowed thickly, knowing it was imperative for the destroyed tissues to be removed. Left unattended, they could be the starting point for a bacterial infection and heaven knew what else… 'I'll go and see what I can find out.' She returned promptly. 'Both ambulances are here,' she said to Callum.

'Good.' Relief showed in Callum's face. 'Theatre is standing by and Max is scrubbed and waiting to assist. The sooner we get Lucas stable and airlifted to the Royal, the better his chances of a full recovery.'

'You're hopeful, then?' Fliss's gaze flew back to their young patient.

'He's holding his own,' Callum said. 'That's about all we can hope for at the moment.'

Within minutes, everything began happening. The ambulance officers arrived with stretchers. Following them along the verandah were the parents of both boys. 'Oh, lord.' Fliss's hand went to her heart. 'They look distraught, Callum. I'll speak to them.'

He frowned. 'We need to get moving.'

She sent him a speaking look. 'I know. I'll be two seconds.'

CHAPTER TWELVE

'HEY, you're supposed to be off duty.' Troy had found Fliss still hovering when he'd come on duty for the late shift.

She gave a helpless shrug. 'They're taking a long time in Theatre, aren't they?'

'From what I heard, the kid is lucky to be alive,' Troy responded with a little shake of his head. 'Why don't you go home?' he suggested kindly. 'I'll call you when Callum's back from Theatre.'

'I'd feel more useful if I stayed here, Troy.'

'OK.' The charge spread his hands in mute acceptance. She looked done in but he couldn't force her to leave the department if she wanted to stay. 'But in this job we can only do what we can, Fliss. The rest is down to whatever god you pray to and Mother Nature.'

She gave him the glimmer of a smile. Troy was right, of course. But in Lucas's case, were even Callum's exceptional skills as a surgeon going to be enough? With this unsettling thought she took herself off to the canteen. Her stomach was already awash with herbal tea—one more wouldn't make much difference.

It was almost an hour later when Fliss managed to catch up with Callum. He was on his way back to his office. 'Do you have a minute, Callum?'

He flicked her a glance and frowned. What the hell was she still doing there? Running herself into the ground wasn't part of her job description. Opening the door of his office, he beckoned her inside, then backed up against the desk with his arms folded. Waiting.

Fliss didn't move close to him but notwithstanding, the space between them felt thick and uncomfortable. And they didn't even speak until he said, 'You look tired.'

She lifted a shoulder dismissively. 'I just wanted to enquire how things went with Lucas.'

'Better than we could have hoped.' Callum's mouth tightened for a second. 'Thank heaven, skin grafting has come ahead in leaps and bounds these days but nevertheless it'll be a while before Lucas is feeling a hundred per cent again. The good news is, his face is basically untouched and his hair will grow back—so, all round, a reasonable prognosis.'

'That must be a great relief for the parents.' Fliss felt some of her anxiety drain away.

He nodded. 'They're in Recovery with him now and I gather his mother will travel in the air ambulance with him to Brisbane.'

A beat of crippling silence.

'Right. Thanks. I, uh, won't hold you up, then.'

They looked at each other helplessly for a second or two, unable to bridge the gap.

Have you nothing else to say to me? Fliss felt like yelling at him. But what was the use? Feeling totally shut out of his life, she turned and made her way blindly towards the door.

Callum felt like ramming his fist through the wall. Why couldn't he have just taken a step, closed the distance between them and held her? His arms ached with the thought of the lost opportunity and now they were empty, hanging uselessly at his sides.

And Fliss was gone.

Moving across to the window, he reached out like a blind man towards the sill, gripping it with both hands, staring out. Had he lost her for ever? Oh, God, why was his throat tightening like this? Whoever said *sorry* was the hardest word had it right. But somehow he'd have to say it. Better still he'd find a way to *show* her he meant it.

Dull depression settled on Fliss like a cloud when she came on duty next morning. All night she'd searched for answers but had found none. She couldn't humiliate herself and try to talk to Callum again. He'd shown clearly enough he wanted out of any involvement with her.

With the benefit of hindsight she guessed she shouldn't have told him about Daniel's phone call. But it wasn't in her nature to be secretive. She liked things out in the open so you could deal with them. But obviously Callum had felt threatened by her revelations. In other words, he still couldn't find it in his heart to trust her enough to let his own doubts and insecurities go.

About midmorning, Maddie caught up with her and said, 'Great news about the funding, isn't it?'

'Funding?' Fliss's brow furrowed.

'The funding for the aged-care facility. We've got it and more than we asked for.' Maddie grinned disarmingly. 'You must have impressed the suit.'

'Oh. Yes, I must have,' Fliss agreed, her voice catching in her throat. And it all seemed light years ago.

'Callum didn't tell you?'

Fliss felt her stomach dive. 'Ah—no.'

The two stared awkwardly at each other and then Maddie took the initiative. 'Must have slipped his mind.'

'Mmm, must have.' Fliss didn't believe it for a second, deciding she didn't need to look any further to realise that, other than about medical matters at the hospital, Callum intended having the least to do with her that he possibly could.

'Oh, by the way,' Maddie jumped in conversationally, 'Callum's got me two days a week in the office at Trail Farm. I've been up to see Tony Buchan. They need all the help they can get, apparently.' She rolled her eyes. 'Their filing system has to be seen to be believed.'

Fliss dragged up a smile from her boots. 'You'll have your work cut out, then, won't you?'

'I guess I'll have to look on it as a challenge.' Maddie grinned. 'It'll be good, though, to be back working full time again. And the extra money will come in handy.' She flicked a hand back towards her office. 'If you've got time, I've just made a big pot of tea. Might even find a chocolate biscuit to go with it.'

Fliss's stomach rebelled at the thought of chocolate at this hour of the day. But the tea and a dose of Maddie's uncomplicated company sounded wonderful.

Next morning, when Fliss got out of the shower she was shaking. Twisting the towel haphazardly around her, she went through to the bedroom and sank down on the edge of the bed, her heart hammering like a drum in her chest.

She'd been afraid of this happening. So afraid. But if it had to happen, why now, when her personal life was in tatters? Oh, lord. Beating back her fear, she picked up her mobile phone and called Jo at home.

'Hi, sweetie,' Jo said lightly. 'This is an early call. What's up?'

Fliss swallowed thickly. 'I've—found a lump in my breast, Jo.'

'Oh, Flissy…when?'

'Just now—under the shower. Can I come and see you?'

'Of course you can,' Jo said practically. 'If you can be at the surgery at eight-fifteen, I'll see you straight away. Do you need to arrange cover?'

'N-no.' Fliss bit her lips together to stop them trembling. 'I'm not on duty until twelve.'

'Good. And Fliss,' Jo said firmly. 'Don't start jumping to the worst-case scenario, all right?'

'Jo—my mother died from breast cancer!'

'And I understand your panic,' Jo said gently. 'Would you like me to come and collect you?'

'No.' Fliss took a long shaky breath. 'I'm OK to drive over.'

'I'll be waiting for you,' Jo said.

True to her word, Jo was there. 'Oh, Jo…' Fliss hurled herself into her friend's waiting arms and was held tightly. Fliss just wished it had been Callum she could have called on to see her through this awful time.

'Come through,' Jo said, slipping her arm through Fliss's and ushering her along to her consulting room. When they were seated, Jo said, 'Let's just have a chat about things for a start, Flissy. Which breast did you find the lump in?'

Fliss closed her eyes for a second. *Did it matter?* 'The left. It was the left breast.'

'And did you find anything untoward in your other breast?'

'I didn't look.' She bit her lip. 'I wasn't game to.'

'And it was a definite lump you felt?'

'Yes—at least, I think so. My breast felt heavy, kind of lumpy. Odd.'

'Odd?'

'Odd—different! I don't know. Dammit, Jo, I'll need a mammogram! I'll have to go to Brisbane. Can you get me an urgent appointment at the Wesley? They have my notes. And Mum's.' Her eyes were stricken. 'How am I going to cope, Jo?'

'If you have to, you'll cope, Flissy,' Jo responded calmly. 'Do you still see your specialist on a regular basis?'

'Of course! After Mum—of course. It's part of the whole thing—regular checks. Could you ring now and see when I can go for the mammogram?'

'Leave it with me,' Jo said gently. 'I'll have no trouble getting you in, if you need one.'

If she needed one! Had Jo lost her marbles? 'Sorry?' Fliss blinked and brought her attention back with a snap.

'I said we'll do a blood test and I'd like you to give me a urine sample.'

'A urine sample? Why do you need that?' Fliss demanded. 'Are you testing for signs of cancer somewhere else? Or sugar? I don't have blood-sugar problems.'

'You probably don't,' Jo said patiently. 'But I just want to start ruling things out, as a precaution.'

'OK…' Fliss drew out the words on a long breath. 'Do you want me to do that now?'

'If you're up to it. But you're obviously tense, so take your time and don't strain. Now, we can go next door to Marika, our practice nurse, and she'll look after you or if you prefer complete privacy, I can—'

'No, no,' Fliss cut in. 'It's fine. I'll see the nurse.' She gave a tragic little laugh. 'It's no time to start being precious, is it?'

'Now, what am I testing for, Jo?' Marika asked when Fliss, armed with a receptacle for her specimen, had disappeared to the toilet.

Jo picked up a jotter from the nurse's desk and scribbled something. Handing the slip of paper back, she said, 'Buzz me and I'll come and collect the results, Marika.'

The nurse looked down at the piece of paper and smiled. 'Shouldn't take long.'

Jo turned from the window when Fliss came back to her room. 'Manage all right?' she asked gently.

Fliss rolled her eyes. 'I'll have a new respect for my patients after this. Sorry if I'm being ratty.'

Jo grinned. 'You're allowed to. Now, while you're feeling co-operative, strip down to your waist and then pop up on the couch and we'll try to get a handle on this lump you think you've found.'

'Is this how you want me?' Fliss asked, wriggling to get more comfortable on the narrow examination couch.

'I can see you've done this before,' Jo said wryly, after Fliss had lifted her arms and placed them behind her head.

Fliss took a shallow breath. 'Once or twice.'

Jo was thorough. Using the pads of her three middle fingers, she palpated Fliss's left breast, beginning at the edge of the nipple and moving out to the rim of the breast. 'Are your breasts feeling tender at the moment?' she asked.

'Not sure.' Fliss bit down on her bottom lip. 'I guess so, yes. And heavy. Different.'

'Yes, you said that before.' Jo continued her palpating up the chest towards the armpit. 'You're right. There is something but I wouldn't bet my reputation on it being a possible cancerous lump.'

'Then what?' Frowning, Fliss half lifted herself up from the couch.

'Don't know yet,' Jo returned with remarkable good cheer. 'Now, let's just compare the other breast, shall we? OK, Flissy, that's fine,' she said after a minute. 'You can get dressed now.'

Fliss put on her bra, staggering a bit as she pulled her T-shirt over her head.

'Oh, help…' She choked a laugh. 'I feel about ninety this morning.'

Jo's eyes ran professionally over her friend. 'Are you feeling faint, Flissy?'

'A bit woozy.' She managed a weak smile. 'I'd love a cup of tea.'

Jo picked up her phone. 'Vicki should be in by now. I'll buzz her and ask her to bring us a pot of tea. And toast,' she added for good measure.

'Thanks.'

Vicki arrived promptly. 'Oh, hi, Fliss.' The younger woman smiled ingenuously. 'I didn't realise it was you in here with Jo.'

'Hi, Vicki,' Fliss dredged up a wobbly smile. The two had met at Jo's wedding and more recently at the McNeals' party. Fliss gestured at the plate piled high with buttered toast. 'This is really sweet of you, but are you feeding an army?'

Vicki chuckled. 'We've one of those four-slice toasters. I'm so used to feeding Brady I just automatically shoved the bread in.'

'Thanks, Vic,' Jo said cheerfully, taking the tray. 'I'll pour. And we could be a while, OK?'

Vicki understood perfectly. Jo wasn't to be interrupted.

'Oh, this is heaven,' Fliss sighed, wrapping her hands around the teamug and taking long mouthfuls of the reviving brew.

Jo eyed her friend narrowly. She was regaining some colour. Poor love. She'd had such a fright. 'Help yourself to toast as well,' she encouraged.

'In a minute.' Fliss gave a wan smile. 'I'm beginning to feel half-human again. How long will Marika be with the test results?'

Jo glanced at her watch. 'She was doing something for Brady as well, but she shouldn't be much longer. That's probably her now,' Jo said, as her phone rang. She spoke briefly and then got to her feet. 'I won't be a tick.'

Fliss nodded, raising her gaze and looking out through the clear glass window beyond Jo's chair. It looked like another perfect day and people would be going about their normal business. Quickly she batted away a couple of stray tears that wouldn't be held back and wondered if her own life would ever be *normal* again…

There was a murmur of voices outside and then Jo returned, squeezing Fliss's shoulder as she walked past. 'Prepare yourself, honey,' she said, slipping into her chair and leaning forward confidentially. 'Do you want the good news or the good news?'

Fliss brought her head up like a startled doe. Good news? How could having cancer be considered good news? But she guessed if they'd caught something early… She swallowed thickly and heaved in a controlling breath. 'Hit me with it, then. And don't dress it up, Jo…please.'

'OK, I won't,' Jo said, spreading her hands in a shrug. 'You don't have a blood-sugar problem.'

'I could have told you that.'

Jo hesitated infinitesimally. 'But you're pregnant, Flissy.'

Pregnant! Fliss's eyes widened as if she could better take it in. The outline of Jo's face went out of focus and then righted itself. Slowly. 'I can't be.' She gave a little whimper. 'Callum always protected me.' She stopped and froze. Except that day when they'd had their picnic by the creek. They'd thrown caution to the winds, leaving open a tiny window of opportunity for Mother Nature to pop in and play her sweet tricks… 'What am I going to do, Jo?' She heard the shocked disbelief in her voice. This was all so unreal. So totally unexpected.

Jo grinned. 'Tell Callum, for starters?'

Fliss ground her lip. 'We're hardly speaking.'

Jo didn't ask why. Instead, she said bracingly, 'All lovers have tiffs and misunderstandings. It comes under the heading of getting to know each other.'

Fliss felt tears burning behind her eyes. 'This is awful, Jo.'

'It's not,' Jo said firmly. 'It's wonderful. Flissy, you and Callum are going to be parents. You'll have to find a way to tell him.'

Fliss shook her head. 'He's away until tomorrow at a rural doctors' conference.'

'Well, that might be a blessing in disguise,' Jo said gently. 'It'll give you time to settle things in your own mind, begin feeling positive about this baby you're nurturing in your body as we speak.'

That brought a new flood of tears. 'This is…so not me,' Fliss wailed, her chest still jerking with ebbing sobs as Jo produced a wad of tissues and helped her mop up.

'Honey, you're pregnant.' Jo's voice held gentle laughter. 'Your hormones are all over the place.' When Fliss had herself under control, Jo asked, 'Now, would you like me to run you home? I can easily stall my patients for an extra few minutes.'

Fliss shook her head, managing to say more or less firmly,' No, but thanks, Jo. I'll just wash my face and collect my wits.' She took a final shuddering breath. 'I, um, need to get my head around this, don't I?'

Jo hugged her briefly. 'You will. And find a way to tell Callum,' she added earnestly. 'He'll want to know. And I'll bet he'll be chuffed.'

'Perhaps he will.' Fliss gave a smile that was almost a grimace. And perhaps he'd jump to the conclusion she'd set out to deliberately trap him into a relationship he neither needed nor wanted.

Fliss drove home slowly, conscious of a feeling of huge relief. She didn't have breast cancer. But she did have a baby growing inside her. A tiny life she was totally responsible for. It was still too much to take in and she felt exhausted, emotionally and in every other way.

Back in her room, she set her alarm and then crawled into bed. She was asleep in seconds. When she woke up, she felt refreshed and marginally back in control. Remarkable how sleep could rejuvenate your body, she thought as she climbed out of bed and under the shower.

Unhurriedly, she dressed for work. She still had time to eat something. And she was starving. Heating some soup in the microwave, she wondered how long she'd be able to continue working in A and E. And if Callum didn't want to know, she'd return to Brisbane. Stay with Dad and Deb, until the baby…

The microwave pinged and she rescued her soup. She got out

some crackers to have with it and then took the tray across to her little table. And thought of the night Callum had sat here with her and they'd eaten pizza. They'd had such anticipation in their hearts then, until it had all gone wrong and he'd stormed out. But they'd found their way back. She blinked rapidly, spooning up the last of her soup.

Perhaps they would again.

'Hey, want to hear my news?' Nick was positively beaming when he met Fliss for handover at twelve.

'Go on, then.' She flapped a hand. 'You're bursting to tell me.'

'Julie and Matty are coming to Mt Pryde for a couple of days.'

'That's brilliant! How come? Is Matty more settled?'

'It's all happened recently,' Nick confirmed, unable to contain his happiness. 'He's been staying for longer periods with Julie's parents and enjoying himself. And last time I was home he actually stayed overnight with them. Jules and I had a night to ourselves for the first time in years.'

'I can see why you might be pleased.' Fliss smiled at the earnest young man, so wrapped up in his role of parent, wanting to do the right thing for his son but trying his hardest to nurture his and Julie's relationship at the same time. 'You and Julie must love each other a lot,' she commented wistfully, wondering whether she and Callum could ever hope to achieve the same kind of commitment. Or was she chasing shadows again?

Nick shrugged. 'We have to stick together for each other and for Matty if we want to continue to be a family. There's no other choice.'

And how lucky for Julie he felt like that. Fliss drummed up a passable smile. 'So, when are they arriving and where are you all staying?'

'This afternoon, and I've booked us into the family unit at the motel. It's larger than the normal units and there's a bed for Matty. And I thought tomorrow I'd take them up to the bluff. There's a great picnic area and Mrs Jones at the motel said she'll do us up a lunch basket.' He grinned a bit sheepishly. 'I want to spoil Jules a bit.'

Oh, how sweet. Fliss felt the tight lens of tears across her eyes. Heavens, she'd have to stop getting emotional about every darned nice thing that happened. But just how, she didn't know. It seemed getting emotional went with the territory of being pregnant. And she still hadn't come to terms with *that* either.

* * *

The department was quiet. Too quiet. Fliss would have preferred to be run off her feet than to have so much time on her hands. Time to agonise over what she was going to tell Callum—*how* she was going to tell him they'd made a baby together. Perhaps she could delay telling him? She felt a lift in her spirits at the possibility but then just as quickly negated the idea. He wouldn't appreciate that kind of information being kept from him. She knew that much.

She looked at her watch again. It was just on early evening. Nick and his little family should be installed at the motel by now. She could only admire Nick and Julie for the mature approach they'd taken towards their relationship after their baby had been born with Down's. Most young couples would have fallen in a heap. Many would have split up with the pressure. Her hand flew to the flat bowl of her pelvis and hovered there. Please, God, she was carrying a healthy baby.

Swallowing the sudden lump in her throat, she went to find Jess, who was acting charge nurse for the shift.

'Hi,' Jess said with a smile, when Fliss finally tracked her down her in the treatment room. 'I thought I'd do a bit of a stock-take. Did you need me for something?'

Fliss shook her head. 'Why don't you take your dinner break, Jess? I'm here and Tammy's about as well.'

'OK, thanks.' She grinned. 'I'm pretty hungry, actually, and it's curry night in the canteen. Have you eaten?'

'Ah, no. But I'll get something later,' Fliss said, suddenly swamped with nausea. Quickly excusing herself, she hurried to the staffroom.

Fliss finished her tea and a handful of dry crackers and felt better, relieved there was no one about to witness her odd little dinner. Taking a long, calming breath, she got to her feet and went across to the sink to wash her mug. So lost was she in her own thoughts it took a moment for her to register the sound of a disturbance outside. Dumping her mug in the drainer, she almost ran to the station, a prickle of alarm teasing the back of her neck, quite certain this was trouble and sickeningly aware of her own new vulnerability.

Violence from the public and patients alike was an ongoing fear for all health professionals who worked in emergency departments around the world. And there was no reason to imagine it couldn't strike here on a quiet night in a little rural hospital.

'Tammy?' Fliss checked her step. The young nursing assistant was white-faced, shrinking back against the wall where she'd obviously been pushed.

'I tried to stop him...' She pointed a shaking hand at a giant of a man in biker's leathers who was systematically thumping open every door in the place. 'He must be after d-drugs,' she croaked through chattering teeth.

'Call the police,' Fliss ordered. 'Tell them to get here a.s.a.p. This person needs to be off the premises.'

Tammy leapt into life and ran to the station.

'You're trespassing, sir.' Moving swiftly, Fliss effectively blocked the man's entrance to the treatment room.

'Sez who? You? Don't make me laugh.' He leered at Fliss from red-rimmed eyes, the smell of alcohol curling off his breath in nauseating waves.

Fliss reeled back but she stood her ground. 'What is it you want? Do you need to see a doctor?'

'No, I don't!' His fist slammed into the wall just centimetres from Fliss's cheek. 'I want my girlfriend outa here.'

Fliss steeled herself to stay calm. 'She's not here. We've had no patients for the past hour.'

'You mob are hiding her...' The intruder shoved his chin with its straggly beard in Fliss's face.

Fliss swallowed thickly. Where was the damned law when you need it! 'Why would we be hiding her?'

''Cos I whacked her one and she took off. Always threatening to—to get to a doctor and have me r-reported...' he mumbled, swaying and suddenly being violently ill at Fliss's feet.

'You disgusting creature!' Fliss banished diplomacy to the four winds, all her sensitivities grossly offended. She made to push past but the man lashed out, his beefy hands catching her by the shoulders. In a haze of terror she felt herself being yanked roughly away from the door and shoved backwards along the corridor, her feet trying in vain to steady her momentum. Fear whimpered out of her throat, ending in a choking sob as she locked her arms protectively over her stomach. Oh, God, don't let him hurt her...or the baby...

It was his worst nightmare. Callum felt the tentacles of fear grip his insides at what he saw. Swearing savagely under his breath, he increased his speed down the corridor until he was running. 'Call the police!' he roared at Tammy, as he sped past the station.

'I have, Dr O'Byrne.'

'Then call them again!' Callum's voice rose to thunderous proportions and Tammy jumped and scrambled for the phone.

White-hot anger spurred Callum on. If the bastard had harmed Fliss in any way, he'd personally see he never walked again without a crutch. 'Hey, you!' Momentarily distracted, the intruder dropped his arms and spun away, rendering him a perfect target for Callum's crash tackle, which brought him to the floor.

Callum was quickly back on his feet, his lean, rugged features stretched tautly as he stared down at his captive. The man groaned and blubbered something into the tiled floor.

'You're not hurt.' Callum placed his boot firmly on the man's behind. 'And don't you dare move,' he threatened darkly, 'or I'll thump you again.'

'Callum…' Fliss heard the croaking disbelief in her voice as she fell into his arms.

'It's all right, Flissy.' Callum gathered her in. 'You're safe, sweetheart. I'm here, baby. Shh now… He looked down at her and frowned. 'Did he hurt you?'

'Don't think so…' But she could feel her legs begin to shake as the trembling raced through her body.

Aftershocks. He held her tighter. 'Relax now. You're safe.' After a minute, he asked, 'Feeling better?'

'Mmm.' She took a breath that was nearly a sob. 'Oh…' she looked bemusedly at him. 'Is that the police I can hear?'

'It had better be,' Callum growled, and then it seemed that people came from everywhere.

'Nice one, Doc.' The young constable grinned as he and his partner manhandled the intruder to his feet.

'I want him charged.' Callum thrust a finger at the prisoner's chest. 'And if he needs a doctor to look at him, get someone else. I refuse to treat him. Is that understood?'

Fliss bit her lips together. Was that ethical? she wondered. But who was going to question Callum's decision? Certainly no one here. She turned in his arms and leaned back against him, feeling his arms tighten about her waist.

Jess and Tammy had come on the scene, both pale and shaken, and slowly they all made their way back to the station.

Simon arrived to take over the night shift. 'Missed all the fun, I see,' he quipped.

Tammy's eyes opened wide in awe. 'You should have seen Dr O'Bryne's tackle!'

'OK, Tammy.' Callum's mouth moved in a dry twist. 'We don't need it in Technicolor.' He looked at Simon. 'Fliss won't be at work tomorrow. I'll arrange cover and Angus Charlton from the after-hours clinic will be on call if you need back-up tonight. And could someone get that mess cleaned up, please, before it smells the place out?'

Jess gave a little cough. 'Job for you, Tam.'

'Oh, thanks!' The youngster made a face. 'I suppose it couldn't wait until the cleaners get here in the morning?'

'Nop, sorry.' Jess was firm. 'You heard what the boss said.'

The *boss* looked at his staff and threw up his hands in appeal. 'Just get on with it, please. And if anyone wants me, I'll be at home, and I'm taking Fliss with me.'

As Callum and Fliss disappeared towards the exit, Jess caught Tammy's coy look and grinned. 'Oo-oo-oo!' they chorused, and offered each other a high-five salute.

Simon looked blankly at his female counterparts. 'Are they an item, then?'

Jess rolled her eyes. 'Are you serious?'

'The doctors are in lurve…' Tammy sang, as she went off to find disinfectant, bucket and mop.

CHAPTER THIRTEEN

WHEN they stepped from the emergency department into the foyer, Fliss stopped. 'I don't have anything with me, Callum.'

'Do you have your key?'

'Yes.' She tapped the little fob pocket on her denim jacket.

'That's all you'll need, then.' Without further consultation, Callum swept her outside to his car.

When they were seated and belted up, he turned to her for a second, before starting the engine. 'I'll check you over when we get home.'

Home. Fliss swallowed thickly, a ray of hope forming a tiny light inside her. Perhaps everything would be all right. 'You're back a day early.'

'Mmm.' He gave a growl in his throat. 'I took off after today's sessions. I decided I needed to be here rather than there, if that makes sense?'

All the sense in the world. She suppressed a shudder. 'I was never so glad to see anyone in my life.'

'Don't.' Callum swallowed against the sharp constriction in his throat. 'I can't bear to think about it.'

A shiver of awareness shafted through her when he reached out and imprisoned her fingers. 'I…guess I'll have to give a statement to the police, won't I?'

'Only when you're feeling up to it.' He raised her fingers gently to his lips. 'They'll have to get past me first. I'm so sorry, Flissy…' His voice roughened. 'I haven't been very kind to you, lately, have I?'

Fliss gave a strangled laugh, blinking through tears. 'I should never have mentioned Daniel.'

'Yes, you should. I should have been mature enough handle it. *You* were, about Kirsty.'

She thought for a second. 'We probably would have worked things out more quickly if I hadn't got that huge bouquet of flowers.'

'And I jumped to all the wrong conclusions,' he added ruefully. 'They weren't from Daniel, were they?'

'No—they were from the lads at Trail Farm. They pooled their pocket money and ordered the flowers off the Internet.' She gave a fractured laugh. 'I can't believe they did that for me.'

'Why wouldn't they?' he said gruffly. 'You turned their lives around.' Callum felt his heart beating hard against his ribs but he couldn't back off again. He had to tell her now, begin to put things right. 'I have such plans for us, Fliss. I hope you'll approve of them.'

And she had such *news* for him. And she hoped with all her might, he'd find it in his heart to accept that now she came with the added responsibility of a child. Their child.

But she still had to find a way to tell him.

When they got to the cottage Callum unlocked the door and drew her inside. 'Mind the step into the kitchen,' he warned. 'I don't want you falling.'

She managed a thin laugh. 'Like I did the first time I came here.'

'When we kissed for the first time…' His eyes were so close she could see the faint specks of silver in the blue. He reached out and drew her to him, kissing her so sweetly she almost cried out with the complete rightness of it. She felt his chest rise and fall in a broken sigh. 'God, I've missed you. Missed us.'

Like someone who had been away from home for a long, long time, she began re-exploring him, revelling in the whole of him, his familiarity. 'I've missed us, too.'

Slowly, she became aware of his palm resting warmly at the nape of her neck, the tips of his fingers playing gently with the strands of her hair. 'I'd love a shower,' she said throatily.

'Am I invited?'

She stroked his face and nodded. It might be the last time they'd share this kind of intimacy. After she told him, perhaps he'd climb back into his hidey-hole and shut her out again. But then, perhaps he wouldn't. She had to hang onto that.

'Do you hurt anywhere?' he asked when she'd stripped off in the bathroom and wrapped herself in a towel.

'Not really. I'm pretty fit.' She stared at him bemusedly as he examined the skin around her shoulders and collar-bone. 'Anything?'

'Don't think so.'

'The thickness of my jacket probably protected me.'

'Still, you might find a bruise or two tomorrow,' he said. 'Don't ever try to confront a lunatic like that again, Flissy.'

She bit her lip. 'I thought it was my responsibility.'

'Your responsibility was to call the police and take yourself and Tammy to a safe place. There were no patients you needed to look out for. If that cretin had smashed the place up before the police got there, it wouldn't have mattered. Inanimate objects can be replaced. Lives can't. Do you understand what I'm saying?' He was speaking softly. curving her back into his arms.

She offered no resistance when his hands continued to move over her body. 'I think I lost ten years off my life when I saw you being roughed up like that. I love you!' The words were wrung from him, and his lips made feathery kisses over her temple, her eyes, cheeks and finally her mouth, his possession fiercely brief. He sighed a ragged breath. 'Do you love me?'

Of course she loved him. How on earth could he think otherwise? Her heart beat faster at the sincerity of his declaration and the words she'd so longed to hear. He deserved to hear them back. Shakily, she stretched out a hand, touching his hair, stroking the outside edge of his ear, the soft hollow in his throat. Then she looked up into his eyes, reading the openness and, unmistakably, the love. Joy, clear and pure, streamed through her. 'I love you, Callum. Please, don't ever doubt that.'

He had a grin a mile wide as he whipped the towel from around her, hastily stripping off his own clothes and drawing her into the shower with him. 'Mustn't get your hair wet,' he said firmly, directing the shower spray away from her head.

She burrowed in against him. 'And why not?'

'Because I want to take you to bed and I don't want to hang about while you dry your hair first.'

'OK,' she complied meekly, and soon he'd turned off the water and lifted her gently out onto the fluffy mat. They dried off quickly and, with towels wrapped loosely around them, went through to the bedroom. Fliss's heart was beating wildly. I have to tell him now, she thought. While we're linked in spirit and before our bodies are joined in the greatest expression of our love for each other. *I have to tell him now. Somehow.* Watching him move automatically to his bedside drawer, she gave a strained little laugh. 'You won't need to use protection, Callum.'

He withdrew his hand slowly, frowning a bit. 'Did you go on the Pill?'

'No…' She hesitated and blinked rapidly.

Callum took her hand and eased her down on the edge of the bed beside him. 'What, then?'

His voice was gentle but it couldn't free her from the stomach-caving fear that this was all too hard and even now, even when he'd told her he loved her, she still couldn't guarantee his reaction would be one of gladness.

His grip on her hands tightened. 'You've got me worried now, Flissy. What is it?'

Fliss drew in her breath and let it go. 'We're having a baby.'

A beat of absolute silence.

'A baby… My God, Flissy, you're pregnant?'

She smiled tentatively. 'I only found out this morning. I thought I'd found a lump in my breast and I went to see Jo.' She went on and unravelled the whole story. When she'd finished, Callum scooped her up on to his knee.

'Oh, you poor sweet girl. I should have been here for you.' His arms went around her and he was rocking her. 'But what fabulous news!'

Fliss felt tears threaten again and resolutely brushed them away. 'You're pleased, then?'

'Pleased? It's amazing. *You're* amazing. We're having a baby…' He shook his head as though he still couldn't quite believe it. He reached out and cupped her face in his hands, his eyes so blue and tender and so full of love that she felt her breath catch in her throat. 'When?' he asked softly. 'The day we had our picnic by the creek?'

'I guess—yes.'

'Are you going to marry me?'

'Oh, Callum,' she whispered through a throat so tight it hurt. 'Of course I'll marry you.'

'That's all I need to know,' he responded huskily, and then he took her to bed and made love to her so sweetly so tenderly she cried all over him and he thought he'd hurt her and kept apologising.

'You didn't hurt me,' she said, half laughing and half crying as

he scooped her in against him and held her. 'I'm just a bit emotional right now.'

He looked worriedly at her. 'But it'll pass, won't it?'

'This is my first time at being pregnant, but I'm sure it will.
Callum?' She ran around a teasing finger around his lips.

'Yes, angel?'

'Could you make me some scrambled eggs?'

He sprang up. 'Stay there. I'll bring you a tray.'

'No.' She waved his offer away. 'I want to get up but I don't
have any clothes. Could you lend me something?'

He gestured to his chest of drawers as he hauled on trackpants
and a long-sleeved sweatshirt. 'Help yourself. I'll get started on
your eggs.'

Fliss giggled. 'I thought you already had.'

He mock-swiped her with the end of the towel. 'Cheeky
monkey.' Then his eyes went soft. 'I hope our kid's just like you.'

Next morning Callum brought her a cup of tea and some
crackers in bed. 'Get up when you feel like it,' he said. 'I've
spoken to Jo. She suggested frequent light meals for a while.
And she wants to know if you'll be staying with her for your
prenatal care?'

Fliss rolled her eyes. 'She'd never speak to me again if I didn't.'
She reached out and took Callum's hand as he hovered beside the
bed. 'Are you going in to the hospital?'

'Later. I've a few emails to respond to and we've a lot of arrangements to make, don't we?'

'Mmm.' She lay back against the pillows and looked
dreamily at him.

A couple of hours later Fliss got up and took a shower and, dressed
in a pair of Callum's trackpants, one of his bulky jumpers and a
pair of his football socks, made her way through the house, looking
for him. She found him in the room he used as his office. He was
finishing off an email. Standing behind him, she put her hand on
his shoulder.

'Won't be a tick.' He reached back for a second, placed his hand
on hers and squeezed. 'There, that'll do it.' He logged off and
swung off his chair. 'Did you sleep again?' he asked, pulling her
gently into his arms.

'Mmm.' She snuggled in against him. 'I'm being very spoilt, aren't I?'

'Just as you should be.' His look was tender.

Arms around each other, they went through to the kitchen. 'Could you eat something now, do you think?' Callum held out the chair for her and she slipped into it and raised a questioning look.

'Do you have any trifle?'

'Trifle?' His voice rose an octave. 'At ten o'clock in the morning?'

She made a face at him. 'I just feel like something custardy and sweet.'

'Ah, right…' He seemed to consider for a second. 'I think I have some yoghurt. And there might be a can of peaches in the pantry—any good?'

'Lovely.'

While she ate, Callum made some tea and they took it outside onto the deck. 'More crackers,' he said with a flourish, and placed the dish in front of her.

She wrinkled her nose at him. 'You're just assuaging your guilt because it's your baby making me feel queasy.'

'You see right through me every time.' He laughed and then became serious. 'I want you to have the kind of wedding you've always dreamed about, Flissy. Posh or simple, big or small. Church or outdoors. Whatever you want. I've only one stipulation and I won't move on it, I'm afraid.'

She swallowed and took a deep breath, wondering what on earth he was about to ask of her. And whether or not she'd be able to comply. And if she couldn't…? 'What is it?'

'I want you to be the most beautiful bride on the planet.'

The tension drained out of her like air from a punctured balloon. 'Is that all?' She rolled her eyes at him. 'No worries, Doc. I'll knock your socks off. And as for where? Why don't we get married here?'

'Here?'

'It'll be lovely.' Fliss was on a roll. 'I'm sure the celebrant would come out from town. And there's plenty of lawn where we could erect a marquee.' She flapped a hand airily. 'Dad'll pay for all that and Deb and your mum could host things. And we could have Jo and Brady to stand up for us and your family could all come from Armidale and we could put them up at the motel. And we'll call in lots of favours to arrange cover for the ED so all the guys can be here with us. It'll be a day to remember.'

Callum's eyes misted, and he blinked and shook his head. 'Your organisational skills never cease to amaze me. I suppose you want to get on the phone now and tell everyone?'

'Shortly. It's just nice sitting here with you.'

He nodded and his mouth worked a bit. 'Uh, I haven't had time to get you a ring, Flissy, but I do have something for you.'

'For me?' Her eyes lit and she wriggled in her chair. 'Can I have it now?'

Callum stood to his feet and went inside. He hoped she wouldn't think it was a crazy thing to have done. But it was all he'd been able to think of at the time to show her how much he cared. When he came back she was standing at the railings looking down towards the creek.

Turning to look at him, she said dreamily, 'I'm just remembering our picnic— Oh, is that my present?'

Handing her the package, he said gruffly, 'I've had it for ages and I got it to show you how much and how far I've fallen in love with you. There'd be no colour, not much laughter and no joy in anything without you by my side.'

'Oh, Callum…' Fliss was so choked with emotion she couldn't find the words to reciprocate. She just shook her head mutely and looked at the package in her hands. It was oblong in shape, roughly wrapped in brown paper and tied with a piece of string. She hiccuped a laugh. 'I see you went to great lengths with the gift-wrapping.'

He lifted a shoulder. 'Open it.'

She did, with trembling hands and slowly drew out a plaque. It had a background of gold and on it were two words: OUR PLACE. 'Oh, Callum…' Her fingers traced the flowing script, her heart overwhelmed with love for this man. He couldn't have thought of anything more fitting to show her how much he wanted her in his life. And if ever she'd had any doubts of that, they were well and truly put to rest now. She raised her gaze and looked at him, her eyes brimming. 'This is the most precious gift you could have given me…'

Taking the plaque from her, Callum placed it carefully on the table and then gathered her into her arms. 'So, is it enough to show my intentions are honourable until I can get you a ring?'

'More than enough…' Her voice broke as she looked up at him and saw the soft sheen of love in his eyes. 'Wherever you are, that's where I want to be—for always.'

Callum let her words wrap round his heart. He couldn't have put things better himself. But, then, when had she ever been lost for words? Their life together was just beginning. They had a baby on the way. They were *home* at last.

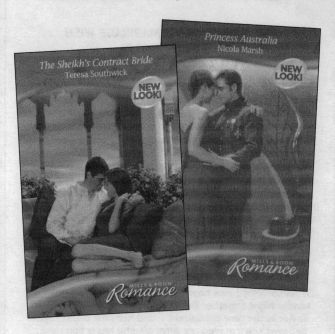

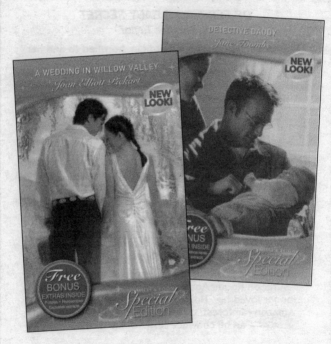

FREE

4 BOOKS AND A SURPRISE GIFT!

We would like to take this opportunity to thank you for reading this Mills & Boon® book by offering you the chance to take FOUR more specially selected titles from the Medical™ series absolutely FREE! We're also making this offer to introduce you to the benefits of the Mills & Boon® Reader Service™—

★ **FREE home delivery**
★ **FREE gifts and competitions**
★ **FREE monthly Newsletter**
★ **Books available before they're in the shops**
★ **Exclusive Reader Service offers**

Accepting these FREE books and gift places you under no obligation to buy; you may cancel at any time, even after receiving your free shipment. Simply complete your details below and return the entire page to the address below. You don't even need a stamp!

YES! Please send me 4 free Medical books and a surprise gift. I understand that unless you hear from me, I will receive 6 superb new titles every month for just £2.89 each, postage and packing free. I am under no obligation to purchase any books and may cancel my subscription at any time. The free books and gift will be mine to keep in any case.

M7ZEE

Ms/Mrs/Miss/Mr...Initials ....
BLOCK CAPITALS PLEASE

Surname ....

Address ....

....

....Postcode ....

Send this whole page to:
The Reader Service, FREEPOST CN81, Croydon, CR9 3WZ